Introduction

'When It Changed', the title of this anthology, is also the title of a story by Joanna Russ. It is my favourite SF short story, and in my mind one of the greatest short fictions of any genre. It has perhaps my favourite short story title: any good story is about when something, or perhaps even everything, changed.

What has recently changed is that science is under threat in a way it has not been for centuries – whether from a loss of hope for a future of ease, comfort, wonder and painlessness, or from economic hardship cutting its funding, or from funding that is focused solely on technological and commercial gain. It's under threat from ideologies that tell people that they need never again think, learn, doubt, imagine, question or do serious mental labour – ideologies that derive their power from making people stupid. It's threatened by well intentioned politicians who have to take science on faith and cannot choose between experts or who are simply hostile to it in order to protect their interests or world views. Science is threatened by its own politicization. It can't help science in the long run if scientists attack religion, even when there are people who preach that New Orleans was flooded for the same reason that Sodom burned.

The debacle over global warming reveals an inability of science to interject its knowledge and methods into political debate. It reveals the continued difficulties, despite tireless efforts, of the sciences to communicate.

And yet, and yet.

Science is the one area of human endeavour where

there is progress. There is progress because the methods of science share one great similarity to the best designing function of all: evolution.

That which does not work is discarded. Great scientists are honoured, but their legacies are refined, superseded or simply thrown out. The scientific method says: test. So great ideas are tested until they are found wanting. Newton describes some things on one level. Einstein shows us how little it helps on a larger scale. Quantum mechanics show how little Einstein helps on the nanoscale. We move on. To read *New Scientist* (or more recently perhaps slashdot. com) every week is to feel some hope for our species. Our thin little layer of cortex is not strong, except in concert, preserving information over time and building on it.

Have the ethical insights of Jesus Christ been roundly superseded? Is there a better explication of the mental discipline needed to face the universe than the Buddha? Has literature progressed from that miraculous age in which both Shakespeare and Cervantes were writing, only to die on the same date, if not actual day? Can we claim that recent history from Auschwitz, Cambodia, Rwanda, Sarajevo, Darfur, or Guantanamo has achieved a lofty political platform from which to lecture the past or build a foundation for the future?

Whatever illusion of progress there has been in daily life, in terms of comfort, longevity or simple relief from boredom has come from technology, the application of science. Our expanded knowledge of where we come from, what kind of creatures we are, what percolates in our cells, what turns the sun, what broils the heart of suns into matter – that comes from science. Though some material gains might just be from sheer weight of human numbers, economies of scale.

Fiction has too often gone off on a tangent from science, portraying scientists as, if not actually mad, at very least cold, cut off, verging on autistic. The lives and work of real scientists are largely absent from fictions ostensibly set in

Praise for *When It Changed*:

"All hit, no miss... thought-provoking at worst, and stunning at best. The book shows that science can inspire anyone and everyone."
- *New Scientist*

"Highly engaging and fascinating... this thought-provoking collection reminded me why I used to like science fiction so much."
- *The Guardian*

"A diamond of compression."
- *Financial Times*

First published in Great Britain in 2009 by Comma Press
Second edition, 2010.
www.commapress.co.uk

The character Mr. Cornelius appears in Paul Cornell's story 'Global Collider
Generation: An Idyll' by kind permission of Michael Moorcock, who'd like to
indicate that that's the only way he should appear.

A CIP catalogue record of this book is available from the British Library.

ISBN 1905583192
ISBN-13 978 1905583195

The publisher gratefully acknowledges assistance from Arts Council England, and
the on-going support of Literature Northwest, as well as the cooperation of the
University of Manchester on this project in particular.

Comma Press and The Centre for New Writing, University of Manchester
acknowledge the help and support of the Manchester Beacon for public
engagement, Professor Dame Nancy Rothwell and all the Manchester Beacon staff.

beacons
for public
engagement

Set in Bembo 11/13 by David Eckersall
Printed and bound in England by SRP Ltd, Exeter

WHEN IT CHANGED

Science into Fiction: An Anthology

Edited by
Geoff Ryman

Whenever you go out there,
you should go out there to save the world.

Actor William Hurt in conversation at the
2009 Arthur C Clarke Awards

Contents

the real world. So has the SF genre lived through a period of such tumultous intellectual change only to ignore those ongoing revolutions?

In fantasies, the scientist's hard fight towards the truth and their endless self-doubt are ignored in the quest to find magic wands to grant our wishes. Faster than light travel, wormholes, AI, immortality of the self, immortality of the species. Sadly, much popular science fiction has become anything other than scientific.

And yet, and yet.

There are so many wonderful science fiction writers now writing whose work is unknown to most people.

There are so many writers who come on the wonders of science by their own paths, unaided by genre.

The science fact pages of newspapers, cult SF magazines, the web or niche-market cable channels are filled with material more imaginative, wondrous, and entertaining than anything found in the mainstream repackaging of SF, franchises the Terminator films or even the delightful *Doctor Who*.

This anthology brings together writers from all over the UK and scientists from the North West just to see what would happen. To see if fiction based in part on the real research being done now by real scientists, could capture the thrill of reality.

With the support of the Manchester Beacon for public engagement, and Professor Dame Nancy Rothwell, Deputy Vice Chancellor of the University of Manchester, the authors and scientists were recruited and introduced to each other. The scientists then answered questions about their fields and research, and went on to provide afterwords about the science in the stories. Both kinds of writing are offered as entertainment of a stimulating kind.

Joanna Russ's story works, not because it gives us great gobs of info-dump, but because it doesn't. Russ has digested science to the point that what it knows is embodied and used.

'When It Changed' gives us a picture of a colonized world in space. All men die in a plague; the women develop a means of reproduction with genetic variation, and over hundreds of years a coherent monosexual human culture develops.

That story could not be told in the fantasy universes of *Star Trek* or *Battlestar Galactica*. These fantasies depend on the universe granting all our wishes. We get to zip across galaxies for free. In these fantasy universes, Russ's world of Whileaway would never have had time to grow. A rescue mission would have arrived. It would have restored the sexual status quo. 'When it Changed' depends absolutely on facing up to the enormous, inhuman difficulties of space travel and the time it takes.

In general bad science is used to save old social norms. In other words, bad science protects us from having to think about real change. The bad science of *Battlestar Galactica* allows its designers to copy Bush-era America onto a setting 150,000 years in the past. The implication seems to be that the natural state of humankind is to be an American in 2003. And when they finally land on our Earth, the characters of *Galactica* reassure us that an American-ish culture developed both the Greek classical tradition and monotheism. Civilization did not come out of the Middle East, the Indus Valley, China and specifically not Africa, not even mitochondrial Eve. The bad science ends up pushing old ethnocentrism.

The bad science of *Galactica* means no one has to develop military structures that suit isolated military cells that will never be able to report back to base. That means the *Band of Brothers*-style characters and storylines are also preserved. Galactica, like the Enterprise, is an aircraft carrier with all its social relations intact.

Bad science is used to copy the past onto the future. The best bits of the past, the stuff we like. We use it to protect ourselves from having to face up to change. That's because, face it, change will take away what we love. Not least ourselves. Then everything we believe in, every person we know.

Russ imagined a world of women, perhaps a fantasy for some people at the time, and then showed that world at the moment of its passing. Anything, however beautiful, is only with us for a while.

Change is heartless and all devouring. Change is also the engine of creation. These stories roll with change rather than fight it.

And they show beyond doubt that any kind of fiction from the fantastic to the mimetic can be made more vivid by a touch of real science.

Carbon: Part One

Justina Robson

The bonds between carbon atoms are the strongest.

They are made in a forging process no less powerful than Thor's hammer on Weyland's anvil; legendary forces. Diamonds, for instance, started life as trees. They fell, slumped into mud, were buried. The earth moved over them and over the aeons its weight pressed them so hard that everything was purged from them, everything, and under this persuasion the atoms joined and became impeccable. What had grown from life eating light became able to refract light, and to cut, not only with its own fine edge but with light that was itself purified as it passed through the crystal and became, through a little monkeying intervention, a laser.

Perhaps carbon is part of the evolution of light. Perhaps carbon is a kind of engine.

I think about this over morning coffee. Many of my colleagues would laugh at this kind of fancy so I don't talk about it. They would bog me down in corrective details: diamonds aren't trees any more, they bear no material relation to trees, and you can refract light with other substances. If light were evolving, what would it be evolving into? How can one speak of the evolution of non living materials? We could have a lengthy chat. I have a KitKat instead. I don't mind talking to you about these things. I know that you, being an imaginary friend, won't mind.

Diamond lasers are very new, as it happens. Most lasers are derived using other gemstones with other colours. I like diamonds because they split the whole spectrum and give that remarkable sparkle; the bling. But the closest I get to one is the blade in the sectioning machine where I cut my specimens ready to make slides that will go into the microscope.

Getting the specimens onto the slides is fiddly. I ruin one in four of them and that's after I've ruined one in six cutting the sections, but my rates are excellent compared to the rest of the department. Years of practice, I say, as they marvel at my beautiful, clean, regular samples, so thin and delicate they are all but invisible. My finger moves on the cutting arm with the regular automated action of a dipping bird or an oil rig donkey and the diamond blade carves through the hard resin in which, smaller than the eye could see, a carbon tube encased in a polymer lies like a strand of Samson's hair. The specimens are so thin you can't touch them. You'd destroy them. A drop of water gets them onto the clumsy, blunt slice of glass, dragging them up by surface tension which is more than strong enough for the job. The glass itself I can handle, hold up to the window, see the catch is good. Then it's into the microscope. It's not like the old days with a tower of lenses that you'd wind up and down. This one bombards the specimen with light and picks up the results: it's the sun and the eyes all in one, a strange beast that lives only to look at very, very tiny things.

This is one of the things that light can do now. It can go where before it was dark, inside the smallest materials.

I adjust the settings and stare at the resulting image, which the microscope puts on the screen. Even knowing what you see takes practice. I see the hexagons of the nanotube holding their six-way shields. The polymer, a much bigger, clumsier galoop of a structure with all the organic awkwardness that the carbon filament abhors, is huddled around in unequal masses, crevassed by uneven tensioning and porous with microvoids. These holes copied their blundering from silk fibres. Their presence is part of what makes this polymer strong and useful just as the absolute order of the carbon makes the nanotube incredibly strong. It's curiously satisfying to see the two things together.

The coffee room is full of snippets from journals about the progress they have had at Sussex, making these nanotubes into beautiful electron emitters that are to become transparent microelectronics. One day they will be mass produced. Magic shall be invisible, printed on plastics, flexible, negligible. We'll all be wearing stick-on patches for computers, says my supervisor grimly.

Stick-on computers? I can't even see things properly on my phone. The idea of looking at an elastoplast to read a book or the news seems strange, although if the text were big enough then maybe I will be the tattooed lady. It's all so exotic, so much like the future, but it's already here.

Meanwhile we have been struggling to make our polymer and the carbon just right, so that the carbon can be spun into lines that are good enough to make cables for a space elevator.

It would be best if the carbon was an uninterrupted line, but making an uninterrupted nanofibre sixty-two thousand miles long seems farfetched, even to me. Our best efforts are a measly four metres. Twisting them around each other in polymer coats has produced workable lengths which carry good loads.

The cost is massive, the project uncertain. The polymer doesn't like huge variations in temperature, or lots of sunlight, or certain kinds of shear. The carbon likes to conduct electricity. If you were putting two and two together on a dinner-dating circuit you would not sit our fibre next to the Earth's atmosphere and expect them to get along swimmingly. There would be sparks and possibly some kind of explosion. The atmosphere would storm off. The fibre would be left as a melting puddle of mixed feelings.

I can't put that in my report findings, though I have drawn this nice picture of it on my notepad.

Instead I have to write in the language of physics, but my message will be the same. Great confidence has been expressed by other materials scientists and enthusiasts about this project, but I have reservations. Draw a line from Earth to space and suddenly the Earth is so small.

I can't say that.

I walked up a big mountain once. The air became thin. I became paranoid. Death stalked me. It had never occurred to me before that we live in a thin skin coating the planet, thinner than the paint on the surface of my pencil. Four miles up, conditions are intolerable. This is what I see when I look in my crystal ball with its six sides.

Some have suggested that the cable, if made, will short out the ionosphere. I don't think our cable would last that long if it tried such a stunt and in any case the interface with the ionosphere isn't going to be that great. But it could carry one heck of a wallop. It will be much more useful as a source of power than a lift to space, perhaps. Anyway, I like that idea better. Unbreakable, conductive cord. Must be useful for more than you think.

I didn't mention the small problems. My student has a piece of the fibre stuck in her finger though nobody can see it. We know that's what it is. It's carbon, so the body doesn't reject it. She feels like Sleeping Beauty who can't wake up, constantly pricking her finger. Another student has an inexplicable rash which turned up a day after dealing with some samples sent over from America. Carbon roses from the invisible thorn. I seem to have escaped so far, but then I treat it as it deserves, with the greatest respect. Rumpelstiltskin spun straw to gold, and this is similar though the gold is black. I wouldn't take any chances with faery work, would you?

I think it will all be dust in the morning.

I can't say that. It would be negative. In the department negative is not seen as a positive, even if it is positively negative. Negatives can't be proven and have no place in science. Also it gets everyone down. I want to write, but don't, that I think this project should have its head chopped clean off, *pour discourager les autres*, personally.

It seems a noble goal, making a cheap lift so as to haul materials up and down from space. How easy then the achievements would follow, the inventions, the discoveries! We can look forward to so much. Memory foam beds – wouldn't exist without the space programme. Pens that write underwater. Ear thermometers, smoke detectors and invisible tooth braces all spun out of mankind's puissant leap beyond the atmosphere. Clearly there's no place for someone like me up there. I look up through the windows which give onto the pavement outside my basement office and watch the shoes passing.

Sensible loafers, laced up, tan. Tights. It's the departmental secretary. My supervisor's brogues are with her. They've gone to a meeting. I should have been there but my supervisor said I am too negative. He is hoping to get extra money. He'll take my points on board. So off he sails. He's right too.

Negativity has its own gravity and I am the departmental neutron star, keeping my distance to prevent others being sucked in. Actually I don't feel that bad. These thoughts really rather run themselves after a while. But I don't approve of the lift programme. I used to dream of a life beyond the stars, in stories, like any other teenager. But then I noticed how far away they were. You can tell that by how small they look.

To any thinking person the vastness of the cosmos, the majesty of the night sky and the rhythms of the eternal round make one's own life and concerns seem overpoweringly important. Some wit said that and I've stolen it. But why would anyone want to spend so much time and money at such high risk with such unknowns for the sake of a few bloated space hotels and moon bases? For deodorant and lightweight spanners and vacuuming robots? Have you seen the moon? Well, have you? And how much of its lonely, arid charm would survive a franchise and another financial disaster? In the future starving children could look up and point out the coloured patch that marks the spot where astronauts, the best of us, are busy digging the lunar dirt for whatever it has that is worth the same as diamonds. They can marvel at the way the world goes round.

Carbon is all straight planes and lines. Rigid. Geometric. I would rather have the moon.

Afterword: How You Look at It

Professor Andrew Bleloch, Liverpool University and Director of the SuperSTEM Laboratory, Daresbury.

The scientific instrument behind the story is the invention of corrective glasses for the electron microscope. You wouldn't think that an electron microscope would need glasses but it turns out that before the invention of these (very expensive, very complicated) glasses the lenses were limited in their ability to focus the electrons. The cover of *Science* magazine for March 27 2009 shows the hexagonal array of a single sheet of carbon atoms imaged directly by a so-called 'aberration corrected electron microscope'.

Recently on the BBC *Today* program one of the presenters asked almost incredulously how mathematics can be beautiful. I feel the mathematician lost the opportunity to point out we find beauty in things like patterns, symmetry and subtly broken symmetry, in harmonies and surprising dissonance. Science has just the same elements of symmetry, harmony, dissonance, predictability and surprise but they are at different levels of abstraction. The simplest level of abstraction is if a musical note is represented as a frequency (A above middle C is 440 vibrations per second) then one octave above is double that frequency – already a mathematical pattern. In addition, one can, in this abstract space start to ask recursive questions about the symmetries of the abstractions which can also give the same kind of pleasure we take in a piece of music or a painting. Justina has captured the ever present childlike (and hence potentially embarrassing) wonder at the intricacies and patterns of the world around us made more so by scientific instruments and scientific understanding.

She also points out the skill and pride in that skill of the researcher. No careers advisor would think to say something like, 'Good at sewing? You should think about experimental physics.'

This story, in its two parts, captures for me the essence of a scientist's life on an average day. Given that it is, at least to a small extent, the result of swapping emails with Justina, perhaps that says more about me than should be completely comfortable. She paints an awkwardly realistic picture of the kind of conflict that occurs frequently in at least this scientist's life. She illuminates the inevitable tension that arises when we try to detach science from the human and then somehow reattach it inappropriately when trying to market our ideas to funding agencies.

Indeed, Justina has used her literary microscope to abstract some of the most important elements of being a scientist.

Global Collider Generation: an Idyll

Paul Cornell

1.

When he first met Li Clarke Communication, lead writer of the Conceptual Design Report, Jerry Cornelius was standing on the back of an elephant that only took commands in French, using a flamethrower on what had been a Hmong poppy field.

The opiate smoke and the screaming masses had been entertaining him only slightly.

A military helicopter had landed, and out she'd stepped, a joyful smile on her face as she'd descended onto the ashes.

'The Short War for Circumferential Survey Completion is over,' she told him. 'The Laotians have capitulated, and enthusiastically embraced particle physics.'

This was back when the Global Muon Collider was still just an idea that required a ring of clear ground around the world.

Back when it was still possible to think, as the Laotian politburo had, that the conclusions of the Circumferential Survey could be ignored by a country that had declared itself neutral in Cold War 2.

Jerry had switched off the flamethrower and sighed.

He increasingly felt that he was doing wild stuff in the name of things that were not, in themselves, all that wild.

'I don't believe there's ever been a machine like this, that's guaranteed to deliver. We know it will discover exciting things. We just don't know what they are yet.'
– Prof. Brian Cox, *Times Online*

2.

Forty years later, Li Clarke Communication was posing for the news crews, letting her pride show. She had adopted a heroic worker's pose, in a fabulous silver-grey dress, the design of which illustrated the design of the Global Muon Collider itself. The dress was not a *metaphor* for the GMC, for in the People's Republic, such metaphors were illegal. Rather, it was a lesson about what was inside the four metre wide concrete arc she was pointing at, the characters printed on the fabric clearly indicating it as such.

She was standing on one of the concrete bulwarks that she had ordered set into the seabed, the GMC behind her, the skyscraper lights of the Chilean town of Concepcion shining through the sea mist behind them both. In the time lapse movie of this section being built, those lights had grown higher as Concepcion became a boomtown.

Exactly where her finger was pointing, the last section of the concrete casing was being lowered into place by one of the giant marine cranes that were normally used to construct thermal vent power stations and carbon sinks. The arc of the GMC vanished into the sea mist to the north.

'The twin fabrics of this dress,' she said, the microphone implanted in her mouth clearly projecting her words to the media crews in their boats and helicopters, 'illustrate the cryostat, the central container of the GMC, inside which run the two beam pipes, each containing a vacuum. Beside these runs the cryoline,' she indicated the silver thread down the left of her dress, 'the liquid helium distribution system. Here we are looking at –' she'd rehearsed this to sound blind to the double meaning, indicating the arc of the GMC with a nod, 'one of the *curves*,' she didn't look at the faces of any of the media she could see, through the displays projected onto her eyes. 'Where the dipole magnets accelerate the beam. Rather than...' she ran her fingernail down her ribcage, as if absent-mindedly drawing a line in the air, 'the straight stretches, where the GMC does not intimately follow the arc of the Earth's surface. That's where we place experiments.'

The collision of seemingly accidental metaphor and politics, of science and glamour, would set them talking all over again. She'd carefully arranged what she'd said so that, picked apart, not all the fragments made sense in any one interpretation. Except the purely literal.

Li loved her job. It kept her young. Literally. All the higher ranking Cold Warriors in the People's Republic were now functionally immortal. Because that way the same people would always be in power, the balance between nations would always remain stable, and there would be no actual war or terrorism or rebellion, except when the major powers needed to let off a little steam. That was how her country did it. The others had their own checks and balances against radical change.

She'd often wondered if Cold War 2 had something to do with the discoveries of previous Colliders. They had shown that what were once called particles were actually the varying oscillations of sheets. Each fluttering appeared as a different particle, and these particles *had* to appear not just in the four directions familiar to human beings, but also in others, imperceptible, wrapped up inside what we knew. Gravity, the everyday business of the universe holding itself together, might only be possible because of micro management inside that fine, unseen, network.

The notion that we were fundamentally *missing the whole story*, that we *couldn't see everything that was real*, had slowly penetrated the public consciousness.

We were all falling in a void, asking urgent questions.

Hence a search for stability. Hence Cold War 2.

But still, one journalist, the other day, had looked at the GMC, going from horizon to horizon, and told her that it proved the world was round.

Li lowered her finger, and moved into her next heroic worker pose, spreading her left hand to indicate the bulk of the tube behind her. She was grateful as always that the world media was no longer in the hands of random individuals, but was once again, in its different ways, civilized and part of the body politic. There would be no stupid questions as she was coming to the big climax.

'We are here,' she said, 'at this important point on the way to GMC First Turn, *because* of Cold War. Cold War is the natural state of mankind. It is the only practical form of global government in which prosperity, scientific advance and human happiness are maximised. Our partners in Cold War do not necessarily share these views: that's the point. Cold War is the only state in which anyone gets anything *done*. It's better for the minds of children, also. Human beings are prey animals, used to being hunted. We have evolved to anticipate death. Better to anticipate a *practical* ending, such as nuclear conflict, that can be easily understood, always imminent, but we all hope never actually arriving, than the many vague and mystical 'ends of all things' that people start to imagine, start to actually *work towards*, in conditions other than Cold War. The creation of the GMC has taken on the resources, and the human urges, that had previously been spent on war. It demonstrates that, in Cold War, opposing ideologies can cooperate to create great things. But this cooperative effort does not mean we should strive to end Cold War, and bring chaos upon ourselves once more. The GMC is not a metaphor for the possibilities of human cooperation. The GMC *defies* metaphor.'

She gently lowered her hand, her head turned towards the future, her face expressing the continuing hope she felt in her changeless old heart.

'*What is the use of knowing things like protons, electrons? this information is utterly use less, half of science is. just made of educated guesses and testable hypothesis, that have been some what proven. Why sit here pondering the origin of the universe? were will it get us? closer to the answer? what is the answer? the satisfaction of knowing? when will it end? what happens happens i guess?....... but hey i'm just some kid in 9th grade who wants to become a dentist some day*'
– *Derek D of San Antonio, Readers Comments, news.com.au, September 11th 2008.*

3.

Jerry also hadn't aged a day in these forty years. Neither had anyone he knew. Well, not anyone fashionable. It was a bit off-putting. He supposed it was down to some spinoff from pure research, something that had happened to him when he was stoned. But he couldn't pin down what. He felt like a national treasure, sometimes, the Queen Mum of Ladbroke Grove. Certainly, Cold War 2 had put some life back into him. Being alive against such a background seemed to be *his* natural state, whatever people said about the planet.

Maybe that was why he was still angry. Because he was still alive.

He watched Li's speech on a black and white television held in the hands of a Yi pedlar on the street in Kunming, the 'City of Eternal Spring', in the Yunnan province of the People's Republic. The pedlar had a boy in the crowd, demanding monies, ideally Tourist Euros, for the privilege of watching. Even though the real show, the Global Muon Collider itself, ran through the city. Shouting sweaty people doing business, shunting around him in both directions, threatened to overwhelm the sound, making his feet slip on the oily cobbles.

The sheer PR of the GMC effort was something to behold, he thought. Some tiny technological news item of such extreme importance, every day. It was like Apollo

13

all over again. Global politics was once more the conflict between Apollo and Dionysus (which had also been, Jerry remembered, how Stephen Fry had once described *Star Trek*). It had ceased to be, as it had become between the Cold Wars, the conflict between Apollo and Starbucks.

Jerry, more of a Dionysian, was wearing a nice black frock coat, with a Ted collar. Retro, but the right sort of retro. Not the sort of coat that implied he was nostalgic for impossible notions of the future like Artificial Intelligence or Indistinguishable Virtual Reality. Beneath the coat he wore a black blouse that had been his dear old Mum's. He was in Kunming on GMC business, working for the Americans. A few minutes ago he'd wandered into the Yuantong Si and shot a monk in the back of the neck with his needle gun. The backlash from that killing would help to further the interests of... well, he almost remembered what the CIA man had told him it would help to further the interests of.

His thoughts snapped back to the television. Li had just said something incredible. That bit about the GMC defying metaphor. Did she really believe that? The Collider was an attractor for metaphor, a sump for it! Colliders always had been. He'd found himself reading, watching and listening to – separately! – the archive material from when the GMC's ancestor, the Large Hadron Collider, had gone online. Metaphors aplenty. The twin beams of life and death, colliding to produce, er, love, probably. That had been his favourite. Because it was so pitifully camp in the face of something real. Almost none of the authors involved had understood the physics. They'd turned the Collider into what they wanted it to be a symbol of, and written about that instead.

Jerry put a hand to his forehead. He would have to do his best to use metaphor wherever he went. This century was getting him down. He let go of the television, and started shoving his way through the crowd, willing himself to getting around to stuff like hiding out and leaving the area in disguise.

'We can say that we develop tools for our difficult business which does not exist in the market. But these tools can be used for the benefit of society.'
– Dr. Lyndon Evans, LHC Project Leader.
www.scitech.ac.uk

4.
Eighteen months later, Li marched through the main hall of Wonderland, in Arica, Colombia. The media followed, as always. They were recording the sights and sounds of the new rainforest that could be seen through the observation walls, water cascading down the transparency, the cries of nature echoing everywhere.

She was enjoying, as always, the ghostly sensations that the huge EM fields here conjured in her brain. It was the closest thing to a numinous experience she could ever expect. And it was one created by science and the people! It felt like that here because of the magnets, 40 Tesla Japanese quadropole monsters, the biggest ever manufactured. The sensations would get even more intense when the magnets were cycled up to maximum, after the beams had been injected into the ring.

'This is one of the four places, around the world, where the beams can be focused and made to collide,' she said. 'These magnets do that. The establishment we call Wonderland was designed to examine the quark gluon plasma that's created when heavy ions, instead of the lighter muons, are collided. That plasma is like the first moments of the Big Bang. It gives us an insight into the moment of creation. It's one of the many other jobs that the Collider will have, besides probing the world of the very small and very energetic.'

There was just over a year to go now until the First Turn, when the beam would complete a circuit of the GMC for the first time. 'You could say all this began,' she said, 'in 2015, when resonances in the scattering of W and Z particles in collision at the Large Hadron Collider in Geneva indicated that there was indeed a new level of reality to be glimpsed. That, as had been theorised, those "fundamental" "particles" were made of "smaller" "particles".' She made all the inverted commas in mid-air, because she knew it looked funny to have someone so serious doing that, and because she enjoyed it.

'Do you think there's any end to that process?' one of the reporters asked. 'Or do you think it's like Russian doll inside Russian doll?'

She winced inwardly at the use of the simile. European reporters often put things to her like that deliberately, to see if they'd get a reaction. 'We don't know. But the end point is the Planck Length, the pixel of the universe as it's been called... by some Europeans–' which got a laugh '–the length under which measurement, and thus science, is impossible.'

The thought of that had lodged in the popular imagination too. It had given the public another mental image: the grainy nature of reality, the possibility that all their experiences were just a... picture. That some pure, ungrained, free-flowing existence beyond their experience was more real.

This was, of course, a feeling humanity had always had, but the quest for the Last Length seemed to confirm it. This new angst wasn't much salved by Cold War 2, but people were at least distracted from it. The prospect of total war, that missiles and germs could one day fall like sparrows, gave people something else to worry about.

'Will we ever get to see that?'

'The GMC takes us five levels of magnitude closer than the LHC did.'

'But?'

'But there are still many decimal points to go.'

'VIEW POLL RESULTS: Will the activation of the Large Hadron Collider have terrible, terrible consequences?
Yes: 50.00% No: 50.00% Voters: 12. You may note vote on this poll'
— *www.geezersphoenix.com*

5.

After eighteen months Jerry had fled only as far as Xining, at the edge of the Qinghai-Tibet Plateau. He'd hitched on the supply trains that ran alongside the GMC. Multinational flags were everywhere, including the one bearing a Chinese ideogram best translated as Annoyed Detente Cooperation. That was usually referred to as the Second Force of Progress. The First Force of Progress was Annoyed Detente *Competition.* That ideogram was painted all over the NASA and RKA ships involved in the space race to Mars.

Jerry was annoyed himself, and the Official Heroin in his bloodstream wasn't helping. Oddly. He felt oppressed by the symbols passing by. Huge thermal buffers had been sunk into the ground for miles around, designed to warp and weft under earthquake conditions. They were a carbon sink too, the Long Solving of Global Warming being another one of those ADCOP things, because none of the sides had found a way to weaponise it.

Almost every aspect of life was now about a limited choice of ideologies. As the ice caps had vanished, so politics had frozen again. Maybe because people had gotten a long hard look at the chaos of the alternative.

That was the heart of his problem. He was a freelancer by nature, but couldn't find an employer that wasn't some vast block of cant.

When he got out of China, he decided, he was going to do something about that.

'We simply want to know what the world is made of, and how.'
– Jos Engelen, Chief Scientific Officer, CERN,
The New Yorker.

6.

Six months later, and Li was looking at America. She was on the walkway that ran along the top of the collider as it passed from the ocean onto the dry land of Nova Scotia. She was in her uniform now, alone, comfortable, checking radiation levels. The sea spray was pleasant on her face. To the West there lay the United States, missing the path of the GMC by just a few miles. The US government had argued and argued about it, in the end only putting in a cursory amount of funding, just enough to say they cared about world peace. Li felt sorry for President Van Lent. As a representative democracy, the USA had to yield to all sorts of conflicting impulses. The trouble was, they had initially thrown their weight behind the notion of a neutrino study project, instead of the GMC. The Super Nu would have run East to West across the continental USA, Route 66 for neutrinos, bringing attention and funds to the flyover states. But that project had collapsed in senatorial wrangling, chiefly because it would have been much more expensive than running the GMC around the world. And perhaps because it looked just a tad selfish.

She was here to supervise the Muon Cooling Experiments at a Canadian laboratory purpose-built on this cold coast. Necessary for the GMC to proceed. Forever causing problems.

She wondered what had happened to Jerry Cornelius. He had been one of her favourite employees. He seemed to take genuine joy in what he did. She'd been fascinated by how old world he was, but that was where their relationship had floundered. He had that British disgust for hope. That 'joy' that was always laughing in the face of something.

18

Collider science was like Marxist synthesis. Clashes between political systems created not just one revolution, but harmonics, resonances that backed up and went forward across time, creating places of understanding, different revolutions. And we gradually make our way towards–

What?

Some indefinable truth. What lies underneath everything. Unseeable by any system.

She liked the feeling of *that* joy.

'<– if the lhc actually destroys the earth & this page isn't yet updated please email mike@frantic.org to receive a full refund –>'
– www.hasthelargehadroncolliderdestroyedtheworldyet.com

7.

It had taken six months, but Jerry had escaped from China. He was now in the middle of nowhere, several hundred miles away from a town called Moron. He was still following the path of the GMC. But it had stopped being an escape route, and started being the focus of a plan.

Mongolian tundra stretched in all directions, the distant bustle of wind broken by the concrete tunnel he walked beside. In some parts of the world it would doubtless have attracted graffiti. Here it was already home to the black moss, the nests of birds, and small animals hiding in the shade.

He was lugging the explosives in a black sack on his back, like some demented Santa. He'd stolen them from one of the construction sites, a dozen miles down the track. He'd attached the first load, with a radio detonator, to the underside of the GMC several miles back. He doubted it would be seen in this empty place. He was hoping to be able to steal some transport before he got to the next bomb attachment point.

Everyone in the world, he thought, was now on one side of the GMC or the other.

Jerry liked to be in-between.

He had no idea why he was doing this.

That was the whole point.

He was just an agent of history. Or against stagnation. Or something.

'Both the LHC, and the space programme, are vital if the human race is not to stultify, and eventually die out. Together they cost less than one tenth of a percent of world GDP. If the human race cannot afford that, it doesn't deserve the epithet 'human'.'
– Prof. Stephen Hawking, BBC Radio 4.

8.

Four months later, Li led the grand ambassadors of the great powers off the bus and into the RF building. With just over two months left before First Turn, she was visiting all the major facilities in such company. The drive had been pleasant. The meadows of the 'Warming Islands' of Greenland got more lush with every visit. The building itself was a mile long, surrounding the GMC tunnel. It had grass growing over the roof and birds nesting everywhere. Here were the Radio Frequency Cavities that accelerated the beams every time they went around the world.

'Ladies, gentlemen,' she said, standing in the great jade hall that shone with polish, 'imagine the future.' She had to speak up over the low ohm ohm of the klystrons that produced the ever-changing electrical field that pushed the muons along when they passed this point. The locals enjoyed tuning in to the sound on amateur radio sets. There had been music made of it, but Li felt ideologically afraid of that, and hadn't taken pains to hear it. 'I can't, because I have no idea what the fruits of pure research might be. But I'd like to hear what you think might result from an inquiry into the nature of the universe.'

The Europeans talked philosophy. Someone brought up Kant. The Russians talked about prosperity, about new technology. The Americans decided that the most important thing was the peace process, bringing people together. The Chinese delegation politely stayed silent, assuming that their view should also be hers.

Li listened to all that hope and felt almost ecstatic.

'CALL YOUR SENATOR, YOUR PASTOR, YOUR IMAN, YOUR BISHOP, YOUR PRIEST, EMAIL, CALL, SCREAM, BESEECH THEM TO STOP THIS MONSTER OF CERN. MICHAEL SAVAGE, RUSH LIMBAUGH, SHAWN HANNITY, LARRY KING , MR PRESIDENT, BARAK OBAMA, JOHN MCAIN, OPRA WINFREY, YAHOO, GOOGLE , CNN, FOX, CNBC, NEWSPAPERS, WHY IS THIS OMNIPITANT THREAT , THIS WORLD ENDING CATASTROPHY NOT TAKING PRESIDENT OVER ALL OTHER NEWS'
– Comment by Dr. Brown on UniverseToday.com.

9.
In that four months, Jerry had got as far as Siberia. Near the town of Tura, to be precise, in Krasnoyarsk Krai, on the confluence of the Kochechum and Lower Tunguska rivers. Mud and insects and endless trees. The GMC looked good running through all that, with the low sun behind it. There was something about it that spoke of Christmas. Or the Soviet Union. Or something. Up ahead was one of the electronics galleries, a concrete bunker that sprang off from the tunnel.

He decided that now was the best time. He had been looking for something more meaningful, like doing it the moment before First Turn, but that might suggest a point to his actions. The last bomb was only a mile back. The blasts would wreck such large sections of tunnel that to repair them would take months. Maybe it would change the thinking of the global Cold War 2 community, create ripples that would change the world.

Or maybe not.

Still, he would have made his No Point.

He took the radio detonator from his pocket. He'd hacked into a communications satellite that stood far enough above the distance he'd travelled to rebroadcast his message to all his bombs at once.

No audience. No need for a big moment.

He pressed the detonator.

Nothing happened.

Except that suddenly he heard engines a mile behind him. Coming after him.

Jerry didn't break his stride. He doubled it.

'Every civilization needs its creation myth. This is ours'
– Rob Appleby, Accelerator physicist at CERN,
Geneva and the Cockcroft Institute, UK.

10.

Two months later, they met in the Arctic. Outside the Samson detector. It stood, black, as big as a cathedral, not reflecting the harsh night of the plain of rock. The black moss was the only thing that grew. The night was clear and the aurora blasted overhead, and you could almost hear the radiation.

Samson was actually a pile of different detectors, containers of gas and liquid argon, silicon semiconductors for particles to slam into, trackers to see where things went, calorimeters to see how hard. It had to be huge, like its sister at the Antarctic, to catch everything that flew from the collisions, and flew so fast.

Right now it was only looking at cosmic rays, only collecting particles that rained down from above. From vast and distant explosions that had happened across the galaxy, even from outside it, back in time to the start, the fireworks of the unfurling of the saddle-shaped flag that was the universe. Streaking into the atmosphere at random, they regularly produced more energy than the GMC did.

Those particles had such an effect on civilisation, thought Li. A tumour here. A mutation there. They were a force that killed great men and started new waves of evolution, accelerating things no matter which theory of history you followed.

Jerry stood like a burnt black stick against the darkness all around. He glowed with malice, charisma.

She had come alone to meet him. Although such weapons were trained on this spot that she could have him reduced to wasted carbon with a gesture.

'One week to go now,' she said. 'Why did you even try to do it, Jerry?'

He nodded at the GMC. 'Why did you try to do *this*?'

'Because relativistic particles, when accelerated, find it hard to turn corners.'

He grinned. White on black. 'You know, I might be on your side next time.'

'Stranger things have happened.'

'Anything *can* happen. Only it never bloody *does*.' He produced his needle gun and brought it up to aim at her head —

Only to find she'd produced her own.

Oh yeah, they were manufactured now. Made in China.

They fired at the same moment.

And for a moment Jerry was sure that the two needles, sparkling in the bright dark night had hit each other, point to point, and that that energy, having nowhere else to go, had forced new particles into being yet again.

But neither of them could be sure where their shots went.

So Li fired again and Jerry fell.

Only a century later, they built the Grand Solar Collider.

It ran in free fall outside the orbit of Neptune, around all the inhabited moons and stations and worlds that then were federated and at another time might be at war, and it shaped lives and gave life, in general, another Holy purpose.

It would take humanity five decimal points closer to the Planck Length.

It would make other discoveries, of which we cannot know from where we are, even here in fiction.

It spoke of where everyone had been, and where everyone would go next.

On the way to something imaginable.

Afterword: It's Real, It's Big, It's Noble

Dr Rob Appleby, Physicist, CERN, Switzerland; Lecturer, Cockcroft Institute and the University of Manchester, UK

The Collider exists, now. It's real, now, here: the CERN, on the outskirts of Geneva, Switzerland. The descriptions of the collider in this story are based on it and are accurate. The real Collider is smaller – only a mere 28 kilometre across – but it too is colder inside than outer space. It too accelerates particles to almost the speed of light, surfing electromagnetic fields. It's one of the biggest projects in the history of science.

We get big so that we can study small. The Large Hadron Collider at CERN produces particles with immense amounts of energy so that we can open up the smallest levels of the universe. We don't spend £8 billion just for the hell of it. Each experiment grows out of the ones that have gone before it.

We have a Standard Model of particle physics, one of humankind's most impressive intellectual achievements and it's been tested to an immense accuracy. But looking at nature shows deviations from this theory, a discrepancy from the model. And that deviation suggests the next experiment. What results is a chain of experiments, each one leading to the next.

In the future of this story, they are very much further along that chain than us: they need a collider that goes round the world. In that future they need immense energies to keep pulling one Russian doll out of another. This requires intense cooperation but intense motivating rivalry, a situation made possible by Cold War 2.

I'm an accelerator physicist at CERN, which means I predict where the protons we accelerate will go, and what happens when they hit each other. At CERN's Large Hadron Collider, we accelerate two streams of protons, pieces of an atom, in opposite directions. The two streams meet at only four points in the underground ring. Sometimes the protons break apart. Often what is produced when they collide are streams of particles which we already know about but sometimes the energy bound up in the protons creates new particles which we hadn't known about.

The Large Hadron Collider exists primarily to see if one particular particle exists, the Higgs boson.

We think the Higgs boson exists because of a feature in our Standard Model, which implies that all particles should have zero mass. But clearly they don't. Particles can be heavy. Some like a photon have no mass, but others, like the electron and quark, do. The theory says the electron interacts with a cloud of Higgs boson and so has mass. The Large Hadron Collider will tell us if this is correct, and it's almost time to find out.

There is no more noble pursuit than trying to understand the universe, and to go on learning. We have to do this as a species, or we will stay still, which really means to go backwards.

Moss Witch

Sara Maitland

Perhaps there are no more Moss Witches; the times are cast against them. But you can never be certain. In that sense they are like their mosses; they vanish from sites they are known to have flourished in, they are even declared extinct – and then they are there again, there or somewhere else, small, delicate, but triumphant – alive. Moss Witches, like mosses, do not compete; they retreat.

If you do want to look for a Moss Witch, go first to www.geoview.org. Download the map that shows ancient woodland and print it off. Then find the map that shows the mean number of wet days per year. Be careful to get the right map – you do not want the average rainfall map; quantity is not frequency. A wet day is any day in which just one millimetre of rain falls; you can have a high rainfall with fewer wet days; and one millimetre a day is not a high rainfall. Print this map too, ideally on tracing paper. Lay it over the first map. The only known habitations of Moss Witches are in those places where ancient woodland is caressed by at least two hundred wet days a year. You will see at once that these are not common co-ordinates; there are only a few tiny pockets running down the west coasts of Scotland and Ireland. Like most other witches, Moss Witches have always inhabited very specific ecological niches. So far as we know, and there has been little contemporary research, Moss

Witches prefer oak woods and particularly those where over twenty thousand years ago the great grinding glaciers pushed large chunks of rock into apparently casual heaps and small bright streams leap through the trees. It is, of course, not coincidental that these are also the conditions that suit many types of moss – but Moss Witches are more private, and perhaps more sensitive, than the mosses they are associated with. Mosses can be blatant: great swathes of sphagnum on open moors; little frolicsome tufts on old slate roofs and walls, surprising mounds flourishing on corrugated asbestos, low lying velvet on little used tarmac roads, and weary, bullied, raked and poisoned carpets fighting for their lives on damp lawns. But Moss Witches lurk in the green shade, hide on the north side of trees and make their homes in the dark crevasses of the terminal moraine. If you hope to find a Moss Witch this is where you must go. You must go silently and slowly, waiting on chance and accident. You must pretend you are not searching and you must be patient.

But be very careful. You go at your own peril. The last known encounter with a Moss Witch was very unfortunate.

The bryologist was, in fact, a very lovely young man, although his foxy-red hair and beard might have suggested otherwise. He was lean and fit and sturdy and he delighted in his own company and in solitary wild places. Like many botanists his passion had come upon him early, in the long free rambles of an unhappy rural childhood and it never bothered him at all that his peers thought botany was a girly subject and that real men preferred hard things; rocks if you must, stars if you were clever enough and dinosaurs if you had imagination. After taking his degree he had joined an expedition investigating epiphytes in the Peruvian rainforest for a year and had come back filled with a burning ecological fervour and a deep enthusiasm for fieldwork. He was, at this time, employed, to his considerable gratification and satisfaction, by a major European funded academic research project trying to assess the relative damage to Western European littoral habitats of pollution and global warming. His role was mainly to survey and record Scottish ancient woodlands and to compare the biodiversity of SSSIs with less protected environments. He specialised in mosses and genuinely loved his subject.

So he came that March morning after a dawn start and a long and lovely hill walk down into a little valley, with a wide shallow river, a flat flood plain and steep sides: glacier carved. Here, hanging on the hillside, trapped between a swathe of ubiquitous Sitka spruce plantation, the haggy reedy bog of the valley floor and the open moor was a tiny triangle of ancient oak wood with a subsidiary arm of hazel scrub running north. It was a lambent morning; the mist had lifted with sunrise and now shimmered softly in the distance; out on the hill he had heard the returning curlews bubbling on the wing and had prodded freshly laid frogspawn; he had seen his first hill lambs of the year – tiny twins, certainly born that night, their tails wagging their wiry bodies as they burrowed into their mother's udders. He had seen neither human being nor habitation since he had left the pub in the village now seven miles away. He surveyed the valley from above, checked his map and came down from the open hill, skirting the gorse and then a couple of gnarled hawthorns, clambering over the memory of a stone wall, with real pleasure and anticipation. Under the still naked trees the light was green; on the floor, on the trees themselves, on rotted branches and on the randomly piled and strewn rocks – some as big as a cottages, some so small he could have lifted them – there were mosses, mosses of a prolific abundance, a lapidary brightness, a soft density such as he had never seen before.

He was warm from his walking; he was tired from his early rising; and he was enchanted by this secret place. Smiling, contented, he lay down on a flat dry rock in the sheltered sunlight and fell asleep.

The Moss Witch did not see him. His hair was the colour of winterkilled bracken; his clothes were a modest khaki green; the sunlight flickered in a light breeze. She did not see him. She came wandering along between rocks and trees and sat down very close to where he slept, crossed her legs, straightened her back and began to sing the spells of her calling, as every Moss Witch must do each day. He woke to that low strange murmur of language and music; he opened his eyes in disbelief but without shock. She was quite small and obviously very old; her face was carved with long wrinkles running up and down her forehead and cheeks; she was dressed raggedly, in a loose canvas skirt and with thick uneven woollen socks and sandals obviously made from old silage bags. Her woollen jumper was hand knitted, and not very well. She wore green mittens, which looked somehow damp. He was still sleepy, but when he moved a little and the Moss Witch turned sharply what she saw was a smiling foxy face and, without thinking, she smiled back.

Tinker? he wondered. Walker like himself though not so well equipped? Gipsy? Mad woman, though a long way from anywhere? He felt some concern and said a tentative 'Hello.'

Even as she did not do so, the Moss Witch knew she should not answer; she should dissolve into the wood and keep her silence. But she was lonely. It had been a very long time. Long, long ago there had been meeting and greetings and gossip among the Moss Witches, quite a jolly social life indeed with gatherings for wild Sabbats in the stone circles on the hills. There had been more wildwood and more witches then. She could not count the turnings of the world since she had last spoken to anyone and his smile was very sweet. She said 'Hello' back.

He sat up, held out his right hand and said, 'I'm Robert.'

She did not reply but offered her own, still in its mitten.

It was knitted in a close textured stitch and effortlessly he had a clear memory of his mother's swift fingers working endlessly on shame-inducing homemade garments for himself and his sister and recalled that the pattern was called moss stitch and this made him suddenly and fiercely happy. When he shook her hand, small in his large one, he realised that she had only one finger.

There was a silence although they both went on looking at each other. Finally he said, 'Where do you come from?' Suddenly he remembered the rules in Peru about not trying to interact with people you encountered deep in the jungle. Uncontacted tribes should remain uncontacted, for their own safety, cultural and physical; they had no immunities and were always vulnerable. He shrugged off the thought, smiling again, this time at his own fantasy. There were, after all, no uncontacted tribes in Britain.

'Gondwana we think; perhaps we drifted northwards,' she said vaguely. 'No one is quite sure about before the ice times; that was the alternate generation, though not of course haploid. But here, really. I've lived here for a very long time.'

He was startled, but she looked so mild and sweet in the dappled green wood that he could not bring himself to admit that she said what he thought she said. Instead he turned his sudden movement into a stretch for his knapsack and after rummaging for a moment produced his flask. He unscrewed the top and held it out to her. 'Would you like some water?'

She stretched out her left hand and took the flask from him. Clamping it between her knees she pulled up her right sleeve and then poured a little water onto her wrist. He stared.

After a pause she said, 'Urgh. Yuck. It's horrible,' and shook her arm vigorously, then bent forward and wiped the splashes delicately from the moss where they had fallen. 'I'm sorry,' she said, 'that was rude, but there is something in it, some chemical thing and I'm rather sensitive... we all are.'

She was mad, he realised, and with it felt a great tenderness – a mad old woman miles from anywhere and in need of looking after. He dreaded the slow totter back to the village, but pushed his irritation away manfully. The effort banished the last of his sleepiness and he got to his feet, pulled out his notebook and pen and began to look around him. Within moments he realised that he had never seen mosses like this; in variety, in luxuriance and somehow in joy. These were joyful mosses and in uniquely healthy condition.

There were before his immediate eyes most of the species he was expecting and several he knew instantly were on the Vulnerable or Critically Endangered lists from the Red Data Book and then some things he did not recognise. He felt a deep excitement and came back to his knapsack. She was still sitting there quite still and seemed ancient and patient. He pulled out his checklist and *taxa*.

'What are you doing?' she asked him.

'I'm seeing what's here – making a list.'

'I can tell you,' she said, 'I know them all.'

He smiled at her. 'I'm a scientist,' he said, 'I'm afraid I need their proper names.'

'Of course,' she said, 'sit down. I've got 154 species here, not counting the liverworts and the hornworts, of course. I can give you those too. I think I'm up to date although you keep changing your minds about what to call them, don't you? My names may be a bit old-fashioned.'

She chanted the long Latin names, unfaltering.

Leucobryum glaucum. Campylopus pyriformis. Mnium hornum. Atrichum undulatum. Dicranella heteromalla. Bazzania trilobata. Lepidozia cupressina. Colura calyptrifolia. Ulota crispa...

More names than he could have thought of, and some he did not even know. He sat on the rock with his list on his knee ticking them off as they rolled out of her mouth; there seemed no taxonomic order in her listing, moving from genera to genera along some different system of her own, but her tongue was elegant and nimble around the Latin names. He was both bemused and amused.

Once he stopped her. *Orthodontium gracile* she sang, and paused smiling. He looked up and she was glancing at him quizzically. 'The slender thread moss.' She looked sly.

'No' he said, 'no, you can't have that here. It grows in the Weald, on the sandstone scarps.'

She laughed. 'Well done,' she said, 'that was a sort of test. But I do have it. Come and see.'

She stood up and beckoned to him; he followed her round a massive granite boulder and up the slope. There behind a hazel thicket and free of the oak trees was a little and obviously artificial heap of sandstone, placed carefully in strata to replicate the scarps of Cheshire and the Weald. And there were two small cushions of *Orthodontium gracile*.

'I like it very much,' she said. 'I like it because it is a bit like me – most people don't know how to see it. It is not as rare as you think. So I invited it in.'

'You mustn't do that,' he said shocked, 'it's protected. You mustn't gather or collect it.'

'No of course not,' she said. 'I didn't. I invited it.' She smiled at him shyly and went on, 'I think perhaps you and your people are more like *Orthodontium lineare*, more successful but not native.'

Then she sat down and sang the rest of her list.

After that she took his hand in her maimed one and led him down beside the stream which gurgled and sang in small falls and cast a fine mist of spray on the banks where rare mosses and common ferns flourished. He knew then that something strange was happening to him, there in the oak wood, although he did not know what. It was magical space. It said a lot for his true devotion to bryophytes and his research that he went on looking, that he was not diverted. But time somehow shook itself and came out differently from before – and the space was filled with green, green mosses and her gentle bubbling knowledge. She spoke the language of science and turned it into a love song through her speaking and the mosses sang back the same tune in harmony.

Sometime after noon they came back to where they had started. He was hungry and got out his lunch box. She sat down beside him.

'Have you got something to eat?' he asked.

'No.'

'Do you want to share mine?'

'I'm non-vascular,' she said. 'I get what I need from the rain. That's why my wrinkles run up and down instead of across. He looked at her face and saw that it was so. She went on, 'And of course it does mean that I revive very quickly even if I do get dried out. That's why I can go exploring, or for that matter,' she looked contented, almost smug, 'sit out in the sun with you.'

None of this seemed as strange to him as it should have seemed. He had reached a point of suspension, open to anything she told him.

'Are you...' but it did not feel right to ask her what she was. He changed the sentence, 'Are you all alone?'

'Yes, sadly,' she said in a matter of fact voice. 'I hoped for a long time that I would be monoicous. Nearly half of us are. But no, alas. I'm thoroughly female and as you can imagine that makes things difficult nowadays.' After a little pause she smiled at him, slightly shamefaced and said in a confessional sort of tone, 'As a matter of fact, that's what happened to my fingers. I was much younger then of course; I wouldn't try it now, but I did so want a daughter, I thought I might be clonal. You know, I'm not vascular, sensitive to pollution, often mis-identified or invisible, all those things; I hoped I might be totipotent as well. So I cut off my fingers and tried to regenerate the cells. But it didn't work. It was a bad mistake. I think we must have been though, somewhere in the lineage, because of our disjunctions and wide dispersal. That's one of the problems of evolution – losses and gains, losses and gains. Vascular was a smart idea, you have to admit, even at the price of all those vulgar coloured flowers.'

He realised suddenly there were no snowdrops; no green sprouts of bluebells, wild garlic or anemone; no primrose or foxgloves. 'Don't you like flowers?'

'Bloody imperialists,' she replied crossly, 'they invaded, imposed their own infrastructure and ruined our culture, stole our land. And anyway they're garish – I do honestly prefer the elegance, the subtle beauty of seta, capsules and peristomes.'

He did too, he realised, although he had never thought of it before.

They sat together, contented, in the wildwood, in the space outside of time.

But he lacked her long patience. He could not just sit all day, and eventually he roused himself, shook off the magic, stood up and took out his collecting kit: the little glass bottles with their plastic screw tops, a sharp knife, a waterproof pencil and a squared paper chart.

'What are you doing?' she asked him.

'I'm just going to collect some samples,' he said, 'so we can get them under the microscope.'

'You can't do that.'

'Yes, it's fine,' he said reassuringly, 'I've got a certificate. This is one of the richest sites I've ever seen. We'll get a team in here, later in the year, but I need some samples now – just to prove it, you know; no one will believe me otherwise.'

'I really cannot let you do that,' she said quietly, still sitting gently on the gentle ground.

But he just smiled kindly at her and moved away up the slope. He bent over a fine little feathered mat: a *sematophyllum* – *S. micans* perhaps; he knelt down, took his knife and scraped along its underside pulling free its anchoring rhizoids and removing a tiny tuft. He opened one of his bottles, popped in the small green piece and screwed up the top. So she killed him. She was sorry of course, but for witches it is always duty before pleasure.

Quite soon she knew, with great sadness, that she would have to move on. They would come looking for him and would find her, and rather obviously the crushed skull where she had hit him with the granite rock could not have been an accident.

Later still she realised that she could not just leave his body there. If they found that and did not find her, they might blame some other poor soul, some solitary inhabitant of wood or hill, some vagrant or loner. Someone like her, but not her. Justice is not really an issue that much concerns Moss Witches, but she did not want the hills tramped by heavy-footed policemen or ripped and squashed by quad bikes and 4X4s.

The evening came and with it the chill of March air. Venus hung low in the sky, following the sun down behind the hill, and the high white stars came out one by one, visible through the tree branches. She worked all through the darkness. First she dehydrated the body by stuffing all his orifices with dry sphagnum, more biodegradable than J-cloth and more native than sponge, of which, like all Moss Witches, she kept a regular supply for domestic purposes. It sucked up his body fluids, through mouth and ears and anus. She thought too its antiseptic quality might protect her mosses from his contamination after she was gone.

While he was drying out she went up the hill above the wood and found a ewe that had just given birth and milked it. She mixed the milk with yoghurt culture. She pounded carefully selected ground mosses in her pestle, breaking them down into parts as small as she could manage; she mixed the green ooze with the milk and culture.

When he was desiccated and floppy she stripped his clothing off, rolled him onto his back among the thick mosses under the rocks and planted him, brushing the cell-rich mixture deep into the nooks and crannies of his body and pulling thicker more energetic moss clumps over his now cool flesh. At first she was efficient and businesslike, but later she allowed her imagination to cavort. She painted *Aplodon wormskioldii* on his forehead and where his toes poked up through her main planting of *Polytrichum* because it grew on the dead bodies of deer and sheep and might flourish on his bones too. She festooned his genitals with *Plagiochila atlantica* because its little curling fronds were so like the curly mass there. She carried down a rock richly coated with the lichen *Xanthoria parietina* because it was the colour of his foxy hair. She looked at her little arrangement; it was clever, witty even, and secure, but she still felt there was something missing.

After a while she knew. She went round the massive granite boulder and up the slope beyond the oak trees and behind the hazel thicket to her artificial sandstone scarp. There she hacked out one of the cushions of *Orthodontium gracile* on a piece of the reddish rock. Back where he lay she uncovered his face again, forced his mouth open and placed the sandstone in it, the little moss resting gently on his smiling lips. It was very pleasing to her, because he had been such a sweet man and knew the names of mosses.

Then she spoke clearly and firmly to all the mosses, the liverworts and the lichens she had planted. She told them to grow fast, to grow strong and to grow where she had told them. Bryophytes are not commonly obedient or compliant, they tend to follow their own rules, coming and going at their own random whim, but she knew this time they would do as she asked because they loved her. Within weeks his body would be part of the moss wood, a green irregular shape among so many others.

Then, sadly, singing all their names one last time, she turned northwards. She climbed high up the hillside and lay down and watched the dawn. When the morning breeze came with first light, she opened her mouth wide and exhaled; and her microscopic spore flowed out between her sixty-four little hydroscopic teeth and was caught by the wind, and carried up into the higher air currents that circulate the Earth.

And then... well nobody knows.

Perhaps she blows there still, carried on those upper airs, waiting for a new and quieter time when witches and mosses can flourish.

Perhaps she walked north and west and came at last to another small fragment of ancient woodland, a tight ravine leading down to the sea or a small island out beyond the uttermost west, and she lives there still.

Moss Witches, like mosses, do not compete, they retreat.

Perhaps there are no more Moss Witches; the times are cast against them. But if you go into ancient woodland and it glows jewel green with moss and is damp and quiet and lovely, then be very careful.

Afterword: Lifeforms

Dr Jennifer Rowntree, post-doctoral researcher, Faculty of Life Science, University of Manchester

I had a lot of chats with Sara about bryophytes and particularly mosses and suggested some books to read. I think she's been true to what we talked about, and has come up with many amusing and interesting things.

The way of finding Moss Witches that she invents, using the website, is brilliant. I'm sure it would work if there were such creatures. Bryophytes need water to complete their life cycle, as the sperm moves to the eggs across a film of water, but they can be found anywhere, even in very dry places. Many species can dry out completely, then rehydrate and start to grow again when water is available. They don't have an internal water transport system like most plants, but water moves over their outer surfaces and they absorb it directly through their cells.

That's why the Witch puts the water on her skin instead of drinking it. The leaves of bryophytes are usually only one or two cells thick and because they absorb water directly, they can be quite sensitive to chemicals in the water, just as the Witch is. With many species, there are protrusions on the leaves that help guide the water around the surface, hence the vertical creases in the Witch's face.

The bryophytes' life cycle has two distinct stages, starting as a spore which grows into a leafy plant, the gametophyte. This then produces male and female sex organs. When an egg is fertilized it grows into a sporophyte, the second stage, which is essentially parasitic on the green plant and which produces the spores.

Some plants are dioicous, which means there are separate male and female plants. Monoicous plants have both sex organs on the same plant. The poor Witch hoped she might be monoicous, but sadly no, she's only female and cannot fertilize herself. The gametophyte has only a single strand of DNA, what we call haploid. The sporophyte has two strands of DNA like us which then divides to produce haploid spores. The witch cannot reproduce so she cut off her fingers to try to grow clonal children. A lot of Bryophytes are very successful at clonal reproduction. Some produce specific structures like little balls of cells or have leaves that easily break off and can grow into a whole new plant. Totipotent means that a whole plant can be grown from a single cell. Bryophytes have the ability to do this naturally.

Sara asked me to name one of my favourite bryophytes. I used to work at Kew Gardens as a conservation officer, managing a collection of threatened bryophytes from the UK. I worked quite a lot on one species, *Orthodontium gracile*, trying to reintroduce it. *Orthodontium lineare* is a non native species, and a more successful competitor than *Orthodontium gracile*. Making a yogurt culture with cut-up leaves is one way to start a colony. I like that the Witch selected some *Aplodon wormskjoldii* to help hide the murder. It's a species that grows on rotting carcasses or dung, a good choice to cover a dead body.

At the moment I'm not working with moss, but with *Arabidopsis*. It was the first plant to have its entire genome sequenced. We're looking at how it adapts to different climate regimes. We grow them in greenhouses or growth cabinets with light and temperature controls and then count fruit, branches or leaves, to see how the plants change over time and under different regimes. It's hoped the work will help us to understand how plants adapt to climate change.

I thoroughly enjoyed Sara's story. It did a great job of imagining an intelligent, human-like creature who works like a bryophyte.

Death Knocks

Ken MacLeod

I hate death knocks.

Fifties council house, eighties right-to-buy exercised, neat front garden. Door painted Forth Bridge red. Not recently, but that hardly matters. The paint wears hard. I rang the doorbell.

A minute went by before a shadow loomed behind the net and the bolt rattled back. The door opened a quarter of the way. Guy looked way older than I'd expected. Thin flat hair, yellow, combed across. Smudges under the eyes and lines on his cheeks that could have been drawn with a burnt match.

'Good morning,' he said, not meaning it. 'Who're you?'

'Good morning,' I said. 'John Kirkland. Sorry to disturb you, Mr Boyd. It's about Gary.'

His face twitched. 'You from the council?'

'No,' I said, showing him my card. 'I'm from Byline. We're a news agency. We write stories that get printed in the papers.' I saw instant objection narrow his eyelids. 'We wondered if you'd like to give us... some kind of tribute to Gary.'

'You've come at a bad time,' he said.

I looked at the step. 'I'm sorry,' I said. 'It's just–'

'What kind of papers?' he asked.

'Any and all of them,' I said. '*Telegraph*, *Express*, the

Sun, the *Mirror*, the *Record*...'

'Don't want Gary's name splashed in they shite papers.'

The door began to close.

'Mr Boyd!' I said. 'If you want to have a word, and you speak to me, we'll have the story out first, and no one else will bother with it. I promise you it'll be respectful. And that'll be the end of it.'

The gap widened again, then Boyd stepped out, leaving the door half-shut behind him.

'Aye. All right. But there's no story.' He shrugged. 'The lifeboat pulled his body from the Firth, down past Hound Point. Jumped off the Road Bridge. No reason I can see. Bright lad, loved his job, loved the Army...'

Soldier suicides are always a story. I've death-knocked a dozen. Always the same. Home on leave. Best mate blown up, IED in Peshawar, ambush in Helmand... something like that.

'Where was he home from?' I asked, scribbling.

'He was never away,' said Boyd. 'No in Pakistan or Afghanistan or that. He bides in this house.'

I looked up from the pad. 'So what did your son do?'

Boyd blinked. 'He's no my son.'

I must have looked confused.

'No story there, either,' said Boyd, sounding angry. 'He's – he was my grandson. I brought him up from –' he lowered a hand, palm out '– that high. His mother, my lassie – well, no story there, or an old story.'

I decided to let that pass, for now. 'And what did Gary do in the Army?'

'Admin or something. No combat.'

'Could it have been anything... in his personal life?'

'He'd no had his heart broken, if that's what you're asking. No regular girlfriend. Played the field, like. He was only twenty-two. Twenty-two.' Boyd shook his head. 'And no other problems. No drugs or money worries or that.'

'And when did you last see Gary, Mr Boyd?'

'Couple of nights ago. He was just going out in Dunfermline. Had a few drinks with his mates in The Californian. Didn't come back.'

At that point his face twisted and he turned away. I waited, asked a couple more routine questions, thanked him and left.

Back on the street, I phoned my editor.

'There's no story, Chris,' I told him. 'Bridge jumper, no background. I'm heading back.'

'Fine,' said Chris.

The papers around Edinburgh don't cover Road Bridge suicides. Not unless there's a reason strong enough to outweigh the danger of giving people ideas. There didn't seem to be one here.

At Dunfermline Station I spotted Alec Lawson, one of my classmates from the journalism course at Telford and now a junior reporter on *The Scotsman*. I ambled over and said hello. After we'd caught up on a few bits of personal trivia we eyed each other warily, not talking about the job. Finally I shrugged.

'Death knock, no story,' I said.

'Same here,' said Alec. He looked away for a second. 'It kind of cut me up, to be honest. A lad younger than us doing himself in like that.'

'Like what?'

'Car engine on, garage door closed.'

'Shit.'

'Soldier and all.'

'That's a story,' I said.

'Nah,' said Alec. 'It's no fucking story. He was some kindae Army clerk. His mum was so pleased he never got sent off to the wars.' He shook his head. 'No fucking explanation. Happy guy. Out of the blue.'

'No background, no story,' I said. 'Ah well.'

'How about yours?'

I lied flat out. 'Sudden death that turned out to be natural. Kid had a congenital heart condition. Might sell it to a medical columnist, but 'no story' is more likely.'

Yeah, I felt bad, but all's fair in this biz. It was up to Alec to check it anyway.

The train came in and we talked indie bands all the way to Waverley. Alec headed south to the *Scotsman* office block in Holyrood. I headed south to Byline's basement place on Leith Walk. Two soldier suicides with no combat stress, similar Army clerical background, same area, two no stories? That was a story!

I hit Lexis-Nexis the minute I got to my desk. Searched on Army and suicide, excluding all the war theatres. No stories. No surprise. Then I started searching death notices, throwing in parameters like age ranges, Army ranks and job titles. I was looking for cases that matched that of young Gary Boyd.

Seventeen across the UK in the past year.

That was actually more than the number of PTSD-related combat-veteran suicides over the same period. In terms of population and occupation, it was way out. I ran the same check for the year before. Two.

I took the stats to Chris.

'Designer drugs,' he said confidently.

That was last year's outcry: designer euphorics that give you a real bad crash when the high wears off. For a month or so every youth suicide was blamed on them.

'I don't think so,' I said. 'Every soldiers and drugs story is about smack.'

'Aye,' said Chris. 'That's combat troops in the fucking heroin triangle. If it's desk soldiers, they probably score the same shit as their mates in civvy street.'

'Anyway,' I said, 'for all the fuss there were three actual deaths, all traced to one bad batch.'

'Three? Where did you see that?'

'*New Scientist* last month.'

Chris didn't look as if he thought much of that source. He's never thought the same of the magazine since it ran a global warming cover piece in the winter of 2014. That was the issue that hit the shelves three days late because blizzards had made the roads impassable.

'See if you can come up with something this afternoon,' Chris said. 'Otherwise drop it.'

I thought of ringing around the police stations, Army bases and coroners' offices for quotes, then I had a better idea: go to the prime source for illicit drug designs. I rang the IT department at the University. Ten minutes later I was on my bike.

★

'The Virtual Man runs on *this*?'

'Not exactly,' said Deepak Singh. He patted the top of the Dell workstation, then brushed the dust from his hands as he settled in front of the keyboard. I pulled up a battered swivel chair and sat beside him. Singh's basement office was tiny, cluttered, decorated only with trade posters. Guarding the Virtual Man wasn't, I reckoned, a plum job.

'It runs on the Grid,' Singh explained, firing up the monitor. 'That's a virtual supercomputer built from programs running in background on thousands and thousands of desktops. Using spare capacity as it becomes available, right? Very neat algorithm – first used for SETI at Home.'

I blinked. 'Settee at home?'

'Search for Extraterrestrial Intelligence,' Singh spelled out. 'Looking for a signal in data from radio telescopes. Still going, as far as I know.'

'And still no little green men.'

'Aye, right. Anyway... the Grid's used for lots of big, resource-heavy calculations. Including –' he waved a hand at the screen '– an integrated software model of every organ and system in the human body, the Virtual Physiological

45

Human, a.k.a. the Virtual Man. And there he is, live.'

All I could see was equations – line after line of them scrolling down.

I laughed. 'It's funny, I sort of expected –'

'A 3D colour graphic? No, that's virtual anatomy, for training surgeons and so on. Different beast entirely.'

'Speaking of anatomy,' I said, 'is there a Virtual Woman?'

Singh looked at me, eyes narrowed. 'That's a very sore point. Actually, there is one, but it's a bodge. They're working on it, OK?'

He sounded defensive.

'Fine,' I said, making a note. 'Now, uh, about hacking...?'

'Oh, right!' Singh brightened. 'I can show you that right here.' He clicked on an icon. 'System scan running... nasty bit of spyware there... gone. It works.'

'But not always,' I said. 'The drug designs...'

'Most of these don't come from hacking the Virtual Man,' Singh said. 'They're straightforward reverse engineering, or stolen off legit pharma research. I have to cover that too, of course.'

'That spyware just now was aimed at the Virtual Man, yes?'

'Oh, sure. Russian hacks almost always are. The pharma design thefts come from China.'

'It's the Russian ones I'm interested in,' I said.

'Here's some I've nailed to the wall,' said Singh, tapping away. The screen changed. 'This file starts last September. Let's take it from the top. Most of the street drug design interest is in euphorics and hallucinogens, for obvious reasons. The black labs sponsor programs primed to look out for any work in the relevant brain functions, or anything to do with opiates. These programs are called sniffers. So... here's an example. A lab at the University of Louvain wants to test an intervention in a molecular pathway in endorphin production. As soon as the model starts running, a sniffer that we hadn't yet detected – they change dozens of times a day – reports back to the Russian Business Network. That's the global clearing house for online crime, all sorts of shit. RBN launches its client's probe: a piece of spyware, again too new for the system to catch in the first seconds. It starts logging the model as the calculations churn through. Now –' he pointed to a line that to me didn't look any different from the others '– that's where we do catch it. Our anti-malware firewall has just been updated. It spots the background logging and – smack! The logger's deleted before it finishes copying.

'But then, just a couple of days later, a request to run a model of rhodopsin function in retinal processing comes in from Manchester University. It runs over a few hours and the results go back – to a server in Kiev. When Manchester runs the daily audit, it finds it's been billed for model it never asked for. I poke around, find a vulnerability in Manchester's requisitioning, into which someone has snuck a neat little program to generate fake requisitions. Manchester IT closes the hole, and that attack isn't repeated. Instead, down here – well, you don't need the details. So it goes.'

With that he put the cursor on the sidebar and scrolled the rest of the file. It went on and on.

'So it goes,' he repeated.

'And eventually, these get used to design drugs that aren't illegal yet.'

'Or make already illegal ones hard to detect. Yes.'

I pushed the chair back and gazed at a dusty Oracle calendar.

'What's the lead time?' I asked. 'From hack to street?'

'Six months or so. It's not like they do clinical trials.'

'How do they test them?'

Singh pinched the bridge of his nose where his specs had left a pair of red marks. 'Moscow street kids.'

'Do they kidnap them or what?'

He looked at me like I was stupid. 'Mr Kirkland,' he said, 'these kids *sniff glue*. They swig Ossetian vodka that *makes them go blind*. They fucking *fight each other* to get a chance to pop a tab that'll make them feel good for a few hours.'

'Could we have a look at your file from eighteen months ago?'

He shrugged. 'Sure. Let's see. July. Hmm... nothing much. It's a quiet period.'

'Doesn't look like it,' I said. The screen was thick with lines that somehow stood out from the rest.

'Oh, that's all legit stuff,' said Singh.

'What is it?'

'Classified,' he said. 'MoD.'

'Ah.' I suddenly felt very clever. 'Torture drugs!'

'I know nothing about the research,' said Singh. 'And there are no torture drugs. Torture has been abolished.' He inclined his turban to one side. 'Haven't you heard?'

I couldn't get any more out of him. I thanked him and left.

*

The Californian – where Gary Boyd had gone the night before he died – wasn't the kind of pub I'd vaguely imagined. Just off Dunfermline High Street, recently built, shiny with neon, low-ceilinged and low-lit. More like a cocktail lounge. I bought a beer in a chilled bottle, labelled with a name I couldn't pronounce, and looked around.

Even for eight on a Tuesday night, the joint wasn't exactly jumping. Four women on extended after-work drinks around one table. The inevitable old guy, sipping one of the unpronounceable lagers from a pint glass and wishing he was in a real pub. Three young guys at a corner table. One of them was in a wheelchair. All of them had short-cropped hair.

I strolled over.

'Excuse me,' I said. 'Did any of you know Gary Boyd?'

'Aye,' said the guy in the wheelchair. 'Who wants to know?'

I introduced myself. They glanced at each other.

'Have a seat,' one of them told me. I sat down and nodded to their names: Phil, Steve, Keiran. Phil was the one in the wheelchair.

'You're looking for some kind of story behind his suicide,' Phil said. 'Right?'

'Uh-uh.'

'Aye, well, so are we. He was sitting right where you are last Friday.'

I shivered.

'You've all, uh, been in the Army?'

'We all *are*,' said Phil, to general laughter. 'Home on leave. Going out again next month.'

He noticed my surprise. 'Aye, they take crips back an' aw.' He held out both hands as if squeezing triggers and made his arms shake. 'Don't need legs to work an HMG.'

'Good for you,' I said.

There was an awkward pause.

'Here's tae Gary,' said Keiran.

We clinked glasses and bottles. I took a sip. The soldiers knocked their beers back in one. Keiran made to rise.

'No, no,' I said. 'Let me get this one in.'

It was the first round of several. The soldiers told me tales. I listened, not caring if they were true or not. A couple of hours had passed before Keiran leaned across the low table and said:

'See you? You don't like the Army.'

'What makes you think that?' I asked.

'You're a reporter. They aw hate us. They're aye sticking up for the Pakis.'

I tried to laugh it off. 'Mind the barman doesn't hear you saying that!'

'I don't mean our Pakis. I mean the Jamaat.'

I shrugged. 'I don't agree with you about reporters in general, but even if I did, it wouldn't mean I didn't like the Army.'

'You lot don't have a clue what it's like out there. You just sit on your arses and sound off.'

That one made me bristle. 'Look, Keiran,' I said, 'I've never been out there, and I've never written a thing against the Army. All the reporters – I don't mean columnists, I mean reporters – who criticize the Army, well, some actions of the Army – are *war correspondents*, for fuck's sake!'

At this point Phil chipped in. 'Aye you have so written against the Army.' He waved his phone under my nose. 'See – five years, ten pieces on soldier suicides.'

'Read them, don't just Google them.'

He leaned back in his wheelchair. 'Aye. When I have the time. The headlines don't look too encouraging.'

The third guy, Steve, spoke up. 'Aw, come on guys. Lay off him. It's no his fault what the papers say. It's no even his fault what headlines get put on his reports.'

'You're right there,' I said with some feeling.

But Keiran swayed forward again. 'I can see it in your eyes, man,' he said. 'When Steve told that story –'

'Give me a break,' I said. 'Anyone would've looked a bit disgusted. Thought that was the point.'

'Here's the thing,' said Phil. 'Nobody who's no been out there has any right to pass judgements on what soldiers do.'

'Not even –'

'Not even. And I'll tell you what's bugging me, John. You've been decent enough company, but you came in here sniffing around for some scandal, some way to blame the Army for Gary taking the high jump.'

This was truer than he knew. My suspicion, after what I'd learned from Singh and from four hours of online research, was that the Army was testing some new interrogation drugs – what the part of the press that my current drinking buddies despised called 'torture drugs' – on its own soldiers, voluntarily or otherwise, and that the spike of suicides I'd detected was a result.

But I shook my head. 'I just wanted to know if there was any explanation, that's all. Looks like there isn't. One of these things.'

'Tell you this about Gary,' Keiran said, in a sudden burst of anger. 'He proved he could take it. He might have worked at a desk, but he showed us he was tough enough to be out there if he'd been sent.'

'How did he do that?' I asked.

I was thinking about something in basic training, or maybe some kind of hazing they'd all gone through.

Keiran stuck a hand in his pocket and held out a blister pack of pills.

'He took one of them.'

Phil and Steve looked at him with dismay.

'Keiran,' said Phil, 'shut the fuck up.'

Keiran held his ground.

'What's done's done,' he said.

He turned to me again. 'See if you can.'

'See if I can what?'

'Take one o' they tabs. It'll no kill you. See?'

With that he pressed one of the pills through the foil, placed it on his tongue, and slugged back a gulp of beer.

'Jesus fuck, Keiran!' said Steve.

Keiran gave him a hard smile, then thumbed out another pill onto the palm of his hand and held it out to me.

'Knock it back,' he said. 'Show us what you're made of.'

Phil and Steve were shaking their heads.

'Don't do it,' Steve said.

'What does it do?'

'It'll give you the worst hour you'll ever have,' said Phil. 'It'll make you feel worse than I felt when they told me my spine was shot through. And I'm not talking about pain.'

'There's no pain at all,' said Keiran, still with the grim smile.

I saw the way they were looking at me. Even Phil and Steve.

I took the pill and knocked it back. I felt the beer wash it down my throat.

Keiran smiled again, opened his mouth, and spat the pill he'd taken into his hand.

'Time for a walk,' he said.

★

I had wanted another drink, but there didn't seem to be any point. We left the pub together, Steve holding the door for Phil to wheel through, and me to follow.

We walked up the High Street of Dunfermline. It was the route I'd have taken to the station, but we passed the turn-off and walked on to where there's a bridge over the motorway.

There the three soldiers stopped, and I stopped too.

'How are you feeling now?' Keiran asked me.

The question seemed strange. The idea that I should turn my attention on myself struck me as bizarre. Of all the uninteresting things I was aware of, I was the least interesting. But I forced myself to inspect what I felt.

What I felt was a crushing sense of emptiness and despair. The back of my throat seemed coated with the fine ash of coal. I could recall no other tastes. I was still seeing colours, but they had no tone. I tried to remember how colours had seemed, in the bar only minutes earlier, and couldn't. In that spasm of memory I saw all my past in the same monochrome ashen light, as a long exercise in futility and failure, with nothing to be proud of or to take pleasure in; and my future dark, with nothing to look forward to.

A moment later, a black wave of misery broke over me. Every loss I'd ever suffered crashed through my mind, every hurt raw and fresh again, every missed chance galling. Life seemed worse than pointless. I didn't feel sad, or even emotional. I wasn't about to cry. There wouldn't have been any point. At the same moment – or, perhaps, a second or two later – I experienced a faint pang: I was obscurely, remotely touched that anyone should have any interest in what I felt. I scanned Keiran's face for any trace of concern. If any had been there, I would have seized on it as a lifeline. I would have answered his question. I'd have answered any question he cared to put.

That thought seemed significant: a pebble on an infinite plain of indifference. A minute upward spike in an endless flat line.

But Keiran's look held only a mild curiosity and a milder malice. I stood alone and bereft. I could not remember what happiness was, and I could not imagine ever feeling it again.

I knew I could end this in a moment. The handrail of the bridge wasn't high, the drop to the road below was. The hour that Phil had warned me of stretched out to infinity. I had no reason, after all, to believe it would only be an hour. I had no reason to believe anything.

Keiran waved a hand in front of my eyes. 'How're you feeling?' he repeated.

Again, a flicker of interest, in the same thought: that I would tell him anything if he showed the slightest sympathy. He didn't. But there seemed no reason not to answer the question he'd asked.

'Fine,' I said. 'Good night, guys. It's been good meeting you.'

I walked along the bridge and turned down the long path through the park to the station. At the platform I watched the Edinburgh train's lights approach, and thought how easy it would be to fall under the wheels. I imagined the implacable rolling edges crushing my skull, crunching through my femurs. A moment of agony, and the misery would stop. I thought about how I could topple forward in just the right way for my head to hit the far rail, and about timing my fall too late for the driver to stop. I thought about it carefully, and for too long.

The train pulled in. The doors thumped open. I got on. I stared out of the window on the right, as lights passed – of the motorway, the Road Bridge, the airport, the town – so distant and indifferent and alien they might have been points in a deep field image from the Space Telescope.

I sat in Waverley station until midnight.

Time enough for the drug's effect to wear off, if Phil had spoken the truth. When the clock numbers turned over, I felt a flicker of hope and relief – and from that flicker, I knew Phil hadn't lied. He hadn't lied about the effect, either. He'd just been mistaken about the effect on me. It wasn't any kind of toughness that kept me going. I'm as sure as I ever was that I couldn't endure what he and his comrades had endured. It wasn't love, or faith, or hope that kept me going. For that hour, I'd had none of them.

What I had was a story.

Afterword: Fantastic Voyage

Dr Richard Blake, Director of the Computational Science and Engineering Department of the Science and Technology Facilities Council

I'm working with the Hartree Centre's SimCell and SimOrg projects. Ken MacLeod's story is a timely picture of actual research now being planned. I compare where we are now and where we're headed to the difference between the discovery of DNA and the mapping of the human genome. We're in the foothills of an international project that will take 20 to 40 years.

We're planning to start with a virtual cell – plant cells at first, and then human. We need to get down to the smallest levels of both time and space, to ensure that we can model how a cell works on a nanoscale. We need to be able to recreate how electrons move about a cell, how chemical bonds are made and broken. We need to be able to model structures in the cell itself, most especially the membrane – for example, to see how drugs enter the cell. We need to be able to characterise the receptors on the outside of the cell, how they can be turned on or off.

We then need to drill up, looking at how cells work together to form tissues and organs inside the body, and recreate how these work. In the case of a drug, we'd model how it is swallowed, broken down in the stomach, passed into the bloodstream, and how it alters synaptic responses in the brain. It's a bit like that film *Fantastic Voyage*.

The first step, the virtual plant cell, will help us with the next generation of crops and biofuels, developing crops that could cope with low water and still give high yields.

Once the virtual human is available for research there will be need for far fewer experiments on animals. The costs of validation programmes will reduce and there should be fewer unwanted side effects to drugs.

Ken's story also shows the importance of new forms of distributed computing, now called Cloud Computing, which combines some of the benefits of distributed computing with large central servers to carry out detailed computations. He mentions the SETI project, which worked using many different computers because the individual computation was relatively simple. Complex virtual modelling requires huge simple computations. Those are less easily distributed across different versions of operating systems.

The project is bringing together people in different fields, from chemists to specialists in fluid flow, from biologists who understand the form and function of tissues, to clinicians who understand the questions that need to be asked. The research necessary for this story would mean, for example, that we have a much clearer understanding of how chemical effects on brain cells would feed through into conscious mental states.

The creation of a virtual human will require that we understand real ones better.

For more on the Hartree Centre and its work, visit www.cse.scitech.ac.uk.

Collision

Gwyneth Jones

Does size matter? You can build a particle accelerator on a desk top, but the Buonarotti Torus was huge, its internal dimensions dwarfing the two avatars who strolled, gazing about them like tourists in a virtual museum. Malin had heard that the scale was unnecessary, it was just meant to flatter the human passion for Big Dumb Objects: a startling thought, but maybe it was true. The Aleutians, the only aliens humanity had yet encountered, had never been very good at explaining themselves.

Nobody would have been allowed to keep the Buonarotti on a desktop on Earth, anyway. The voters were afraid an Instantaneous Transit Collider might rend the fabric of reality, and wanted it as far away as possible. So the aliens had created the Torus, and set it afloat out here in the Kuiper Belt as a kind of goodbye present – when they'd tired of plundering planet Earth, and gone back from whence they came.

Wherever that was.

But the Aleutians had departed before Malin was born. The problem right now was the new, Traditionalist government of the World State. A fact-finding mission was soon to arrive at the Panhandle station, and the Torus scientists were scared. They were mostly Reformers, notionally, but politics wasn't the issue. Nobody cared if Flat-Earthers were in charge at home, as long as they *stayed* at home. The issue was survival.

Malin and Lou Tiresias, the Director of Torus Research, were checking rad levels after a recent gamma burst, using high-rez medical avatars. There was a gruesome fascination in watching the awesome tissue damage rack up on their eyeball screens... Luckily the beast needed little in-person, hands-on maintenance. Especially these days, when it was so rarely fired-up.

No transiters would ever take any harm, either. They weren't flesh and blood when they passed through this convoluted way-station.

'At least they're scientists,' said Lou. 'My replacement, the Interim Director, is a high-flying gold-medal neurophysicist, *and* a media star.'

'Huh. I bet she's a Flat-Earther of the worst kind,' growled Malin. 'What d'you think's going to happen, Lou?'

The World Government was supposed to leave the Panhandle scientists alone. *That was the deal.* In return, it must be admitted, for past services the researchers would rather forget –

'I'm afraid they're going to shut us down, my child.'

Lou gave a twirl, and a crooked grin. Hir avatar wore a draped white gown, a blue-rinsed perm, rhinstone wingtip glasses and a pantomime beard: an ensemble actually quite close to the Director's real world appearance. With some members of the Torus station community, you had to ask them if they preferred 'he', 'she' or the unisex pronoun. Lou, the funky, reassuringly daft, all-purpose parent figure was obviously a 'hir'.

'It's a question of style,' he explained, ruefully.

There were few of Malin's colleagues who hadn't fooled around most *un*-traditionally with their meat-bodies, and few who respected the boring notion of mere male or female sex.

Malin digested the thought that Lou was to be replaced by some brutal, totalitarian, politicised stranger.

'Will we be black-listed?'

'Not at all! They'll send us home, that's all.'

Malin had glimpsed movement, on the edge of her screen: sensed a prick-eared scampering, a glint of bright eyes. Who was that, and in what playful form? People often came to the Torus: just to hang out in the gleaming, giant's cavern, just to delight in the sheer improbablity of it... They say deep space is cold and bare, but Malin lived in a wild wood, a rich coral reef, blossoming with endless, insouciant variety. It thrilled her. She loved to feel herself embedded in the ecology of information, set free from drab constraint: a droplet in the teeming ocean, a pebble on the endless shore –

'I don't want to go home,' she said. '*This* is home.'

To the Deep Spacers, mainly asteroid miners, who used their sector of the Panhandle as an R&R station, the Torus was a dangerous slot machine that occasionally spat out big money. They didn't care. The scientists were convinced their project was doomed, and terrified they'd never work again once the IT Collider had been declared a staggering waste of money. The night before the Slingshot was due to dock they held a wake, in the big canteen full of greenery and living flowers, under the rippling banners that proclaimed the ideals of Reform, *Liberté Egalité Amitié...* They toasted each other in the Semillion they'd produced that season, and talked about the good times. It all became very emotional. Dr Fortune, of the DARPA detector lab, inveterate gamer and curator of all their virtualities, had arrived already drunk, attired in full Three Kingdoms warrior regalia. He had to be carried out in the end, still wildly insisting that the Torus staff should make a last stand like the Spartans at Thermopylae and sobbing –

'*An army of lovers cannot lose!*'

Nobody blamed him. The DARPA bums (the lab teams were all nicknamed after ancient search engines) had switched off their circadians and worked flat out for the last 240 hours, gobbling glucose and creatine, trying to nail one of those elusive *turnaround* results that might save this small, beloved world; and they had failed.

The 'fact-finders' arrived, and immediately retired to the visitors' quarters, where they could enjoy stronger gravity and conduct their assessment without bothersome personal contact. The Interim Director herself, alas, was less tactful. The science sector was a 4-spaced environment, permeated by the digital: Dr Caterina Marie Skodlodowska didn't have to signal her approach by moving around in the flesh. You never knew when or where she would pop up – and her questions were casual, but merciless.

She asked Lou could 'he' envisage building *another* Torus. (Dr Skodlodowska didn't buy unisex pronouns).

'Of course! Eventually we'll need a whole network.'

Lou was wise, but 'he' lacked cunning.

'Eventually. Mm. But you've analysed all those esoteric Aleutian materials, and you can synthesise? Strange that we haven't been told.'

'We don't have to synthesise, we can *clone* the stuff. Like growing a cell culture, er, on a very large scale.'

'So you don't yet know what the T is made of?'

'But we know it *works*! Hey, you use Aleutian gadgets you don't understand all the time on Earth!'

She asked Lemuel Reason, the fox-tailed, clever-pawed technical manager of the Yahoo lab, exactly how many lives had been lost.

'Very few!' said Lemuel, glad to be on safe ground. 'Er, relatively. We don't fire-up unless we're pretty sure the destination is safe.'

The Deep Spacers were volunteer guinea pigs, in a lottery sanctioned and encouraged by the World Government. They could apply for rights to a sector of Local-Space, and transit out there to see what they could find. Some went missing, or returned in rather poor shape, but a respectable minority hit paydirt: an asteroid rich in gold or exotics; an exploitable brown dwarf. These sites couldn't yet be exploited, but they were already worth big bucks on the Space Development futures market.

'I was thinking of the so-called Damned, the political and Death Row prisoners shipped out here for so-called Transportation. I believe you'll find the losses were 100%, and the numbers run into many hundreds.'

Skodlodowska was referring to a sorry episode in the Panhandle's history. The 'Damned' had been despatched to supposedly Earth-type habitable planets, the nearest of them thousands of light years 'away' by conventional measure. They'd been told that their safe arrival would be monitored, but that had been a soothing lie, for only consciousness, the *information* that holds mind and body together, can 'travel' by the Buonarotti method. Did Lemuel have to explain the laws of neurophysics?

'The mass transits were recorded as successful!' cried the Yahoo.

Dr Skodlodowska smiled sadly.

'The operation was successful, but the patient died, eh?'

They did their best to look busy, to disguise the fact that the great Collider had been more or less in mothballs for years. It was useless, Skodlodowska knew everything, but they had to try. Malin was a JANET, a wake-field analyst. She worked on her core task, sifting archived bit-streams for proof that non-Local transiters had actually arrived somewhere: but she couldn't concentrate. She was poking around in an out-of-bounds area, when her screen flagged a warning and switched to the Buonarotti video, digitised from analogue, that she was using as a safety net... One of the few records of the real Buonarotti to have survived, and quite possibly her only media interview.

'You're going to break the speed of light this way?' asks the journalist.

'Break the what?' says the direly dressed, slightly obese young woman, in faux 4D: twisting her hands, knitting her scanty brows, speaking English with a pronounced, hesitant

European accent. 'I don't understand you. Speed, or light, neither is relevant at all. Where there is no duration there is no *speed*.'

Coming over as both arrogant and bewildered –

'Terrible combination,' muttered Malin, shaking her head.

'The shiny blue suit and the hair? Or the genius and the journalist?'

The new boss was at Malin's shoulder. Dr Caterina Marie in the flesh, slender yet voluptuous in her snow-white labsuit and bootees, and (you betcha) absolutely darling lingerie underneath. The female lead for a C20 sci-fi movie: brave, maverick, beautiful lady scientist. *But there's a Y chromosome in there somewhere*, thought Malin, malignly. She didn't have the genemod for detecting precise shades of sexual identity, but she had friends who did, and something must have rubbed off –

'The format.' Shame at her secret rudeness made Malin more open. 'Imagine how it sounded. Kirlian photography. Auras. Breaking the mind-matter barrier. All those ideas, totally bizarre to the general public of the time. But TV interviews aren't everything. Give her a smartboard, let her turn her back on the audience, she'd dazzle you.'

'I think you like her,' remarked Caterina, in a voice like dark honey.

'What I know of her, I think I like. But Buonarotti is ancient history and we don't have her notes. The important thing is that our Torus *works*.'

'I keep hearing that. The Torus does *something*,' corrected the Director, 'It makes people disappear, *very* expensively. I grant you that.'

Malin forced a smile: it hurt her face. The Transportation episode had been before her time, but she still felt that guilt. So now it was Malin's turn to get fried, or to win the boss over. Ten seconds to save the world –

They didn't have Buonarotti's notes. Everything had been lost in the chaos of the Gender Wars: all they had were

fragments, and the prototype 'device' that had been rescued by the Aleutians from the wreckage of battle. To Malin the truth was still self-evident: but Skodlodowska and her bosses might well feel differently. They were Flat-Earthers, after all—

'Peenemunde Buonarotti invented a means of sending human beings, translated into code by her scanner-couches, around a big collider buried under the rocks of Europe. She split those transcendental packets of code into two, and ramped up the energies so that when they collided, they broke the mind-matter barrier. Nobody understood her, but the Aleutians *did*, and that's how we got the Torus. For an instant, transiters are where speed, time, duration, distance don't exist. If they've been programmed with a 4-space destination, then *instantly* that's where they'll be. No matter how far —'

She took a deep breath.

The Torus was a black box that seemed, fairly definitely, to take people instantaneously across light years. But proof was elusive.

'You can't shut us down!' Malin began to babble, unnerved by Dr Skodlodowska's silence. 'This is the gateway to the stars! We have gas giant moons, asteroid areas, planetoids, where the prospects for mining are *fabulous*. We have the habitable planets, where you could move in next week. Okay, okay, it's all in need of development, but what we do isn't magical, it's *proven*. There's absolutely no doubt that instantaneous transit happens. We see the event. The only thing we don't have —'

She was out of breath, out of time.

'Is a repeatable experiment,' said Caterina, dryly. 'Isn't that what divides science from pseudoscience? Oh, don't look like that —' She laid a hand on Malin's arm, and the touch was a shock, warm and steady. Her dark eyes glowed. 'Your enemies are back on Earth. *I'm on your side.*'

Yeah, right, thought Malin. That's why you're asking all the awkward questions, and sending our stupid babbling straight back to Earth. But when Caterina had gone she thought it over, staring at the movie of Buonarotti: and then, with sudden decision, opened the file she'd been working on before the boss appeared. Not exactly *secret*, but a little hard to explain.

The DARPA team, as their nickname suggested, were all about destination coordinates: how the linkage between consciousness and specific 4-space location happened. The Yahoos and the Googles studied the human element, the transiters themselves. The possible JANETs (named for a long ago academic and science network) looked for news from nowhere, postcards from Botany Bay... Somewhere in the wake of the monstrous energies of collision, there should be buried fragments of sense-perceptions from the other side. The S-factor, the physical organism, had arrived in another place. Eyes had opened on alien scenes, skin had felt the touch of another planet's air. There must be some irefutable trace of that landfall, leaking back from the future. The JANETs hadn't found it yet but they lived in hope.

Malin had been figuring out ways of reducing the P-factor interference (essentially, stray thoughts) that disturbed the wake of a collision. It had been observed that certain transiters, paradoxically, seemed to *dream* in non-duration. There were brainstates, neuronal maps that cognitive analysis translated as weird images, emotional storms, flashes of narrative. It was rich stuff, but all useless crap, since everything had the signature of internally generated perception. But *why* were some transiters having these dense and complex dreams? What did it mean?

What if you flip the gestalt, see the noise as signal?

Malin searched in forbidden territory, the personal files of the Damned. Alone in a virtual archive room, in the middle of the night, she felt herself watched. She looked over her virtual shoulder and, inevitably, there was Caterina – leaning against a filing cabinet, dark hair a shining tumble: hands in the pockets of a white silk dressing-gown.

Malin's avatar wore nubbly old Rocketkid pyjamas.

'Of course, you can explain yourself,' said the vision. 'You wouldn't be doing something so illegal and unprofessional if you didn't have very good reason. Do you know how much trouble you're in?'

Malin nodded. 'Yes, but these files are banned because of data protection, nothing scientific, and I'm not looking at personal information. I think I'm onto something. See here –' She shared her view. 'See this? Hyper-development in the *anterior insula*, and the *frontal operculum*? That's not uncommon, it indicates a natural-born, life-experience augmented talent for handling virtual worlds: a gamer, a fantasist, a creative scientist. I have a group of these people, all showing the same very unusual P-stream activity in the event-wake. The backwash of the collision, that is. Like layers of new neuronal architecture –'

'What's that extraordinary *spike*?'

'That's what I'm talking about.'

'But these are induction scans, decades old. Are you telling me that what happened in the Collider retroactively *appeared* in their files?'

'Yep, it's entanglement effect. We get them, spooky effects. In terms of intentionality, we're *very* close to the Torus.'

Ouch. Traditionalists, Malin reminded herself, were *repelled* by the strangeness of the new science.

The boss did not flinch. 'What d'you think's going on?'

Desperation generates blinding insight. Back in the JANET lab, Malin had seen, grasped, *guessed*, that Caterina Marie Skodlodowska really was on their side. Her questions were tough, but that was because she had hardliners to convince at home. She wanted the Torus to live!

Malin drew a breath. 'I've been trying to eliminate 'stray thoughts' from the information-volume where we'd hope to find S-traces from the remote site. Probability-tunnelling back to us. In certain cases I'm seeing P-fragments of extraordinary complexity. I think they're mapping the equation of the transit. When you have a problem that's too big to handle, subsituting imagery for the values is a useful technique.'

Caterina paid attention. 'You mean, like a memory palace?'

'Yes! I think I'm seeing prepared minds, impelled by the collision with the mind/matter barrier to *know* what's happening: where they're going and how. They're experiencing, processing this knowledge as a virtual world!'

'That sounds dangerously like meddling with the supernatural.'

It's a bit late to worry about that, thought Malin, exasperated, and forgetting that Cat was not the enemy. Down all the millennia, people like you have said science is 'challenging the Throne of God'. The funny thing is, your 'God' doesn't seem to mind. Your 'God' keeps saying to us, *Hey, wonderful! You noticed! Follow me, I have some other great stuff to show you –*

'Not supernatural, purely neurology. Brain-training. We could do the work here on the Panhandle. We need to be able to handle complex virtual worlds, so we have the equipment. We're just not allowed to ramp it up, because of that 'destroying the fabric of reality' thing, you know, creating exotic brainstates close to the Torus.'

'I see you've given this some thought,' said Caterina, without a sign of alarm. 'There would certainly be some risk.'

'I think it's worth it. What's happening here, in these files, is involuntary and uncontrolled. If we could get people to do the trick voluntarily, we'd have your repeatable experiment! I could be a candidate myself, I've spent enough time in virtuality –'

'You could turn yourself into a quantum computer?'

'I *am* a quantum computer,' said Malin (and heard herself, arrogant and bewildered as Buonarotti). 'That's what consciousness is, like the universe: a staggering mass of

66

simultaneous, superimposed calculations –'

Caterina's avatar was ripping through the data. 'You're saying that some of the Damned made successful transits. Why didn't they come back?'

'Would you?'

'Good point.'

'Theoretically there's no problem about 'coming back'. Imagine a stretched elastic. It *wants* to rebound. The difficulty should be *staying*, at the remote site, I mean. That is, until we have a presence there, to anchor people in the new reality. Another station.'

'What about the Lost? Why didn't they 'rebound'?'

They died, thought Malin. They were annihilated, unless they had this fortuitous ability; or at least someone in the party did.

'I don't know.'

That strange glow rose in Caterina's eyes (her virtual eyes); which Malin had seen before and could not quite interpret.

'Well... I think you've set us a challenge, Malin.'

So they were off, Malin the possible JANET and her polar opposite. Skodlodowska chose the destination. She decided they might as well go for the big prize: one of the Transportation planets, where they should find Earth-type conditions. Maybe they'd meet some of the Damned! The science teams, in a fever of hope, prepared to fire-up the Torus. The fact-finders stayed in their quarters, and communications with Earth (as far as Lou could discover) continued undisturbed. It looked as if Caterina wasn't telling her Flat-Earth bosses that she planned to take this crazy leap into the void.

Malin spent hours in the neuro-labs, getting her brain trained under the supervision of Dr Fortune, gamer-lord of the Panhandle's virtualities.

'You're fraternising with the enemy,' he warned her.

'Fraternising's a dirty word. I'm offering the hand of

friendship.'

'You'll be sorry. You don't know what she really wants.'

'She wants to make a transit, obviously. It's her secret dream.'

'Yes, but *why*?'

'I'm hoping it's the everlasting fame and glory,' said Malin.

The mystery bothered her, too.

All transiters, even the humble 'prospectors' had to do some brain-training. They were schooled in handling, visualising, internalising their survival kit: so that the pressure suit, rations, air supply would transit with them, imprinted on the somatosensory cortex; and they wouldn't turn up naked in hard vacuum. Malin had to do a lot more. She was building her memory palace, a map for the equation of the transit. They had decided, playing safe, that it should be a starship. Visualise this, Malin. Choose the details and imprint them. Internalise this skin, this complex exo-skeleton. The ship is the journey. You are the ship, and you are with your crew, inside the ship −

'Conditions for supporting *human* life?' wondered Caterina. 'Is that necessary? Why not a completely new body and chemistry?'

'Maybe it could be done,' said Malin. 'Not easily. We unravel S from P by mathematical tricks in the lab, but consciousness and embodiment evolved together. They're inextricable, far as we can tell.'

'So on the other side, it's the real me, who I always was?'

'Yeah, I suppose.'

They had lain down like prospectors, in the Buonarotti couches in the transit chamber: and they had 'woken up' on board. Malin remembered the transition, vaguely as a dream, but she'd forgotten it was real. Reality was the ship, the saloon, their cabins; the subliminal hum of the great engines. Malin's desk of instruments, the headset that fastened on her cranium, sending ethereal filaments deep into her brain. She was the Navigator.

Caterina, of course, was the captain.

They lived together, playing games, preparing food, talking away the long idle hours, as they crossed the boundless ocean of information –

'My name isn't really Skodlodowska,' Cat confessed.

'I didn't think it was!'

'I liked you straight away, Mal, because you're so *normal*, except kind of unisex. I'm sorry, but I find bodymods unnatural and repulsive –'

Oh yeah?, thought Malin: but she understood. Caterina hadn't chosen her genemods. She had been compelled, by pressures no Reformer could understand, to make herself into a beautiful, risk-loving woman.

'My *thoughts* are very perverse,' she said, solemnly.

Caterina snorted. They giggled together: and Malin shyly reached out to take the captain's hand.

A shipboard romance, what could be more natural? What could be more likely to anchor them in the faux-reality, and keep them safe? Dr Fortune had warned them that they would be scared, that what was 'really happening' was utterly terrifying; and it would bleed through. But what frightened them most, even in the closing phase, when Malin never left her desk, and the starship, rocked by soundless thunders, seemed to be trying to fall apart, was the fear that they would be enemies again, on the other side.

Landfall was like waking. Malin was lying on what seemed to be a mudbank, among beds of reeds as tall as trees. The air smelt marshy, acrid. She turned on her side, she and Cat smiled at each other, rueful and uncertain.

They got to their feet, and stared at each other.

Skodlodowska's beautiful white scientist-suit was somewhat altered: wider across the shoulders, flat in the chest, narrow in the hips. Malin wore her ordinary station jumper, a little ragged at the wrist and ankle cuffs.

'Oh my God,' gasped Malin. 'We made it!'

'I'm a *man*,' whispered Caterina, in tones of horror.

'Yeah, and I'm a woman. Shame, I always hoped I was an intersex in a woman's body, deep down. It's much *cooler* to be an inter! But hey, nobody's perfect. Cat, pay attention, we're here, we did it!'

Malin had started skipping about, wildly excited.

'I thought breaking the barrier would give me my *true* body –'

'Oh for God's sake, come on! We've done it! The repeatable experiment! Interstellar scheduled flights start here!'

Four slender bipedal figures had appeared, beyond a gleaming channel that didn't quite look like water. Scanty golden fur covered their arms and shoulders, longer fur was trained and dressed into curls in front of their ears, and they wore clothing. They kept their distance, murmuring to each other.

In that moment, still in the penumbra of the collision, Malin saw the future. She knew that she would be the first Navigator, carrying unprepared minds safely through the unreal ocean. She would see the Buonarotti Transit become a network, trained crews an elite, and these weird voyages frequent; though never routine. She saw, with a pang of loss, that the strangeness of the universe was her birthright: but there was another world, of brittle illusions and imaginary limits, that was forever beyond her reach.

But Caterina was shaking fit to tear herself apart, and Malin suddenly realised that what had happened to the Lost could *easily* happen again, to the two of them. Quickly, rebound. Set the controls, the mental switches.

Return.

Afterword: No Final Word

Dr Kai Hock, Lecturer in Accelerator Physics at Liverpool University. He designs small accelerators that can be used for cancer therapy.

The things we think are true today will not be true in one hundred years time. If you used a mobile phone a hundred years ago, people would have thought it was magic.

It is possible that the physicists of today are wrong, that even Einstein's relativity is not completely correct. Newton was considered the authority in physics for hundreds of years. He was right in most of his theories, except for some things. For example, he assumed that an object could continue gaining speed without an upper limit. Einstein's equations show that there is an upper limit, which is the speed of light.

Yet, this limit remains an extrapolation. It is based on the prediction that the amount of energy needed to accelerate an object to light speed is infinitely large. Since it is not physically possible to have an infinite amount of energy, physicists often think that the speed of light is like an infinitely high barrier that cannot be climbed. Many other things in Einstein's theories of relativity have been tested. It's a theory, a good one, but theories are overturned. The fact that particles have never been observed to go faster than light does not mean that they are not able to do so. No one has seen the Big Bang.

The Large Hadron Collider at CERN collides particles, creating new, exotic ones. The theory is that these recreate conditions just after the beginning of the universe, often known as the Big Bang. The theory is an extremely good one, but we still need to spend billions of dollars to build the accelerator. The accelerator is used by particle physicists, and their results are in turn used by cosmologists and astrophysicists to test this theory to see if it fails.

I think it's unlikely that we will have interstellar travel with our current technology. There would need to be a new, unknown science. In Gwyneth's story human technology has left us trapped at the very outer edge of the solar system, but an alien technology we don't understand and can only barely operate, seems to be able to send us to distant star systems. It works by reducing us to elements, splitting us and then colliding those elements.

Gwyneth's story reminds us that science has not yet said its final word because so much is still unknown. *Dr Who* with his TARDIS or *Battlestar Galactica* with its jumps across space still retains a place in our imagination. What if we could somehow tunnel through the 'light barrier' without having to climb over it?

Without a Shell

Adam Marek

The taste of porridge was still in Bucky's mouth when he saw the guy explode. First there was a flash, like fireworks on the ground, then the crack and boom of the soundwave rolling out across the pavement, flipping cars up onto their backs, throwing kids against the school railings. For the briefest moment, Bucky saw the guy come apart, his insides effervescing, continuing in the direction he had been running before he detonated himself. And then the explosion picked Bucky up, rattling against his visor, and dumped him into a privet hedge.

There were shouts and the roar of fire exhausting itself on the inside of a pizza van. Teachers calling everyone inside. The sounds that always came before the sirens.

In assembly, they all lay on their backs on the gymnasium floor with their eyes closed. The place stank of smoke and static and shoe leather. An old CD of nineties pop hits played through the PA system. The voice of the singer repeating the invitation 'come on Barbie, let's go party' almost smothered the sounds of their uniforms working.

All around Bucky, the uniforms purred against the battered bodies of the students, teasing out their bruises, anaesthetizing their cuts, sewing back together their skin. Bucky's collar worked at his neck, licking out the stickiness where a branch had torn into him.

The teachers sat on chairs at the side of the hall. A

chunk of Mrs Abernethy's frizzy white hair was missing at the side, the ends blackened where it had been. Her eyes were closed and her little fists were on her lap.

When all the uniforms were silent, the sound of the music was faded out slowly, easing them back into themselves. They sat up, crosslegged, as Mrs Abernethy took to the podium. Here, backlit by the screen, the bite taken from her bonnet was obvious to all, and a murmur spread among them.

'Yes,' Mrs Abernethy began. 'A warning to me, to us all, to never be without our full guard.' The murmuring grew louder, but she stopped it just by straightening her neck.

Next to Bucky, Dill whispered, 'shame it didn't take her bloody head off.'

Bucky lifted the fingers of one hand, a signal that silenced him.

'Once when I was a girl,' Mrs Abernethy continued, 'I was putting on a pair of dungarees, which I'd taken fresh from the airing cupboard, when I felt a strange buzzing sensation and then a sharp sting in my side. A bee had flown inside them while they hung on the line, and then my mother had unknowingly folded the bee inside the clothes, where it had stayed silent all night until I disturbed it. It was the first time I'd ever been stung, and the shock made the pain much worse than it really was. I made a terrible fuss and brought my mother running upstairs who thought something truly awful had happened to me. Once I was out of my dungarees, my mother shook them, and the bee fell out and crawled across my bedroom carpet. My side was throbbing, the most ugly pain I'd ever felt. I was so angry with this bee that I picked up a book to dash its little brains on my floor. But before I got to it, the bee flew up and out of the window. My mother told me not to worry, that it was already dead, because a bee's sting, once thrust into skin, remains, and is tugged from the bee's body. It would soon be dead, and no longer had the means to harm anyone else.' She paused and looked across at the students, her fingers coming to the edge of the lectern for emphasis. 'At least the bastards always die,' she said. 'At least we have that.'

The first time Bucky put the uniform on, his mum had cried as she smoothed the fabric over his arms and squeezed his shoulders. He asked her what was wrong, but she shook her head. He never understood what was going on with her. Was she proud of him because of everything the uniform signified, or was she afraid for him, knowing that the uniform would make him stand out, would incite jealousy and rage?

Before Bucky's school had the uniforms, the attacks were few and randomly spread among all of the city's schools. But giving these children special protection made them a special target. The suicide bombers knew exactly whom this country least wanted to lose. And even better for them, any bomber with a shred of conscience could continue with their mission, knowing that it would achieve the objective of increasing terror and newspaper columns while doing no permanent damage to the kids. It was like they said, if there was a nuclear strike, the only things left standing would be the roaches and the kids of Aleksander Academy.

The attacks had got a hundred times worse since they started wearing the uniforms, and now they could never go back to not wearing them.

Gym class. They played football in their house teams for points. Bucky was in Radcliffe, the blue house. At the other end of the gym, the five Skinner kids in green were on the balls of their feet, ready to move.

The whistle blew, and Mr Castle chucked the ball into the centre. Bucky ran for it. His mirror position on the other side, Gayle, ran too, something fearsome in the way her mouth guard lit up her face. He saw only her, charging forward, the ball forgotten. This time he would not let her take him down. He could not look at her without feeling the familiar cold slam of his back hitting the gymnasium floor.

His heart was thumping, his breath loud in his throat. At the last second, he switched direction, ducking to the side, his arm oustretched to whack her in the chest and knock her to the ground. But she stepped up onto his thigh, leapt high into the air, spun round as he ran past her, and kicked him in the back of the head, sending him sprawling.

His face hit the floor. The ball rolled past. Plimsolls squeeked just in front of his nose. The whistle blew, and in that immediate silence he felt his glove tighten with brutal force, and the crack and fizz as it began to set his broken meta carpel.

'Ten points Skinner!' Mr Castle announced, and then blew his whistle again. 'Someone get him off the court.'

'You suck, Fuller,' Gayle said, grabbing him by the foot and pulling him to the side. Bucky tried to get up, but the room was swirling. He lay there, focusing on a Kit-Kat wrapper under the bench, willing everything to stop so he could get up and rejoin the game.

Gayle Hopper. Whose symmetry was flawless, whose socks were always pulled up, who had once killed a kid.

That's what she told him anyway, the one time they went out on a date. And it wasn't really a date. He had not asked her, and she had not accepted. They just walked together after school, taking the long route, and sat on the old railway bridge throwing stones at the abandoned greenhouses below.

They sucked fizzy lemon sweets, smacking their lips around their stories. She asked him if it was true about his dad getting his head cut off, and he said that it was, knowing that she had already watched the whole thing on YouTube. Everyone at school had. But that she had asked meant she wanted him to think she hadn't watched it, which meant she wanted him to like her. And that made him excited.

'How do you even cope with something like that?' she asked.

'You just do,' he shrugged.

She'd rested her chin on her folded arms on the railings and looked out across the rooftops.

'So is it true that you killed someone?' he asked.

'I don't like to talk about it,' she said, loftily. But after a moment of noisy sweet-sucking, she relented.

Just after they had all been issued their nano-tech military-grade uniforms, there were almost daily clashes between Aleksander Academy and the local comprehensive, known as St Fuckwit's.

A schoolbus had been blown up at St Fuckwit's a few months before, but they were offered no special protection. Battles were played out on the local news between parents and school governors, and on the playing fields behind Sainsbury's by the pupils themselves.

Bucky had not been at this particular clash, but he'd heard that one of the kids had tossed a hub-cap like a Frisbee, and it had smacked Gayle in the visor and made her stumble. Gayle never stumbles. She was mad. She picked the hub-cap straight back up again and grunted as she threw it at the kid. Gayle's aim was perfect. She got the kid straight in the throat and he went down like a sack of shit. They all cheered.

At these battles, there were always more kids from St Fuckwit's than from Aleksanders – Fuckwit's had 800 pupils, compared to Aleksanders' 60, but their aim was rubbish and they had regular uniforms. The first scrap Bucky ever went to, when he got a freckled kid right in the forehead with a pebble and he went down, Gayle had patted his arm and said, 'good one,' and then told him not to worry, that these kids didn't cost their parents anything to make. If any of them didn't get up again, their mum and dad could make another one for free.

Bucky didn't ask Gayle how come she didn't get arrested if she'd killed a kid. It would have popped the bubble they were blowing together.

After Bucky had walked Gayle to her house, he got home two hours late to find his mother standing in the open doorway, the smell of chicken soup pouring out into the street. He tried to explain that his phone had run out of charge, that he'd had his first date with a girl, something which he was certain she'd be proud of. But she didn't hear. Her ears were stuffed full of madness.

Whenever Bucky's mum had to punish him, she did it with the bamboo handle of a broken fly-swat. The swatting bit snapped off years ago, but she kept the handle tucked down the side of the fridge. When it needed taking out, she would brush off the dust with her fingers first, a habit which always puzzled Bucky, as his trousers would clean off the dust anyway. It bothered him that this made no sense. Maybe if he understood it, he would understand a lot of other stuff too.

Things were rarely explained to Bucky, and he suspected that this was because people were afraid of finding out they were less smart than he was.

His mum's cheeks were always red after she'd given him a beating. He didn't know whether this was because it pained her to have to punish him, or if it was a biological reaction to the effort needed to damage him through the uniform.

After a beating, the walk upstairs was always a slow one, and his mum watched him climb, one step at a time. 'Make sure you sit on it for half an hour,' she would say. This was to make sure the suit had time to repair everything, for the little nanotubes to identify the damage and begin their healing regime. If Bucky took his uniform off before the damage was healed, the evidence would remain on him until the next morning when he went to school.

When he sat on his bed, he could feel the seat of his trousers weaving everything back into place, an itchy, buzzing sensation, like he was sitting on a nest of angry ants. From here, he had a clear view right across the common to the school clocktower with its broken face. At dusk, its silhouette was a forlorn shape, hunkered down atop the gymnasium, its head tucked into its shoulders.

In the queue for lunch, Bucky was standing next to Dill. There was a desperation in Dill's eagerness which most of them found repellent, but Bucky was too polite to ignore him. Something about Dill's enthusiasm always drew him in eventually. Dill kicked Bucky's shoe and grinned. 'Where did you tell your mum you're going tonight?' he asked.

'A birthday party,' Bucky said. He took a bowl of green jelly from the fridge and put it on his tray. He'd split his lip when he kissed the gym floor, and couldn't face eating the spaghetti Bolognese, which he knew would make it sting like crazy. His reflection wobbled within the jelly's surface.

'I told mine I was coming to your house,' Dill said.

Bucky chewed the inside of his cheek, wondering whether Dill's parents had his phone number, and whether they might call for any reason. He pictured his mum picking up the phone, and her jaw going tight as his lie was revealed.

He and Dill sat with the other Radcliffes. At the table opposite, Gayle made the face that they made when they were pretending to be Fuckwits, stabbing her knife up and down.

Dill laughed beside him, spitting Bolognese onto the table. 'Better hope you don't get her tonight.'

The speed at which Gayle's affection for Bucky had soured astounded him. For a week after they walked home together, she'd sought him out at breaktimes so their phones could mate, swapping their favourite music and pictures of themselves. They sipped from the same paper cups. One time she'd even feigned stupidity for him, the most selfless gift in an Aleksander's courtship. She pretended she could not identify the third nominalization in a given sentence during the inter-house quiz, allowing Bucky to win that round.

Inter-house competition was encouraged with spit-flying fervour at Aleksander's. The captain of Radcliffe, Valdez, was insane with it, whipping them up into a frenzy of excitement with his legendary pre-competition rhetoric, then giving dreadful beastings in the bogs to anyone who messed up.

Valdez was huge, so Bucky really had no choice but to tackle Gayle at that football match. He'd tried to ease her down as gently as possible. He hadn't meant to knock her out. His head just kind of got in the way.

She'd remained unconscious at the side of the field while Radcliffe roared with celebration, piling into each other. Bucky, dripping with mud, experienced true regret for the first time, and nothing in his uniform was able to heal it.

In study period, Bucky was reading Weschler's *History of the Use of Metaphor and Hypnosis in Warfare* when Gayle elbowed him in the back of the head.

'Fuckwit,' she said, and her fellow Skinners tittered behind her.

Bucky imagined the troops in Kyrgyzstan, and the terrifying hardship they endured. On the frozen mountains, they were attacked with projectiles made of intelligent stuff that burned long after impact, that was trained to sniff out flesh and eat through nano-fabrics to find it. These soldiers did not lie down to allow their uniforms to heal their bodies, they continued to fight while their uniforms worked. It made the attacks that Aleksander's suffered at the hands of Kyrgyzstani sympathisers seem infantile.

Our soldiers had minds trained to resist sleep, to act without hesitation, to attack with relentless spirit. The officers who were Aleksander's graduates had a reputation for stretching the capabilities of the ordinary soldier until they began to act like specials themselves. Bucky found it fascinating what people were capable of.

Already, the officers particularly skilled in Neuro were beginning to specialise. Mr Wotek, Bucky's Neuro-

Linguistics teacher, said that by the time Bucky was ready to graduate, there would be positions for specialist Neuros who would never step onto the battle ground, but would work in labs creating Think-Weapons – something that was science fiction now but on the cusp of reality. Mr Wotek said Bucky had a natural flair for Neuro. He didn't know if it was natural or not, but it was definitely what he wanted to do.

If Bucky's dad had been better trained, if he'd been wearing the second generation of nano-uniforms and not the first, he would not have been captured. He would not have appeared on YouTube surrounded by Kyrgyzstani terrorists with a bag over his head. The same bag that minutes later they would put his head into.

In the last class of the day, Bucky could see the other kids' feet jiggling under their chairs. They couldn't wait for the bell to go. In his head, these little foot tappings, which the teacher's ears were too weak to pick up, were like drumbeats.

The school bell rang. They stuffed their notebooks into their bags and clattered their chairs under the desks. There was excited chatter which no teacher bothered to stifle. Bucky saw Gayle give another Skinner a covert thumbs-up. Their shared anticipation made Bucky's hair crackle.

The alley that ran alongside the playground was filled with the clicks of spinning bicycle wheels. The youngest person present, Taylor, a girl from Mattock who was eight, stood on the back of another Mattock with her arm thrust deep into the glass recycling container at the corner of the car park. As she pulled out each wine bottle, she passed it back to another girl, who set them out in a straight line.

One person from each of the houses was selected with Ipp-Dip-Dog-Shit. They stepped forward and faced each other. Little Taylor put an empty red wine bottle in between them and spun it. It stopped first at Cal Thomson from Radcliffe and then at Huck Yama from Pearson. There were gasps and chuckles because Yama was a monstrous fifteen-year-old built like a bison who had never been knocked off his bike, whereas Thomson was thirteen and had yet to win a round.

Thomson and Yama each took a bottle from the line and smashed off the bottom against the side of the recycling bin. They took bikes from their housemates and cycled up to either end of the alleyway, where they faced each other, waiting.

The kids from Aleksander's clung to the wire-link playground fence, shaking it and shouting the names of the opponents.

Little Taylor looked across to both ends of the alley to make sure they were ready, then called, 'Ichi, ni, san!'

Yama was fastest from the start. Reflections of the buddleia which overhung the alley whizzed across his visor. Thomson's feet rattled against the pedals as he missed them.

Speed was the key to bottle jousting. The playground entrance was directly central between the two start points, so if they travelled at the same speed, the clash would happen there. If one of the combatants could cover more ground though, they would force the moment of clashing inside their opponent's half of the alley. If you managed to do this, it was a huge psychological advantage.

Yama and Thomson met half way up Thomson's run. Yama lanced him in the chest with the broken bottle so hard that it took him off the back of his bike. Thomson's back hit the ground first, his unused bottle smashing beside him. Yama continued on, cycling over Thomson's arm, and chucking the bottle down so it cracked on his helmet. He thrust his fist up into the air to wild cries of excitement from his housemates. Thomson's bike, as if only just realising its rider was gone, fell sideways and scraped against the brick wall.

Three Pearsons ran up the alley to grab their unconscious housemate and lifted him inside the playground. They put him on the roundabout, where he lay, his uniform fizzing against his bruised chest.

The kids had to move fast now. They usually only got two or three rounds in before the police sirens sounded and they had to run. Bucky was picked in the next four, as was Gayle. When little Taylor spun the bottle, it stopped at her. When it span a second time, Gayle stepped on it so that it stopped in front of Bucky. To argue would have been cowardly.

Gayle picked up two bottles and clashed them together to break the bottoms off. She threw one of them to him and he jumped aside rather than attempting to catch it. It shattered around his feet and the Skinners laughed at him, and called him chicken-shit. Bucky picked up a bottle, whacked it against the container, and wondered how one simple mistake on his part could have turned Gayle into this snarling wildebeest who couldn't wait to gore him.

Bucky cycled up to his end of the alley, looking at all the kids' fingers poking through the fence.

Was it always going to be like this with her? Did he have another two years of it before he graduated?

They faced each other. Gayle was salivating over her handlebars. Little Taylor took her position and held her arm in the air.

Bucky stuck his hand up to stop little Taylor. He put the bottle down, then began to undo the buttons of his jacket. He ignored the confused murmurs from behind the fence, and stared at Gayle as he pulled his arms out of the sleeves and dropped the jacket to the ground. Gayle did not move at all until he started on his shirt buttons, when she stood up on the pedals of her bike, perplexity showing in the tilt of her head.

Through the fence, the Radcliffes began to shout. Valdez, the Radcliffe captain yelled at him to put his uniform back on. Bucky knew why he was angry – if Gayle really messed him up, the teachers would have to take notice.

Maybe they'd even put a stop to it.

Bucky took off his helmet and placed it on top of his jacket and shirt. He sat on his bike, bare-chested, with a mad grin on his face. Valdez grabbed little Taylor and pulled her back so she couldn't start the race, causing the Skinners to jeer.

Bucky picked up his bottle, flipped it once in the air, caught it by the neck and began to peddle.

Gayle looked at her housemates, confused, angry. She grunted as she set off, shouting, 'Come on!' She swung the handlebars from side to side with the effort of braking the bike's inertia. When the kids from Aleksander's realised Bucky wasn't going to stop, they roared like they'd never done before.

The sound of them, and of the fence bashing against its posts filled Bucky up. The rough wall of the alley blurred and he pushed harder and faster. Gayle was shouting too, showing her teeth. But Bucky was not afraid. He had already won. Like Mr Wotek always says, the person willing to lose the most always wins the battle.

The distance closed between them. Bucky crossed into Gayle's side of the run. There was a moment, just before they met, when he wanted to stop, when he saw spit flying from Gayle's jaws. But nothing could stop him now, not breaking, not even leaping from his bike.

Gayle cocked her bottle-arm back, ready to lance Bucky. Bucky threw his bottle to the ground. It exploded under his wheels. He grabbed his handlebars, put his head down and pushed as hard as he could go. If he was going to let Gayle sting him, it had to be hard enough that she'd never be able to sting him again.

He couldn't watch her in the final moment, he stared at the fence shivering back and forth under the hands of the Academy kids.

At the edge of his vision he saw sunlight flash against the green glass of the bottle, and then... nothing.

Gayle swore behind him and her brakes squealed.

Bucky dragged his feet along the ground to stop the bike and turned to look back.

Gayle threw her bottle against the wall.

'What were you thinking?' she said, then got off her bike and kicked it over.

The Radcliffes cheered and charged out of the playground entrance to slap his bare back. Bucky smiled. That she hadn't lanced him could mean only one thing.

Afterword: Beyond the Military

Dr Vinod Dhanak, Senior Research Fellow in the Physics Department at the University of Liverpool. He has published research in nanoscience and on the use of nanotechnology in body armour, and is currently working on the use of nanostructures on metal surfaces.

Adam's story, though futuristic, represents what researchers in nanotechnology are actually working on.

Most body armour worn by police consists of Kevlar or similar material. Our research has shown that the incorporation of nanoparticles – very tiny structures – into Kevlar reduces the thickness of the material and makes it more resistant to sharp objects. Tests on new polymers incorporating nanoparticles, and known as nanocomposite materials, show that a bullet fired at them spends more time going through the material and loses energy. So these new materials give greater protection against stabbings, shrapnel and bullets.

I've attended conferences in which Chinese and Japanese researchers have discussed facial creams that contain hollow nanoparticles. These are spherical and hollow and, in the event of injury, release drugs. Adam's healing suit could incorporate such creams, as well as carbon nanotubes. In the event of blunt force trauma, they would release chemicals for healing. I'm not a biologist but there are people who are looking at the use of nanotechnology for drug delivery, or to administer nanoparticles into the blood stream so that they deliver drugs to cancer sites.

Another aspect of Adam's suit: it would have sensors that would send information to a doctor about injury, so that treatment can be prepared before the patient arrives. Something like this already exists with the iPod Nike. The shoe senses if you are running and transmits information to your iPod about the calories you are burning or how far you've run. The next step would be to have nano-sensors woven into the fabric of clothes where they would monitor vital information from the wearer, such as heart rate, and transmit the information remotely to a PC in a doctor's surgery.

My current research looks at fullerenes, molecules containing 60 carbon atoms also called Bucky Balls. One of their many interesting properties is that their electronic structure can be altered to make them superconducting. That means current can be carried with less resistance. This reduces the energy needed for devices, making them more portable, and reduces their impact on the environment.

At our university we have colleagues looking at the use of nanoparticles to deliver hydrogen in fuel cells in small, safe, controlled amounts. This would make us less dependent on fossil fuels for our energy needs, and help the environment.

The applications of nanotechnology go well beyond the military ones shown in this tale.

You

Geoff Ryman

The first time you switch on your lifeblog, your eyes feel bigger, heavier. Your eyes are your portal to both worlds, real and virtual. You blink, and see your own present life, as if through the eyes of a fish, rounded, clear and smooth.

You see your own hands. To occupy them, you are knitting, blue yarn with biowires sparkling in it.

That number to the right is a date and time. No, inside your eye. Focus on the middle distance. See it?

The little glowing virtual anatomy is you. That one there, bottom middle. Your physiome. It shows us if you are in pain, under stress or ill. It has a series of recognized emotional states. Right now you are in A: very alert, interested – alive we would say.

Everything you see and hear is recorded and shared. That graph on the left shows how much data has been saved, compared to the amount published on your social server.

You wear the computer and the computer wears you. In a sense your lifeblog is you. It's who you are socially. Trimmed, edited, it's how people see you.

Most of us talk over our lifeblogs, explain as we live like we're telling a story. In a sense who you are has always been a story that you told to yourself. Now your self is a story that you tell to others.

So small, so light, so capacious, the appliance that you

now call your blog not only records but lets you live in other lifeblogs. You can share the day of a celebrity. Share the day of someone long since dead.

So. The lights go on, in someone else's life.

★

You're looking at soil, red soil bare of plants.

You look up, and falling away in layers of tan, ochre and bronze are the silhouettes of cliffs, one growing out of another, going further and further back. There's a small and misty sunset scattered through dust. The shadows are long and cold.

See the date? See the identifier? JoyAnna Haven. Her physiome shows perfect heart and lung capacity, though her age is 39. She's been in training.

This is JoyAnna on Mars.

The sky is the colour of tarnished copper saucepans and the frozen ground underfoot crackles with a thin noise. That's the ice as JoyAnna walks. Numbers dance in her eyes; something is feeding data all the time.

Someone else says, right up close to your ear. 'You know, we never would have the funding for this without you.'

'Naw,' says JoyAnna. 'It's Assumpta Ciges you want to thank.'

All of you start to walk determinably. You see something like a white tent ahead, but it doesn't flap.

JAH: 'She's the one who cracked all this for us.'

'We wouldn't know that but for you.'

'Me? I was just a little info-miner. I didn't even do the basic Software Archaelogy to retrieve it. All I knew was that she'd done some work on the cylinders. So I got a grant to go through her blogs. I thought I'd just blip through at high speed, see what was there.' JoyAnna's chuckle sounds pained. 'I was very young.'

You come to the entrance of the tent, duck and push aside layers of plastic, and then look down in a dimmer light.

A pit has been dug into the Martian surface, its sides supported by plastic battens. A ramp of earth slopes to the floor of the dig, which is perfectly level, though slightly rippled like the floor of a sea. Thousands of tiny objects, a bit like bullets are arranged in the form of a giant spiral with arms, like a galaxy.

JoyAnna says, 'She'd have loved to see this. She died you know, 2030, right in the middle of the big storm. I've got an edited version of her blog stored, if you'd like to go through it.'

The other woman says, 'Yes please.' She sits down cross-legged on the mat.

Bam

You see a street. It's white: the pavements, the asphalt, the rooftops – everything is white, with seamless blue above it, no clouds.

Numbers dance. That's the temperature. It's 29 Celsius, a beautiful summer's day. The air is full of misted light. Find the date. See it? This is 2027. That indicator on the left? JAH to JAH to AC?

That means you're looking at JoyAnna's blog from 2073, but she's looking at her own blog from 2058. And that one is looking at the lifeblog of Assumpta Ciges.

You're seeing Manchester, as it was, one hundred years ago. Next to you is some kind of park – grass, trees, all a livid green. The software archaeologists have done a superb job, resolution, colour, 3D, and sound, all just superb. The eye-camera is rocking from side to side. Assumpta Ciges walks with a limp. See? Six physiomes. Yours. Mine. Assumpta's with her arthritis and replacement hip, two of JoyAnna's, and of course the woman listening on Mars.

That's why they call this vortexing. You just spiral down through layers of other people's lives.

A young voice says, 'Trees! Look at those trees, they're huge!'

The same voice when old says, 'This is so embarrassing!'

JAH: 'I'm looking at private trees. People had trees of their own. It's all so green that it hurts my eyes. And the houses, and the roadway, everything, it's all painted white! I thought it was snow. But Access has just told me, it's paint, they painted everything white, I guess that's to reflect sunlight, increase albedo. And it's so clean, everything. Nothing on the pavements, no horse manure anywhere. Ow! What's that?'

It's a bus. It roars past you all. There's an interesting sign on its side, *Fuelled by biotechnology*. It creaks to a stop, and waits rumbling at a shelter.

JAH: 'Whatever it is, it looks medieval, like some kind of war machine, only so blue and polished, bluer than the sky. And look at the clothes. I mean I don't know what I was expecting. I guess, stupid extravagance, but these are really nice clothes. I mean if it's this warm, they're going to be wearing light stuff, but look, it's all printed in colours. They're functional but also so, so pretty. Why shouldn't things be pretty as well? And all those bicycles, and funny shoes – I don't know what they're made of – and the white is just blinding, against the blue. Everything white, blue, green and then pink, red, yellow on the people, and all the bells from the bicycles. Oh! She's getting on the bus!'

The eye–cameras lurch and sway, and Assumpta's hand holds up a blue card. You can see the sleeve of her coat: it looks as thin and light as leaves. She swings round into a seat, and the camera begins a light continual shiver that makes everything shimmer in white light. Rows of old brick buildings jolt past. Bio-lumescent signs look in daytime like green lichen. Rows of stalls and carts, and all along the eaves, the rooftops, thousands of tiny buzzing windmills.

The bus stops. The cameras limp off it, one step at a time. An Asian gentleman helps her down.

Assumpta says to him, to his crumpled face and his neat grey beard. 'Oh thank you so much!'

JoyAnna old: 'All those beautiful people. Dead.'

Blip

You're looking at red soil again.

JoyAnna old: 'So this is when Assumpta got time with the robot on Mars.'

From someone's life, Assumpta's or one of the JoyAnna's, a toy is playing Handel's *Water Music.*

JAH: 'Outgoing messages to the bot take 9 minutes and the answer takes 9 minutes so we're on an 18 minute cycle. Right now, Assumpta is waiting for the bot to respond.'

All of you wait looking at soil. Handel adorns.

JAH: 'I don't think Assumpta talks enough. Judging from the date, this is just over five years since the cylinders were found. A bot took a core sample, baked it as usual, only it turned out to be full of perfect little cylinders. All with marks on them, in a spiral going round it like a piano roll.'

Someone shows you one of them. Inside your eyes, a cylinder turns. It's tiny, two centimetres long, burned black, flat at both ends. Spiralling round it, are recurring patterns, swoops and swirls.

JAH: 'They look a bit like Arabic, don't they? Everybody was hoping that they were a *cultural artefact.*' She has a horrible regional accent and slices those last two words up into precise little tranches.

Something pings, and with a sudden smoothness, the bot on Mars lifts up its head. Inside Assumpta's eyes, then JoyAnna's and yours, the image comes to life. Broken rocky ground out to a very near horizon, and looming over that bronze cliffs looking just like Utah, a bronze sky, that's dust, but deep purple just overhead. The bot rolls towards a small crane, printed from scratch out of poly on Mars. It's a rough lattice of material.

Assumpta says, 'Rendition.'

JAH: '*Chren-dee-shon*. I love the way she talks. I didn't expect her to sound so Spanish. That's the order to the bot to scan the excavation site. They'll make a laser print of it, so it can be printed in poly back on Earth. We won't begin to see that for 18 minutes. I hope nobody minds if we skitter ahead.'

JoyAnna old: 'Oh no, why would anyone want the experience of walking in a botblog on Mars? We'd much rather hear you, JoyAnna.' Handel skips and jumps; images flicker.

JAH: 'It's a rendition bot. So it will take a laser impression from different angles for the print-out. After that, infrared for compositional analysis. Then we'll get ground-penetrating radar just to confirm that there is nothing else below the one level. Then x-rays to stimulate ultra-violet and other light emissions to help with dating. And EXAFS for structural detail. It's amazing what they were able to do.'

The bot looks down into the trench at a small intelligent digger. Nothing reinforces the sides, and the dig is open to elements. The Spiral opens up its arms to you in natural light. There is a buckling sound from behind the bot, thin in the Martian air.

Suddenly the bot is hoisted up and swings out over the dig. It hangs suspended over it, the cylinders in a neat arrangement, like stars.

There is a blast of light, blanking out the cameras. Colour swirls. Handel plays.

People in those days thought of time as straight. For you now, time spirals.

Blip

And a room trills suddenly into place.

One of the JoyAnnas says, 'This is Assumpta's house, that evening.'

Electric lights blaze. They look like miniature suns. Assumpta has a big box, Refrigerator Access tells you, and the floor is covered in red, fired tiles. Assumpta's hand pours a whiskey rather unsteadily into a glass and she passes it to a man. He's her age, and wearing some kind of absorbent sports wear, though he doesn't look like he runs much.

JAH: 'This is just after the botshare with Mars. The gentleman is Assumpta's client, Tomas Schelling. He paid for the botshare. He's Director of the University's Meridiani Crescent project. Assumpta was already Professor Emeritus at this stage; so she's working for him on a contractual basis.'

Two glasses clink together. Assumpta says, 'The surrounding clay has iron it. The cylinders do not. I don't know if that is significant.'

Assumpta swivels in her chair, to look at a screen on the kitchen table. They were still using terminals. She points to an image of a cylinder, a series of marks at one end of the spiral. Suddenly the marks are highlighted, gold against black.

AC: 'Marks like these appear at one end of all the cylinders.'

TS: 'Some kind of starting point?'

'Assuming that the marks are indeed deliberate. I think they're numbers.'

'Oh.'

JAH: 'He's sounding so un-surprised. His face is absolutely still.'

AC: 'Here look. They differ each time in a very regular way.'

TS: 'You've been able to translate them?'

JAH: 'That's a very careful sip of whiskey that Tomas is taking.'

AC: 'Well. The first is a single mark of a kind I'll call

a twirl. And another twirl and below that, two twirls close together. It could show us one plus one equalling two. The next cylinder in the sequence should be, and yes it is: two plus two equalling four!'

JoyAnna when young makes a coarse little laugh. 'Look at his eyes. It's love. His risky little commission has just come up trumps.'

TS: 'Then they're not numbering the cylinders?'

AC: 'No, but they may be establishing mathematical patterns.'

Tomas Schelling tosses back his head and drains his glass in one.

There is a thin sound of ice and wind. An older JoyAnna says. 'I was privileged to live through Assumpta Ciges's first great mistake. Establishing numerical patterns is what Americans did on the bronze plates on Voyager. That was to show that the plate was a cultural artefact. And because that's what we'd done, we expected something similar from aliens.'

On the screen the cylinder turns, the marks spiralling.

JAH: 'Mysterious little buggers, aren't they?'

Blip

The same kitchen, only now with the sound of rain on windows.

JAH old: 'After that she worked on them for about seven or eight months. Mostly from home; she wasn't very mobile. She drank way too much. It's not a fun blog. I'll just show you this part. Though it always makes me sad.'

Assumpta is feeding sliced chorizo to a tortoiseshell cat. It winds itself around her legs. She looks up, cuts a slice from the dried sausage for herself. On a plate, mozzarella, some lettuce. She eats with her fingers.

In her eyes a cylinder turns.

JAH: She's just called up the 47th cylinder again, turning

it over and over in her eyes. Now she's calling CGIs to help visualize tools that might have made those marks.

On the kitchen terminal, you suddenly see something like a metal corkscrew.

But it's far too inflexible. It obliterates any chance for the more narrow strokes that follow.

So now Assumpta calls up a kind of pen with a soft tip. It flips bits of wet clay, which would account for the prickly-pear nodes that appear on the surface sometimes. She's comparing them. Yes, there's an approximate match.

And for the first time, she's trying to imagine what might hold a pen. So, she's finally begun to imagine aliens, if that's what they are, and how they work. There's a kind of mouth holding the cylinder still, and she's pulling the image like taffy, to create a kind of tentacle that holds the pen.

And now she's laughing at herself. She gives up and just shows a pair of hands. She knows she's come up with a tool for two-handed bipeds. Us.

So she makes the corkscrew flexible. She shows it stretching, thinning, shortening, and fattening. How flexible does it have to be? In the end, she has to make it as flexible as mist, fitting the curlicues.

Assumpta makes it more solid and it looks like a worm.

JoyAnna old: 'This is as far as we'd known for certain that she got. I feel very strange. I really want her to get it, I want her to solve it. She deserves to. But not yet.'

Assumpta twists the worm and shows it grasping the cylinder at one end and turning it like a corn cob. The other end bites out a mark, then turns it, shifts, and bites out the next.

Assumpta turns off the CGI. She's magnifying an image of a cylinder to microscopic scale.

You see the marks at almost nanoscale. The bites are smooth with gliding streaks in them, but nothing like tooth marks or cuts. It's like they've been sucked out of the clay.

Assumpta calls up a CGI of a mouth and she's now making it fit the streaks and smears. She pulls back, and there we have it.

A worm with a mouth.

Assumpta's turned off all imaging. Her physiome shows her bowing. She's put her head in her hands. She says, 'The possibility is that the marks are simply a trace of something eating the clay. The nodes left on the surface are probably just faeces.'

Assumpta tries to laugh. The sound seems to be coming out of the bottom of a well.

JoyAnna young almost shouts. 'Except for the numbers! Assumpta! The numbers. She can't hear me.'

Numbers flip up, tones bleep. That is Assumpta calling up a blog share. Access tells you that that is Shelling's blog ID. She's calling him.

'Dear Tomas.'

She sounds as though she is sending condolences for a funeral.

'I will of course be writing a full report. But as you will see from readings and images attached, I am fairly certain that the marks are simply the result of something feeding on the clay cylinders, probably for the iron content. So the marks are repeated probably because they tended to scoop the clay in a limited number of ways. I wish I had something more satisfactory for you. But I think we can consider the consultancy at a close. As always, it has been a pleasure. I hope you won't mind, but I will continue working on the problem and if there is anything further, I will be sure to let you know. A hard copy will follow for your records, along with my last invoice and record of expenses, which in any case will not be large. Yours as ever, Assumpta Ciges.'

The cat mews; unseen, rain prickles windows, Assumpta stares. Her breath wreathes in the cold.

They were so isolated. They only had one self.

Blip

And then all you see is a floor. Poured concrete, and a sleeping bag full of knees, and next to that a bowl.

Can you guess where you are? Look at the indicator, it says JAH, nothing else, so this is just one level of one blog. Look at the date: 2058. And Handel is playing.

JoyAnna is inside a sleeping bag, and venturing a chill hand out to a bowl of soy crisps. You hear them crunch and a mug goes up to her lips. If this were a modern blog you could at least taste it. From JA's physiome, she's drinking some kind of homemade hooch. Maybe she thinks being slightly tipsy will get her into Ciges's mindset. She looks up: a bare room, with charcoal drawings direct onto a wall. There are windows, which at first look like pixelated screens. The strange popping sound is actually the clucking of hens.

JAH: 'I'm freezing cold. Even with the sun out. They call this our summer. There's a cloud of mosquitoes outside. They just kamikaze into my window screens.'

The windows have a fine mesh across them and we can see mosquitoes swirling around outside. Some kind of alert is flashing inside JoyAnna's eyes.

'My cows' lifeblogs are giving warning signs. They need milking. Their virts usually herd them back from the park to my stable, but I think there's a glitch in their eye receivers and they are not being triggered to hook themselves up to the milking machines. That's not such a huge problem. I just need to get up and walk to the stables. I need to feed my hens, too; the feed is in my backpack. I should just haul it over there and TCB. But I don't want to.'

Her physiome shows a clear X state. JoyAnna in despair. She sits in silence. You look hungrily at the uneaten soycrisps, out of your reach by 80 years.

Then she says just one word. 'Mystery.'

You're probably thinking, well the young JoyAnna was such a little gold digger. She'll just do a search, blip to the end, find the solution, and go off and make her fortune. You haven't been paying attention. No. She goes back inside, to be with Assumpta.

Blip

> She goes right back to the end of that phone call.

> Assumpta strokes her cat, and slowly finishes the chorizo.

> 'Yes, Bertie, yes, I shall feed you in moment.'

> She heaves herself up from the table, finds the cat food, cuts off a slug of it and lumps it onto a plate.

> Then Assumpta thumps upstairs. Rain on the roof. Stockings peel off wearily. She rolls under the covers and finds her book.

> JoyAnna young coughs to clear her throat. 'The Professor Emeritus and ex-President of the British Academy spends her nights reading fanfic gardening slash.'

> Young JoyAnna is content to read with her.

Love in a Changing Climate

Denim's eyes were still fixed on her, as Julie squatted to feel in the soil for potatoes. She knew her jeans were too tight and rode down at the back. It was a bit shameless of her. In the cleft of her exposed butt, a tattoo spelled out the word in Samoan that only Denim could read: LOVE.

> *'Come on, you're supposed to be helping me dig,' she said, and only then realized that it sounded like an innuendo.*

> *Denim's glossy, long black hair whisked against her cheek as he crouched beside her. His great thighs were as smooth as her own. She could smell him, a mixture of sweat and spice and something delicious all his own.*

> *'Do you miss home?' Julie asked.*

JoyAnna whispers, 'My husband left me too, Assumpta. I've got too many keys as well inside my eyes, for the stables, for the dispensary, for my files, my grant ID. I don't spend my days on the phone talking to friends like you do. I've let your friends become my friends. I somehow want the dead to live again, your nephew to get his scholarship; your students to find jobs. I sometimes believe that I could turn a sudden corner and find all the roadways painted white.'

She starts to read again. You're the one who wants to blip now. You try to push Assumpta's blog, can't, then locate the right version of JoyAnna's. OK we can blip.

It's a rickety table in a forecourt on a sun-flecked day. Assumpta is lowering a tray full of cake and coffee. Her physiome is an almost even grey: you feel as though she's in a moment of respite from everything unlovely and harsh. Under her trousers, electric bandages, filaments with wires, keep her ligaments warm and give her muscles a neurological boost. The camera motion shows that she no longer limps.

At the table sits a much younger man: Asian, handsome, with black hair, black eyes. He is cherubically plump and he moves like a little boy, shrugging with pleasure. 'Assumpta, you are lovely. Lovely, lovely.' He tucks into his cake.

Assumpta sweeps into her chair and watches him eat. His cheeks bulge with cream. He swallows. She asks, 'Now?'

Then everything swims unfocused, and in your eyes physiomes line up, yours, JAH's, Assumpta's and now Gudu's. A report is offered. It flowers open, full of details.

JoyAnna says, 'They've just descraped privacy.'

His name is Gudu and he's 42. And he will be able to see that Assumpta is 68, suffers from arthritis and an hereditary heart condition. She is of course no longer fertile. He on the other hand has what someone's Access tells you is an extraordinarily high sperm count. A small article starts to explain: reduced pollution is improving male fertility. He has a slight predisposition to baldness. Self-cured of appendicitis and... what is this? Damage to the frontal lobe. All of your physiomes seem to thump in unison.

Gudu says, 'Oh, all of that is lovely.'

JAH: 'I'm tempted to say of course he doesn't want a child. I mean, he wouldn't want a rival, would he?'

Numbers flow into a grid, and Gudu says, 'Now this is my equivalent. An Indian horoscope.'

JAH: 'He's explaining, and I'm talking over him and I feel bad about that, but I can't be bothered. Assumpta, I have to say, selfishly, that I'm dreading that I'll have to spend the rest of our time together with this man. My mother's lifeblog is full of an annoying twit she met online.'

The numbers boil down to a very high fraction.

'That means we are very compatible.' Gudu beams. 'I remember when I was young my parents tried to marry me, though the incompatibility was high, and sure enough, we didn't get on from the moment we met.'

Assumpta chuckles. 'That is very reassuring.'

The last of the cake crumbs pinched together, Gudu puts his hands down flat on the table.

'The Financial Advisers Guild needs to see that I have twenty thousand euros in my account before they will let me register. Would you be able to transfer that sum into my account?'

Assumpta's physiome pulses once. It lights up, red blue yellow, and continues to coruscate.

JAH: 'Don't give it to him!'

G: 'I will pay you right back the moment they see it.'

JoyAnna rails, 'If he had a brain in his head, he would have waited six months until you couldn't live without him. A brain in his head and he wouldn't need the twenty thousand. And he wants to give people financial advice?'

The whole image seems to twist in harness, and Assumpta draws a deep breath. 'It really is very difficult.' Her voice creaks like leather being stretched. 'I really don't have a spare twenty thousand.'

G: 'Oh! You have time. You can think about it.' He's still smiling and he waves everything else away. 'Thank you.'

JAH: 'It sounds like what he says to all the old women who turn him down. Old men as well I reckon. He likes a finger up his arse.'

You live through Assumpta paying for the coffee, and

kissing him on the cheek, and then the bus ride from the Northern Quarter. Would it be so very bad, you wonder. Buying someone? When you're 68 and alone?

White Manchester, green trees, bicycles, home.

JAH: 'I want to hug you and I can't.'

Assumpta gets home; she allows herself to limp and she goes straight back to that box of a computer. She takes down her dating profile. She enters codes and webcams her retina to the bank. She waits looking at her own reflection on the screen.

'You fool. You idiot.' The cat springs up onto her lap, and hides his head under her forearm, as if sheltering from the overhead light.

Blip

Your lifeblog tells you this is summer, a year later. You see a marble floor. Assumpta has apparently twisted round her bare foot so that she can see the sole. It's dusted with fine white powder.

Someone, another aged female you can't see, says something in Spanish. Access tells you: Assumpta's sister, Bella. This is Barcelona. Someone's blog, yours or JoyAnna's translates. The voice has said, 'I wish you would wear shoes! You're not a child!'

Assumpta is humming a childish song; you've heard it before. She looks up to a sink full of water and plunges her hands into it. 'This marble is beautiful. It really does cool down the house.'

The sister's voice echoes, 'Not if you keep opening windows.'

Still, Assumpta does not look at her. Instead she holds up a soup plate. Light reflects on its moulded edges which are a faded green with gold. A bubble slides down it.

Up from Access comes an image of a Meridiani cylinder. Assumpta is thinking of work.

AC: 'These beautiful plates.'

Bella says, 'We need to talk about Mother's legacy.'

AC: 'Of course.'

Assumpta slots the plate into a rack full of crocks and cutlery. She shakes the water from her hands, and walks out of the kitchen, looking at the pattern of the rug in the hall. She goes into a parlour or sitting room and strokes the polished surface of a mahogany table, and admires heavy candlesticks with cherubim.

BC: 'Assumpta! Assumpta, where are you going?'

She limps across the room, opens the French windows, pushes back the shutters. Noise from the street floods in. Barcelona booms, crackles, wheezes, clatters. Summer solstice, 32 degrees, St Joan's Day. In the street below children are setting off firecrackers. They're crouching under long-needled pine trees that run straight down the middle of the medieval road.

'Assumpta, Assumpta please! They're setting off rockets! They fly in through the windows!'

Assumpta grunts.

Bella's voice sounds querulous and old. 'One of the apartments across the road was set on fire last year! This is too much, too much!'

The image jerks. The sister is perhaps trying to pull her back. Someone who may be JoyAnna makes a piteous sound. You glimpse Bella's black trousers and shirt; you see Assumpta's hands flinging away hers.

'All right! You close the shutters. I'll watch from outside.'

The image pulls back from the French doors, its attention fixed on the cracks that run around the edge. The shutters thunk shut, and the green handle turns as if by itself.

Assumpta looks out; the rooftops are now dark, street lights shining. There is a fizzing from below. The children scatter and a rocket squeedles like a mouse, shooting up into the trees. It gets stuck in the branches. It sprays glitter and then suddenly the image blanks out with a boom. When the cameras adjust, the tree is on fire, burning like a torch.

Assumpta says to herself. 'Car paint. So. Peels. Some fades. Lately all grey, perhaps puritan. No one wants to look fancy, though more intelligent than their owners. We preserve, the trees root us too in the old shapes. Firewood in winter.'

Something wrong with the translation? Cars, those ancient monstrosities, still swollen and polished, line the street.

And JoyAnna says as all of you watch, 'Why is the past glamorous? I mean, it was everyday to them. But I love all those shiney things, and the beautiful cloth, it looks just like coloured fog, it's that thin. It makes everything here look grey and cold. I'm so sick of digging in cold mud. Your trees and sunsets aren't that much more beautiful than mine. Except to me.'

A particularly huge rocket bursts overhead, its dancing light, its illuminated smoke for a moment imitating a nebula.

'This is what books only aimed to do and never could. Give you the glint of someone else's sunrise, or what getting old is really like: you can't swing your forearm very far; your friends start to die; you can't get fresh fruit in the shops.'

All of you watch in silence until the fireworks die.

The cylinders turn.

JoyAnna no longer sounds quite so young.

Blip

It's autumn 2030. Assumpta has a phone call in her head. It rings with the sound of blackbirds singing. A name comes up in the eye: Magda Parentes.

JAH: 'Oh no! It's the Horrible Serb!'

A new voice says, 'Assumpta my dear, are you very busy? Can you talk?' She sounds polite, sugary.

AC: 'Yes of course.'

MP: 'You must feel so dreadful. So sad.'

'Must I?'

Assumpta summons up the cylinders again, the same one, number 47, the one that begins with 16.

MP: 'Well, with Tomas not there any longer.'

The walls and ceiling seem to nod. Assumpta pauses only briefly but sails on. 'Well, I finished my work on that over a year ago, so though it's sad...' She lets her voice trail away in what sounds like wisps of relative unconcern, but the physiome shows her heart is thumping.

'You're being very brave. But still. It must rankle just a touch to have someone take over your work on the cylinders. At the 3D print. And for it to be Herr Kurtmeier?'

Assumpta's voice manages to chuckle and be icy at the same time. 'Which is the point of your call, obviously.'

'You don't mean to say you didn't know?'

JoyAnna hisses. 'Lie, Assumpta. Tell her they consulted you. Tell her that you and Kurtmeier patched up the quarrel.'

MP: 'Personally I've never cared for Kurtmeier, but his work isn't bad. And people so want to be told that the artefacts are cultural, don't they? They'll keep hiring people till they find someone who will.'

AC: 'Are you working on them as well? If you don't mind my asking.'

Magda sighs. 'Well yes, actually. I hope I can keep his fantastical streak in check.'

'So kind of you to call.'

'Well you were always so good to me in the past.'

End.

Her physiome roils. She calls Tomas. His Turing answers, sounding just enough like him to be maddening. Hearty. 'He's away on holiday. How are you, Assumpta?'

'You can tell him that I'm not well. That I'm sorry he's lost his post. He must feel dreadful. I'm mystified that no one had the grace to tell me what is going on. Have him call me.'

She paces the house.

JoyAnna says, 'I wish I could get you to let go. They're

right, of course, the young people, right to want a chance of their own. But there's nothing to stop you working on them.'

Assumpta stands up with a sniff. 'Yes.'

She scrapes her chair towards the terminal and the keyboard. There is a ping. Her news feeds automatically begin to chime: a story about the salt pump and the Gulf Stream. Assumpta switches it off, muttering. 'Get out of my head.'

Something disappears from your array. Your date, JoyAnna's date are both there, but the blogdate for Assumpta is missing. You want to ask JoyAnna: what day is this?

AC: 'Earthworms subsist on rich organics in soil. But there is no loam or hummus on Mars. So why no other finds of cylinders if they are the remains of food? Otters leave heaps of abalone shells, Neanderthals leave gnawed bones. But there is no other similar find.' Assumpta makes her rustling, breathing-out sound. 'Not even the faeces.'

She steadies her nerves with a small sherry.

AC: 'All right. Then we must assume it is some other kind of purposeful activity other than feeding and look at it again.'

She makes a lunch out of cheese and salad, but doesn't eat it. She reads papers and listens to taped lectures on earthworms and cuttlefish, then a very bad popular book on possible alien biologies.

She turns her newsfeeds back on. It talks to her as she works. It's a blog from a young Reservist overseeing the evacuation of Phoenix. He's heard gunfire on the other side of town. Vehicles are running out of electricity while idling in the jam; people are walking in the heat towards California; there's no water. JoyAnna's blog offers her the option of following his lifeblog instead.

Assumpta's date has come back on. JoyAnna goes still. A file opens, flowers, the research grant application, and a date, a year. JoyAnna's voice quavers. '23rd December? You only have five days left!'

Ping.

Assumpta receives an RSS report. The newly established dates from the Martian mass extinction match those of the cylinders. The Spiral and the climate tipped at the same time.

They've been picking raspberries in December. That night Assumpta reads two gardening romances.

The next morning, Assumpta wakes up hungover and immediately begins to do housework. She has a long handled feather duster to reach up into the corners to get the cobwebs. She then washes dishes and the eight soupbowls that arrived from Spain. Her physiome shows she is dehydrated.

She gets herself a whiskey. Sitting at the table she says, 'The only thing I have is the numbers. If that is indeed what they are. If I can understand why they are not in sequence, then I will understand something at least.'

JoyAnna says something and you realize that she's been silent for hours. 'I think Assumpta's understood that life blogging counts as publication. If she makes a discovery and it's logged, she'll get the credit.'

The flickering stops, once again at cylinder 47, where the Spiral gets stuck on the number 16.

The cylinders move in order inside Assumpta's eyes.

First, cylinder 47, in which there are four groups of four. Is that indeed a representation of 16?

Cylinder 48 starts off with two sequences of eight swirls, also 16.

Forty nine repeats that but follows it with several prickly-pear nodes.

Assumpta then stops, and orders a system check and special back up. *Ping.* The blog has been published, but also backed up.

JoyAnna says, 'Good girl. I was right. She's in a race and she's making sure the blog is being backed up, saved, and registered. She's got it.'

Fifty shows 16 individual swirls piano-rolling the length of the entire cylinder.

Fifty-one repeats that pattern and follows it with a single very large node.

And Assumpta begins to laugh.

At first she laughs like Oliver Hardy, everything bouncing up and down, her hands patting the table in unison. Then a happy, gentle sound, through teeth, like rain.

'It's... a... ha... ha... TURD! They *shat* to hoo hoo hoo say NO!'

Assumpta stands up to do a little dance. Her hips roll in a perfect figure eight and her feet trace a samba.

JoyAnna laughs aloud a hearty, British baying laugh, and that knocks her back into blogging mode. 'That's a samba.' Thanks, you think. 'Assumpta lived in Brasil for a while, years ago, taught at the State University of Para in Belem.'

The arthritis intervenes, Assumpta stumbles, goes ooooh, and then finds that funny as well. She starts to sing a song in Portuguese. It's a laughing song, the chorus consists of the sound of laughter. Translated the title is 'Who's Laughing Now?' Aha-ha-HAH-HAH-HAH.

She calls Schelling. The Turing says, 'Sorry Assumpta, but he's away for Christmas now.'

She chuckles. 'Just tell him I have something to report on the cylinders.'

The cylinders with their numbers flutter back and forth. 'Well my darlings. What were you up to?'

Then she says, 'Hmm. It's chilly in here.'

The cylinders dance all day long. Assumpta keeps pouring herself a whiskey to celebrate. By 6pm it's dark and she is asleep.

Day three starts very late. The blog records snores, then the slow waxing of light on the walls. But Assumpta is not conscious to see it.

Up come the feeds with news from Bangladesh, and

the American Southwest, and now trouble on the border between India and China.

Assumpta groans, she stomps her way out of bed and goes downstairs to the refrigerator. She surveys it for a moment before taking out the sherry, but what she says is, 'Nothing can survive just eating iron in clay. What else did they eat? They must have eaten something!'

Still in her nightie, she puts in a round robin call to biologists in her network. She magnifies the signs again, to see how they were made.

AC: 'All right. I think we can say that the worms definitely did not have teeth.'

She has a continental breakfast of cheddar cheese, oatcakes and raisins. She calls on the CGI package. 'So let's just try to imagine what they were like.'

She tries to imagine the worms in a colony. She pastes them onto a Mars whose surface is not red, but streaked with ice or tiny melted puddles. In the end it looks like grass, a lawn of worms, reaching up toward the light.

'They photosynthesized.' That's JoyAnna. 'Rhodopsin. It's protein in the human eye, it photosynthesizes, and it's red, like Mars.'

And Assumpta says, 'Yes, that's it.'

And it takes you a moment to realize that the two of them cannot be in discussion.

AC: 'If they photosynethsized they might eat clay only when suffering iron deficiency. So we might not find any other cylinders. They wouldn't need them that often.'

She checks to make sure the lifeblog is still saving and registering. She goes upstairs, puts the blog on block. Presumably she showers.

When it comes back on the time is 15.37 and the sky has gone ominously dark. Assumpta is bundling herself up in sweaters and a coat, and goes outside. She has difficulty opening her French doors, steps outside and gasps. The air looks like solidified crystal. The sky overhead is clear pale blue, except for a bank of cloud to the north that is being pulled over it like a blanket.

You see the outside temperature is minus 15 degrees. Assumpta's breath sidles out of her nostrils like thick steam. She shivers her way to the clothes line and starts unpegging a shirt. Her hand shakes and fumbles it. A solid sheet of cotton, the shirt tumbles to the paving.

And shatters like china. It lies in shards.

AC: 'What is going on?'

She turns and hobbles, quivering, back inside. She closes the French doors and then lumbering, rolls up the kitchen rug against the lower edge of the door. She collects bread and bananas, a tub of yogurt, all the food in the house, and then retreats into the sitting room. She rolls up rugs against the doors there too, and turns on the heater at full blast.

Then she checks to make sure that the lifeblog is continuing to save.

'I'm afraid we are having some unusual weather.'

She goes back to the CGI. She uses the blog to tell the University computers what she wants. Worms, two centimetres long. Photosynthesising. Capable of movement. The CGI system goes to work.

Turings begin to call, delivering automatic Christmas greetings. *Hello (slight pause) Assumpta, Ted's calling to wish you a merry season!* She turns them all off.

Overhead, the sky begins to make an ominous grinding sound, like pepper being milled.

JoyAnna suddenly yelps. 'Shit! The date of your death is actually the day they found you. But you'd been lying dead for two days. This is it. It's now. You're going to die now.'

The worm resolves as an image.

Assumpta; 'For the sake of neatness. Make them the same size as the cylinders.'

The machine takes over, and the worm is there, wrestling with a cylinder in clay, and it is clear: one is a simulacrum of the other.

Assumpta breathes out. 'Of course.'

The sky grinds. The heat blows.

'Any system of writing must mimic the main original kind of communication.' Then she says to her system. 'Make them both worms.'

Two worms roll together, mouthing each other's bodies.

'They communicated by touch. By kissing the lengths of their bodies. And the cylinders tried to record that process of whole body touching. We'll never translate that language without a Rosetta stone. But why the debate over numbers?'

She calls up a gathering of worms, and then superimposes the Spiral. A Sprial of worms.

They are passing the cylinders along its length. Passing them out, passing them back.

AC: 'The definition of writing is that which preserves information across both space and time.'

The worms seethe; the university pseudo-AI starts to improve the image. You see a Martian sky, slightly blue from the presence of water vapour, you see the congress.

AC: 'They were trying to invent writing. They started with numbers. The Spiral was a debate about how to write numbers. Todd told me they couldn't be intelligent, their whole body size would not allow for brain complexity. But what if they had some kind of neural interface when they touched?

'What if it started to go cold and dry? They knew they needed to measure that?'

And she starts to cry. It must be all that booze at work. 'Deaf dumb blind. But they could feel the cold!'

JoyAnna says, 'You don't have to feel that we are like them.'

Two of the worms dance together, turning each other, kissing in spirals.

Then with a soft click, all the lights go out. You can hear the blow heater die. The room is as dark as the inside of the brain. Assumpta's physiome fluxes in panic. She yelps, stands up, thumps against furniture. She checks if the lifeblog was being saved.

JAH: 'It's OK, Assumpta, the Library has its own generators, it has saved all of this.'

A clumping of furniture. No light at all. Garments rustle and slither. A clatter in the dark, a fumbling and finally a battery-operated torch snaps on. Assumpta now wears an overcoat.

Her front corridor is spotlit all around us. She steps outside her front door, and her breath is pulled out of her making a noise like the counterstroke of a cello. The numbers for temperatures rattle through her eyes. She tries to call Tomas.

NO NETWORK COVERAGE.

The phone system is down.

Outside there is only driving snow, like stars shooting past at warp speed. They swallow up all the light; there is nothing beyond. Gasping for breath Assumpta tries to advance but the wind is extraordinary, pushing her back. From somewhere up the road peoples' voices echo, shouting. Assumpta tries to shout too but it is too cold; she can't.

A voice from down the street calls, 'The radio says to stay inside!'

Assumpta turns and the wind harries her back. Hinges squeal as the front door opens. They resist being closed against the gale. The lock won't click shut. She rams her body against it. Her knee gives away and she cries aloud, but she falls against the door and it finally shuts. On the floor, she pushes the welcome mat against the lower edge of the doorway and crawls along the corridor.

'Stupid!' She'd left the sitting room door ajar, and much of its saved heat will have been sucked up the staircase. As if praying, on her knees, she pushes the sitting room door shut behind her. She crawls across the floor onto the sofa and pulls the sofa cushions on top of herself, and curls up. To save the batteries she turns off the flashlight

The air outside growls like a wounded beast. She sits chill in the dark.

She calls Schelling again. This time she gets through to his Turing.

'Hello Tomas. Things are pretty serious here; there really is the most terrible storm. All the lights and power are out and of course I have no heating. Please call.'

She rings Bella, but her sister has put her on block.

She waits in the dark.

JoyAnna says, 'How did your pretty little sister, the one everyone adored, the one you used to dress up, how did she get so mean? Maybe it's better never to be adored, like us. Momma never called me pretty; I could see I wasn't pretty. I'd go to the movies and pray for the lights to go down so that people wouldn't see what a dump I was, and that I had to go to movies alone. I was too brainy, I brought in my files to the class and showed my favourite saved things: planets and starfish and ancient architecture and that popular girl tossed her hair and said what's so interesting about all of that stuff? Papa: "You'll have to get by on brains."'

Still no image, except for three glowing physiomes and losta numbers, so many numbers and icons, that they almost crowd out the world.

Her voice constrained, Assumpta calls up a number code and clearance information. She turns on the torch and points it into her eye, and the darkness disappears in light.

JAH: 'You've just retinaed Mars. Can that work?

Nine mintues to wait. The image of the worms comes back. The worms turn each other like corncobs, talking in a spiral.

Then they begin to make love.

JoyAnna murmurs. 'You spent the last quarter century trying to find love. You believed in progress too, I bet, the advancement of science. The world is folding in on itself. Your Martians died just as they invented culture.

'Our world isn't dying, Assumpta. I know it feels like that now. Because of Gudu, your mother, that cat, your work, everything that's on the news, but it isn't the same as those little bits of brain on Mars. We already have writing

114

and numbers; we have more than writing. We have wireless and blogging; we can reason; we didn't fight a war, we won't; we're all still here, Assumpta.'

The flashlight snaps on. The temperature in the room is still above freezing. Assumpta opens a wooden cabinet, and gets out the whiskey, and starts to drink. Alcohol is a food. But it opens the circulation system near the skin and speeds freezing. Assumpta climbs back into her shelter of sofa cushions. She puts all her name list on auto dial.

NO NETWORK CONNECTION.

The power for the network is down. Only military channels are open now. You have those because of your contract: to the Rylands Library. To Mars.

JoyAnna: 'Assumpta, do you sense me in the future, sitting next to you, reading with you, drinking with you, hell, even peeing with you. You got love, Assumpta. Me.'

Wind batters the roof.

'You might still have been alive after I was born. I might have met you as a little girl. I could have sat on your lawn, or looked at your 20,000 books and said "Why would anyone want so many books? Just keep em on your pod." I could have called you Aunty.'

Assumpta sits up again, and reads out new parameters for her blog.

JAH: 'She's trying to make this last sequence have a wider distribution; it will be stored in a different inbox than usual. That's one of the reasons it wasn't noted. Also, nobody thought that anybody's blog was saved with the power down. It's the military channels.'

Assumpta says, to the lifeblog, her audience, her people. 'The Spiral is the record of a process of invention. It was an attempt to turn a system of communication through touch into a system of writing. They photosynthesised but ate clay for mineral content. They wrote with their mouths. They did not finish developing their system of numbering and writing. The Spiral was a debate about how to record numbers and something like words. We now know climate change comes quickly. It tips. This change happened in four Martian years, as it is coming upon us.'

'Record and post,'
ENTRY POSTED
Ping.

And suddenly, there is a bronze plain, bronze sky. All three of you now stand on Mars, with the bot. Assumpta tells it, 'Please show me the Spiral.'

Nine minutes to receive, nine minutes to answer. The image is frozen. Somewhere Handel plays.

All three of you sit and wait.

Assumpta says, 'All my books are upstairs.'

Her physiome shows pains around her chest. There's a burble, and she looks down; she's coughed up whiskey.

JAH: 'I bet it's like this for angels. They just have to stand by and watch it happen as we make a mess of everything. Mouth useless, God's love useless, freedom useless. Freedom is the enemy – it just lets us make mistakes. *Love in a Changing Climate.* Love without words. Love as angels love, beyond comprehension, outside words, beyond hope or any objective correlative. You don't know I'm here, but I'll stay here and I'll keep listening. I'll keep watch.'

The cold sinks in. The physiome starts to shut down. Time rolls down, the numbers decrease.

'Your blog still keeps going on. Your eyes still get data. The blog's still there. And me. For a while.'

Elsewhen, on Mars, JoyAnna when old has finished her tale, and is being buckled in. There is a jerk and she is swept up, swung out over the dig. The Spiral opens its arms wide.

'Rendition,' she says, with the accent of Assumpta Ciges. The cameras blank and you, and me, and they and us, we hang with her in the very centre of the light.

Afterword: Egyptian Parchments and the Mary Rose

Dr Manolis Pantos has been leading heritage and archaeological science research at the Science Technologies and Facilities Council (STFC), Daresbury Laboratory for the last ten years.

The story begins with a discovery on the surface of Mars. Clay artefacts imprinted with a spiral design look 'intentional'. Is this evidence of some ancient intelligence recording messages for other intelligent beings in the future? Or was it a natural process that led to the creation of these highly organised designs?

The story posits that in 2027 in-situ scientific examination is possible with some expert backup from Earth. Very plausible, as similar kinds of investigations have been planned or even been carried out by robotic instrumentation already in our times.

In the case of these inscribed clay objects the first thing established by archaeological science methods is the composition of the clay and whether it has been subjected to high temperatures. These methods are based on the same techniques that are in use by geologists to characterise materials on Earth or even originating from the neighbouring planets. The mineral and chemical composition can be analysed with the use of x-ray techniques, diffraction or fluorescence. Portable instrumentation for in-situ studies is available for first assessment and before other, more sophisticated laboratory-based instruments are employed for more detailed analysis and identification of molecular or crystalline constituents. All fired clays normally contain iron and minerals, the amounts of which can be linked to the type of clay and if any heating has taken place.

For the case of oxygen-poor Mars, the discovery of hematite would indicate great antiquity when the atmospheric composition could have been very different. In fact, the characterisation of the objects as clay implies that processes leading to the formation of clay were once present on Mars. A rather exciting aspect as this would necessitate the presence of water. This in turn enhances the possibility of presence of life, in some form. To extrapolate this to the presence of intelligent life takes us further into the realm of fertile science fiction.

The interpretation of the inscribed designs can not be performed by instruments alone. Comparison with similar designs is needed. If the designs represent some sort of code, then the code needs to be broken. If a message is coded, then a language has to have been used, even if it's only a semantic language, based on assumptions of universal iconology and meaning. This is in the broader area of anthropology, linguistics, art history and development of intelligent communication systems. Geometric decorative motifs or even number symbols used for simple recording purposes preceded attempts to tell a story through art or literature. Spiral and other geometric motifs are often found in prehistoric art, and without a contemporary record of their meaning archaeologists rely on their imagination to interpret their significance.

What could be learned from Assumpta's objects using today's scientific methods? A great deal actually, assuming that the objects could be transported back to Earth. There's a whole battery of techniques that can elucidate the origin, age and composition of objects of this kind. Some of these techniques rely on the use of cutting-edge technology employing synchrotron light sources, international facilities producing a wide spectrum of very intense light, from the infrared to high energy x-rays. The objects could be studied at a resolution of a few micrometers, in 2 or 3 dimensions, non-destructively. The chemical composition could be studied to concentrations as small as 1 part per million. Crystalline minerals and non–crystalline organic inclusions could be identified with a high degree of certainty, using techniques that are now applied routinely at several synchrotron light sources around the world to study Van Gogh paintings, Palaeolithic bones, Roman pottery, Egyptian metal objects, ancient textiles or medieval parchment.

But the meaning of the spirals would require the imagination and knowledge of a scholar, not a mere scientist, a philologist or linguist perhaps, with cultivated insight into human thinking processes. At least as far as present day knowledge allows this cannot be done by any robotic instrument, however intelligent.

Studies on heritage materials undertaken in the past at Daresbury Laboratory are now pursued at the UK's new synchrotron light source, Diamond, in Oxfordshire. The most recent work carried out by Daresbury scientist Dr Andy Smith and colleagues from the Mary Rose Trust was concerned with the chemical pathways of iron and sulphur compounds that affect the long-term preservation of the Mary Rose timbers. Alteration processes in other materials, such as metals and glazed ceramics is another topic of current interest.

In The Event Of

Michael Arditti

What wording will you use on my death-site, Mother? *Much loved daughter of Edward and Alice...* that is your prerogative. *Sister of the late lamented Sarah...* that would be more contentious. *Aged twenty-two* or *twenty-two squared... Cruelly taken from us in a freak accident...* that depends on your credit with your fellow arbiters. *Family messages only...* that may solve the immediate problem but could encourage heresy sites and we all know where those lead.

History does not repeat itself. All life extends to infinity. Those in the Top Bar can expect to regenerate themselves while the rest can look forward to painless non-existence, their experience filed in the collective memory. Suicide is said to have been eliminated from the Controlled World, along with misery, despair and God. So what went wrong? For me, for you, for Sarah? She is the unseen factor in our family equation. Her death-site was unaccountably deleted, but her death remains the bedrock of our lives. You will ask yourself through your tears – I do not speak lightly – how we could both have chosen this savage, antisocial way to die.

Your friends will rally round you. Once the alerts have been posted, your mailboxes will be packed with condolences. I trust that you will remember to warn the authorities and prevent another crash such as the one after Father's gold service bar. It will be hard for people to come up with suitable messages, even with the aid of the sentiment check. As they speak of your grief, they will doubtless be thinking of my ingratitude: how you might have used your loyalty bar for a place on the Lazarus list but preferred to secure your immortality by another route... one that has proved to be a dead end.

I do not deny that I was born with every advantage. Our dom was on base two of the Bunker, a floor above the Primes. Your Top Bar status entitled us to optimum nutrition and access to all levels of Life Service. We had exclusive use of two sub-Saharans, which I know that many of your friends regarded as risky, but I shared your view that, while they might not be as reliable as animations, they brought their own distinction. Besides, you claimed that, as an arbiter, you were obliged to take a lead in helping aliens just as you were in recycling waste. To allay any lingering qualms, you added that, before they came to us, they underwent a strict six month quarantine and were both sterilised and sterile.

As far as I can recall, my early childhood was happy. You introduced me to playgroup at the age of three. You told me later that, unlike most children who shrank from the strange faces on the screen, I instantly began making friends. The group was, of course, restricted to the children of Top Bar parents: arbiters, innovators and tribunes. Even there, however, I was privileged. Father's job ensured that I was among the first to be given one of the new generation playtrons. This unleashed a storm of jealousy in the group, with one mother threatening to withdraw her son unless I kept the toy off-screen. Father guaranteed my compliance, apologising for any trouble we had caused, although I suspect that he was secretly pleased at having the chance to show off his influence. Such local difficulties aside, you were both free to devote yourself to your work, confident that my time was constructively occupied.

I would be the last to complain of parental neglect. The balance between my intellectual and psychological development was constantly monitored. While you were no doubt influenced by your experience with Sarah, most of my friends reported a similar routine, mocking the over-protectiveness of Top Bar parents who scheduled them for repeated sessions with various behavioural, medical, nutritional, social and technical assessors. You even employed image enhancers to retouch my avatar every two months to be sure that I was making the best of myself. For all of which I thank you.

Constancy, contentment and control were the watchwords of our world, and I had the good fortune to enjoy all three. I remember the first time that I felt pain, an experience sufficiently singular to sear itself on to my brain. One of the sub-Saharans – who had, after all, been chosen for their dexterity – dropped a plate on my foot. My screams brought you running from your desk. I can still picture her distress when you sacked her on the spot, refusing to reconsider even after the medical assessor had declared that no bones were broken and the behavioural assessor that, with skilful counselling, I would suffer no long-term trauma. I would swear that her replacement arrived the very next day, but I know that I must be mistaken since you would never have hired anyone who had not been rigorously decontaminated and reprogrammed.

An even more tenacious memory, one that resisted concerted attempts to dismiss it as a figment of my imagination or an early screen story I had muddled with time-life, was of my first meeting with Arthur, a meeting that remained unexplained until now. I was playing in the hall when a sub-Saharan let in two strangers. She later swore that she had taken them to be neighbours but, even though the interrogator was inclined to believe her, you had her excluded. The pair were a boy, not much older than myself, and a man who might have been his father. They were oddly dressed with old-fashioned breathing equipment, like fish-tanks. His clothes apart, the boy looked much like any of my friends, but glimpses of the man's wrists and scalp revealed pronounced wrinkles and blotches. I know now that these were signs of age but, in our stories, even Merlin had smooth skin and thick hair.

'It's uncanny,' the man said. 'You're her twin.' The boy stepped forward to touch me, at which point the sub-Saharan realised her mistake and pressed the alarm. The man grabbed the boy and ran off before the custodians pounced. I was less frightened by the intrusion than by your subsequent panic. You claimed that the pair were surface people who had infiltrated the Controlled World by bribery or through some crack in the ventilation system. I soon realised that I must stop asking questions or risk causing you further anxiety. I tried instead to discuss the matter with my friends but, as though I had used a trigger word, the screen immediately shut down. You made me promise not to speak of it to anyone. I kept my word, but I hadn't promised not to think about it. For all the air of mystery, it thrilled more than it threatened.

That incident presaged the end of my innocence. Soon afterwards, one of my friends, Judith, broke the secret of my identity. You have since told me that I should never feel ashamed of being cloned. In which case, why did you conceal it for so long? According to the site – and you have always done everything by the site – parents should tell a clone the truth at the age of five, yet you left me to hear it from Judith who had eavesdropped on her parents. We were chatting as usual when I said something to provoke her. She replied that she didn't care because I was going to die young. Instantly the screen went blank. I knew about death and dying from stories, of course, but my direct experience was limited to a series of extinctions when my playtrons short-circuited and, despite their being rapidly replaced, I was left with a deep sense of loss.

I had never pictured anything like that happening to me, so I questioned you during the evening nutrition. The sad, shocked looks on your and Father's faces testified to the seriousness of the matter. You refused to discuss it that night, but you both took the next day off work, ushering me into the screen room where you accessed a specially coded site... the first of the many specials to which I was about to be introduced. We listened while a woman with a voice like ice-cream outlined the basic facts about clones. She insisted that, far from being freaks of science, we were double expressions of love and even a double elite since the treatment was both genetically and socially exclusive. She urged us to be grateful to our parents, since you had not only undergone an exacting assessment process and a range of invasive tests but made a great financial sacrifice.

I myself was subject to such frequent assessment that the assurance was not as compelling as it might have been. The knowledge that you had been exposed to a similar process served to reduce your authority rather than to guarantee your competence. Nevertheless, I sat quietly until the end of the talk when you asked if I had any questions. 'Yes! Yes, I do. Yes, I have. Who am I? If I'm not me and your daughter, then what am I? Am I a unique clone or one of many? Are there other Sarahs scattered about the Bunker?' For I soon found out that you had given me not just my sister's genes but her name, which was a thought that both comforted and appalled me.

No doubt at the time my questions were not so neatly phrased, but, however much I overstate my articulacy, it is impossible to overstate my hunger for the truth. To be fair, you did not equivocate but declared that you and Father were indeed my biological parents. Having lost a daughter aged twenty-two to a rare virus, you had been so heartbroken that you had devoted all your energy and resources to bringing her back.

My inevitable response was 'Why didn't you have another child?'. Top Bar parents were authorised to have two children and, while I was happy enough with my playtrons, I longed for a time-life brother or sister. You explained, as fully as you could to a seven year old, that you had been unable to conceive again. Like most Top Bar women you had opted for a uterine pregnancy, but Sarah's birth led to complications which damaged your supply of eggs.

I did not deny your assertion that no child had ever been as loved, although over time I was left wondering whether you loved me for my sister or for myself, not least since I was increasingly confused as to who that self was. Given that you had been so determined to create an exact clone that you not only harvested Sarah's DNA but used it to impregnate one of her own eggs, then surely, in loving me, you were simply loving her?

Once the truth about Sarah was out, you licensed other people, notably Grandmother, to talk about her. The consensus was that she had been an exceptional girl: loving and kind, intelligent and beautiful, all attributes designed to encourage me but all, except for the last, having the opposite effect. One of my friends used to complain of being compared to her older sister, but it was far more unnerving to be compared to my older self. I was afraid that on the one hand I would fail to live up to her and invalidate your sacrifice and, on the other, that I would surpass her and invalidate your memories. While my biology set studied the respective influence of nature and nurture on human development, I felt myself to be a prisoner of both: not only created to the same genetic pattern as Sarah but living in the same environment with parents who treated me in the same way.

My greatest fear was of dying young, not because, as Judith had hinted, very few clones have so far lived out their natural span, let alone been eligible for a place on the Lazarus list, but because I was convinced that my replication of Sarah would extend to dying at the same age. I was particularly alarmed by the mention of a virus. I knew of course about screen viruses – the Moderator regularly declared them to be our number one security threat – but I had never heard of their affecting people. You sought to reassure me, insisting that Sarah's death was the direct result of having moved to her own dom. You and Father had vehemently opposed it, not least since she could only afford somewhere on base eight, but she had been resolute, alternately threatening and pleading (so much for Little Miss Perfect, although I knew better than to point it out!). She had joined two friends, another girl and a herm; but, as Father explained, like so many young people they neglected to look after themselves. There had been a problem with the screen filtration system; a virus mutated and Sarah died.

Conscious of the distress it caused you, I took care not to raise the subject again. Instead I questioned Grandmother who, initially evasive, described Sarah's death in a term unfamiliar to me as *a tragedy*. When I looked it up in the dictionary, I found that it had been blacked out. So I asked you – perhaps you remember? – but, rather than explaining, you demanded to know where I'd heard it. To protect Grandmother, I said that it was in one of the stories I'd been watching. You seemed sceptical; after all you spent your life ensuring that such archaisms were excised from the screen. Nevertheless you gave me an explanation of sorts, describing it as an old-fashioned word for *sadness*, with violent overtones, that had no place in the Controlled World.

I am sure that you suspected Grandmother since you carefully monitored our next few sessions of inter-generational chat. My biggest worry was that you might stop me going to her eightieth birthday party in the summer. I was wild with anticipation since it would be only my third ever journey out of the dom. The first, of course, had been to watch Father collect his gold service bar at the Tribunal, and the second to make my vows in the Junior Citizenship ceremony at the Grand Rotunda. It was my good fortune that, for propaganda purposes, the Moderator had decided to hold the ceremony in public that year. It remains one of the most memorable days of my life, marred only by my failure to meet up with any of my friends, either because their image enhancement had been too extensive or because, despite the pack of custodians, their parents refused to let them linger outdoors.

The new trip promised to be even more momentous, since we were not only travelling to another bunker but staying for a whole week. Despite the discomfort and delays of the transit, the repeated decontamination checks, the chafing of our biosuits and sniffing of the custodians, I relished the journey. My excitement grew on reaching Grandmother's dom, which was larger than ours though far less efficient. It took me a while to realise that when she talked of housework, Grandmother meant the things that she did for the house rather than the other way round. Her only help was an old-fashioned serviteur, about which you were scathing. 'Let's have one thing or the other,' you said, 'a sub-Saharan or an animatron. This is the worst of both worlds.'

No sooner had we entered the dom than Father started to cough. He blamed it on the dust but I felt sure that it was due to Grandmother, who seemed to irritate him far more than she did on screen. I was embarrassed that he should make his feelings so plain, but I had to admit that Grandmother was a disappointment. Although her image enhancement had been crude and often out of synch, it was a shock to find her so grey and gaunt and smelling faintly of a waste disposal. I whispered to you that the best birthday present we could give her would be a cell regeneration course, but you hissed back that, even if we could afford it, she was a bar two person and therefore ineligible. She had asked for a cat – a time-life cat to replace one that had died, but you said that it was perverse of her to want something that was expensive to feed, difficult to control, bad for the environment and prone to disease, rather than a low-energy, low-maintenance petron. When she refused so much as to look at one, you replied that her taste for the primitive had blighted your life.

The most fascinating feature of Grandmother's dom was that it was on two floors. I was forbidden to go upstairs, ostensibly on account of the poor ventilation, but more probably, as I soon discovered, because it was full of books. At first I was confused by the strange setting for the familiar names: *Pollyanna*; *Jane Eyre*; *Pippi Longstocking*; *Cold Comfort Farm*. Instead of uniform files to click on and scroll down, they were unwieldy objects with pages to be turned by hand. Moreover, on opening them, I did not hear a friendly voice telling me the story but had to struggle alone with print stretching across the page. Then, every few lines, I needed to put down the book to let my thoughts catch up with the words.

Even so, I knew that I had stumbled on something of great value. I sneaked three of the books down to my room and, putting on my playtron at full blast to distract you, seized every spare moment to read. I began with *Jane Eyre*, which I had enjoyed on screen but found so much richer on the page. I was surprised by the scale of the differences. Far from being pretty, Jane here described herself as plain, which had the unexpected effect of making her more likeable. Then, on returning to Thornfield after the fire (a fire that had been started on purpose), she found that Mr Rochester was not simply suffering from heatstroke but was permanently blind.

I was startled and disturbed, confused and elated, and curious to learn how Grandmother had come by such treasures. I questioned her one day when, for all your criticism of the quality of Life Services in Bunker J, you and Father were both in conference with your offices. She was reluctant to speak out for fear of offending you but, when pressed, she explained that she had preserved her parents' library from a time when books were read for the words as well as the stories. She added that, as a girl, you had loved them and so had Sarah. Your name came as a surprise, but Sarah's was an inspiration, her interest licensing mine.

Grandmother allowed me to take *Jane Eyre* home, along with *Ballet Shoes* and *Anne of Green Gables*, provided that I kept them hidden. Finally and most precious of all, she gave me the links to three heresy sites which published books unarbited.

My efforts to conceal the contraband were no match for the scanners. You were outraged, although you chose to focus on the danger of the books themselves rather than on my duplicity. Father spoke of the selfishness of hoarding paper at a time when the last remaining trees in Constitution Square were dying. You spoke of your deep hurt that your daughter should so denigrate your life's work as to choose to read stories that had no status in the Controlled World and were inimical to personal growth and civic harmony. When I mentioned that Sarah had enjoyed the same stories, Father accused me of having no decency and you accused me of having no heart.

This marked the start of my rebellion. I know that I am passing over scores of smaller events, but a suicide note demands a certain succinctness. Grandmother died before I could sound her out further, but her revelations about Sarah had confirmed my suspicions that the dutiful daughter existed only in your mind. She too had defied the parental veto on unarbited books. What had they meant to her? With no one to ask, all I could do was explore the sites for myself, finding a mystery even in books that were too remote for me to relate to and a beauty even in those that I could not understand. Taking my cue from the sites, I created alternative histories to cover my tracks. I was growing ever more secretive and withdrawn. Was this unique to me or a feature of adolescence? There's a word that you didn't expect me to know. Why have you and your colleagues excised it from controlled speech? How can you hope to understand the feelings if you deny the words?

Death haunted me. I was terrified of an afterlife: not of punishment (I never became so influenced by my reading as to give any credence to God) but rather of the prospect of your cloning me again. I posted letters in a special mailbox, which I made you promise to give to the next Sarah to spare her from similar agonizing. You pleaded with me not to torture you. You swore that you would never survive the death of a second child, let alone be able to carry a third. Ever practical, I pointed out that that was no obstacle since you could opt for a laboratory birth or else hire a sub-Saharan. Which was when Father intervened, declaring that, even should you want to, you could not afford it since you were still making the final payments on me. Then you added in a calculated whisper that anyway you had learnt your lesson; it would be throwing good money after bad.

You nevertheless found the means to send me to a clone support group, commending it as one of the smartest in the whole Life Services, as though that were a mark both of its efficacy and your love. I logged on for my first session with a mixture of truculence and curiosity. It was the first time that I had knowingly come into contact with any of my fellow clones. I had often speculated as to whether any of my friends were like me. With more than three thousand names in my address book, the law of averages dictated that some must be, although it had always seemed insensitive to ask.

On this showing my fellow clones were not the best balanced of people, but then I suppose, if they had been, they wouldn't have needed the support. There were five of us. Our convenor, Jeremy, who also ran a group for Surviving Twins, said that he wanted to keep the sessions intimate, but Joe1luckless (not his real name) declared that it was rather that no one else could afford the fees.

Joe's donor had been an actor in the era before animatrons, a notion that the others found bizarre but which, having read the unarbited *Cold Comfort Farm*, I knew to have been the norm. Joe's story made mine seem commonplace. A tribune's widow had fallen in love with his donor after secretly screening his films. Sparing no expense, she sent a pair of gene-jackers to the Surface World and had him illicitly cloned. She raised Joe as her son until he reached eighteen, when she demanded that he become her lover. He was appalled. Not only did he think of her as his mother but he felt a strong, albeit unexpressed, attraction to her nephew. He was at a loss to explain it until he read on a heresy site that, despite his screen persona, his donor had been a herm. He told the widow, who accused him of lying and threatened him with exclusion.

My closest ally in the group was Jean, who had been cloned by her own daughter. She claimed to have loved her mother so much that she could not bear the prospect of living without her but, according to Jean, her actions told a very different story. Nothing but bitter hatred and a desire for revenge could explain her rigid control of Jean's nutrition prescriptions and monitoring of her Life Services, let alone her leaving her, at seventeen, with the avatar of a twelve year-old, which made girls her own age reluctant to talk to her and boys afraid of breaking the law.

Our remaining members were Ruby, a twenty year-old, who defied image enhancement to display her deeply scarred face, and Stanley, a twenty-three year-old, who appeared in silhouette. It turned out that both their donors had been treated by the same backstreet geneticist. Stanley's donor had been a famous boxer before the ban on blood sports. About twenty-five years ago – I presume that you have the details in memory – there had been moves to relax the ban, and he had had himself cloned in readiness for a comeback. In the event, the ban was upheld and he took out his frustration on Stanley who, instead of feeding his hopes, now mocked them. When Stanley grew old enough to fight back, the man threw him out, leaving him to live in the Hinterland until he was taken in by an anti-cloning campaigner who signed him up to the group.

I had never met anyone as angry as Stanley, whose repeated threats against his donor fuelled Jeremy's warnings that the group would be shut down. He did, however, form a close bond with Ruby, whose story neatly chimed with his. Her donor, an avatar model, had brought her up with exceptional strictness, aiming to control her every impulse, even denying her solo access to a screen until the welfare assessors intervened. When Ruby was ten, the donor began to dress them both alike in a vain attempt to bridge the age gap, but she waited until she was eighteen to reveal the full extent of her plan. This was to train her for another three years and then kill herself, enabling Ruby, who would then be at the peak of her beauty to take over her career. Horrified, Ruby grabbed a knife and gouged her cheeks. Deprived of her future, the donor did indeed kill herself, leaving Ruby steeped in guilt.

Without telling the rest of us, Ruby and Stanley began to chat outside the sessions until one day, with respective diffidence (her) and defiance (him), they confessed that they had fallen in love and intended to quit the group. Whether because he feared that he would never again achieve such success or else that their romance was doomed to failure, Jeremy chose to wind up the group, assuring Joe, Jean and myself that, while we might feel particularly threatened as clones, our concerns about loss of self were shared throughout the Controlled World. I later heard that he went on to run an animatron dependence group, but I have never been able to access it.

I hardly need remind you that the next two or three years were hard. Like Ruby, I was deeply disturbed by my dual identity, although I turned my anger against you rather than myself. To everyone's relief, when I reached eighteen, you and Father allowed me to move to my own dom with a girl and boy from my citizenship group. I would have preferred a herm, not least for symmetry, but, with the success of the realignment programme, they were harder to find. I lost my hymen to a junior innovator and built up my immunity to the opposite sex. I made friends in time-life and joined a group of tectonic explorers who made unauthorised climbs to the Surface World. My dom-mates urged caution, citing the dangers of capture by the custodians and exposure to surface disease. I don't know whether it was the Sarah in me or just the 'me', but I scoffed at their qualms and embarked on a rigorous fitness regime.

The night of my first sortie arrived. We broke into Transit Depot Three and clambered on to the freight rail buffers. As we hurtled through the labyrinth of service tunnels and out to the Hinterland, I felt like an avatar in a heresy game. We stopped at a large purification complex, where our leader (no names, no scapegoats) ushered us into an unscanned ventilation shaft. I climbed up the icy ladder, my senses alternately heightened and numbed. Suddenly, I felt a drop in pressure. My head was filled with light and someone yelled at me to close my eyes. Two arms grabbed my shoulders and lifted me to the surface. I gazed up into infinity. The landscape was vast and varied, but all I could see was the sky. I realised how constricted my life had been in the Bunker, where the only freedom was on screen. I felt an intense desire to tear off my mask and drink in the air, but a warning hand restrained me. It was no time for suicidal gestures... at least not yet.

We trudged over cratered roads to the meeting-point, a cracked concrete pillar the colour of a screen on standby, that was incongruously known as the flyover. Sitting on a broken block in the biting wind, I felt a twinge of regret for our ergonomic chairs and regulation 22.5 degrees temperature. It vanished when a group eleven or twelve strong emerged from behind the pillar. Although they outnumbered us three to one and were on home ground, they did not feel at all threatening. Despite everything we had been taught about surface people, it was immediately clear that they were no different from us. Physically, of course, they were bulkier, even though we were wrapped in protective suits and they were wearing skins. Their flesh was darker, not sub-Saharan but tanned. Their faces were more expressive than those of the people I knew, time-life people as well as avatars. For all that they would have benefited from style – and, though it pains me to say it, hygiene – assessors, they exuded a vitality and strength that were hugely attractive. One man in particular stirred feelings in me that I had thought existed only in books.

It soon became plain that these feelings were mutual. After an initial awkwardness we talked as frankly as old friends. I listened in fascination as he described his daily life: the ever-present danger from hostile gangs, feral dogs, and caches of unreleased chemicals. One of his group overheard and teased him. 'Come off it, Arthur. Anyone would think you were trying to turn the girl's head.' He blushed (something else I had encountered only in books), which I now count as the moment when I fell in love. He spoke of his struggle to build a new world from the ruins of the old, disowning both the technologies and the ideologies that had caused so much harm. You might claim to be doing the same but, whereas you have retreated into a tomblike security, creating a world so balanced that it has become bland, he was ready to suffer, even to die, to preserve freedom.

He invited me home to meet his father. Although I suspected that a social call was the last thing on his mind, I accepted without the least misgiving. Perhaps there was something in my blood, as there had been in Sarah's, that drew me to strangers or perhaps – irony of ironies – some dim recollection of childhood left me with a lifelong fascination for surface people. Either way I quit my companions with the promise to be back by five and walked with Arthur through the rocky wasteland into a wood called the Dean. I was amazed to see so many trees, not lasers or cybernetics but time-life trees with substance and shadows. Ignoring the risk of bites and rashes, I pulled off my gloves and stroked the bark, at which Arthur took my hand and raised it to his lips, gently kissing each of the fingers in turn.

We reached his hut, where he introduced me to his father who, to my surprise, was blind. 'You have a beautiful voice,' he said, 'it reminds me of someone I knew long ago.'

'Even through the mouthpiece?' I asked, distressed by the distortion.

'She came from the Controlled World too.'

He seemed to know at once why we had come and disappeared behind a screen of skins with such discretion that I felt no embarrassment. Arthur tossed some tools off a chair but otherwise seemed unaware, or at any rate unconcerned, by the mess.

'I'd like to offer you something to eat,' he said, 'but your stomach couldn't take it.'

'I'm not hungry,' I replied truthfully. 'I doubled my nutrition before I left.'

He kissed the nape of my neck and my shoulder, moving slowly down to my breasts. My flesh thrilled to his touch and I longed to rip off my mask and reciprocate. As if reading my mind, he placed his hand firmly on mine. 'No,' he said. 'No. I won't make love to a corpse.' He continued his advance down my body, tracing a circle around my stomach until he reached my groin. Reeling from pleasure, I raised his head. Unable to kiss him, I willed all my desire into my fingertips and, thankful for once that they were moist, ran them down his throat to his nipples, across his chest and on to his thighs. No sooner had I released his springy penis than he pulled me towards him and we made love. We made love three times, and I hope that somewhere in your heart you will find a speck of gratitude that your daughter tasted such passion before she died.

I laid my head on his chest and closed my eyes.

'We have such a short while together,' he said. 'Don't let's waste it in sleep.' I gazed into the gathering darkness and felt the strangeness of a world where light was linked to time. 'Our lives are so different... so distant,' he said. 'Are we ever going to meet again?' I made no reply, afraid to sound either trite or despairing. I wanted to cling to his skin forever so that the issue would not arise.

'Tell me about yourself,' I said. 'Everything. I've met your father. What about your mother?' I scanned the hut for a trace of feminine influence. 'Do you have any sisters or brothers?'

'No, to both. Just Pop. My mother came from your world. She died when I was born.'

'What was her name?'

'Sarah. I know... I know.' He laughed. 'Now tell me that I've slept with you because I'm searching for my mother.'

'What did she die of?' I asked, unable to echo his laughter. 'That's if it's not too painful for you.'

'A virus. Her parents disowned her when they found out she was pregnant. She came back up here but her body couldn't cope. There were problems with the birth. She was very weak and caught something. I don't know what exactly. No one was in a hurry to tell me.'

'Did her parents – your grandparents – never get in touch?'

'Only to ask for the body back. Pop agreed. He felt that he owed them that. Once, when I was a kid, he took me down there to meet them. I don't know what he was after. Maybe he wanted me to see where I came from? But they threw us out. They set these mechanical dogs on us.'

'The custodians.'

'One leapt at Pop and mauled his eyes.'

'That was what blinded him?'

'Yes. He was in agony, but he picked me up and we managed to break free. My face was covered with blood. His blood. At five, you remember the blood.'

'You were five?' I asked, and we both looked at my watch. I longed to end an encounter which now felt sinister. 'I must go.'

We barely spoke as we trudged back through the Dean, although the reasons for our silence were very different. We reached the flyover, where my companions' ribaldry made Arthur unexpectedly coy, and I was grateful to escape with nothing more than a quick hug and the generalised hope that he would see me again soon. I said nothing – not even for form's sake – that might lead him to wait for my return.

The ribaldry increased as we made the vertiginous descent of the ventilation shaft and took the cramped and perilous journey back through the tunnel. I returned to my dom and, scarcely acknowledging my friends' relief, shut myself in my room where I am now writing this.

You might argue that I have no proof of Arthur's parentage. There may have been other Sarahs who ventured up to the Surface World twenty-four years ago; there may have been other fathers who brought their sons down to visit their grandparents. We will never know. The only man able to identify me lost his sight on your... that is, on the grandparents' orders. But, in my view, the evidence is irrefutable. It may not be technically a crime. Mine was not the womb that bore him, although the womb that bore him was identical to mine. But I refuse to be saved by a technicality. So did some mysterious – not to say, mystical – force lead me to him? After all, even in our depopulated worlds, the odds were heavily stacked against our meeting. Or should we see it simply as a fact – not an irony, not fate, and certainly not retribution – just a plain, biological fact that two people were attracted to each other who shared something of a common past and rather more of a genetic inheritance?

I am afraid that I cannot live in a world of such facts, and I certainly cannot live in a world where such facts have no meaning: where you and your associates are so determined to shield us from tragedy that you even delete the word from the dictionary; where Father and his associates have substituted novelty for wisdom. Sarah died as a consequence of love, but I shall die of despair or the closest thing to it in our Controlled World. Perhaps at last I am escaping from her template.

In a few minutes I shall leave the dom and walk quietly to the Transport Depot. I shall climb back up to the Surface World, taking care to avoid the flyover. This is not one of your arbited stories, where love conquers all; I love Arthur too much to allow him to share my guilt. Yet it will comfort me to know that I am close to the one person who has ever wanted me for myself. I shall take off my mask and breathe the air that he breathes even as it kills me. I shall die alone in the wasteland and trust that my flesh will soon be devoured by dogs, leaving no trace of my identity – not, whatever you may say, out of spite but, rather, because it is the only way that I can be sure of your not harvesting my DNA to create another child, the third in this wretched line of Sarahs.

I should also warn you that I shall be posting copies of this mail to everyone in my address book to prevent your effecting another cover-up. I realise of course that this runs the risk of a delay mechanism malfunction leading someone – not you perhaps, but one of the three thousand other recipients – to read it at once and activate the custodians to intercept me on the journey. That is a risk I am prepared to take. So, as my finger hovers above *Send*, let's leave it to the Fate in which neither of us believes.

Afterword: Clones are Still People After All

Professor John Harris: Lord Alliance Professor of Bioethics, and Director of the Institute for Science, Ethics and Innovation, University of Manchester. He is also author of On Cloning *and* Enhancing Evolution.

Nobody now clones human beings. It's illegal though you can clone embryos for research purposes and keep them until 14 days development or indefinitely frozen.

Michael Arditti's story does a good job of sticking to the facts as we now know them from cloning animals. He assumes that the abnormality and failure rates would be about the same as for animals. Clones may also have a foreshortened life, but this is less clear. Dolly the sheep had problems with her joints, but we don't know if she actually died too young. Apart from anything else, we haven't done enough research on what the natural lifespan of a sheep is.

It's possible that in this far future, foreshortened life and other problems of cloning might have been solved. Sarah's mother would also have had the option of using stem cell technology to create new eggs of her own, and replace the lost child that way. The story depends on Sarah's mother wanting an absolute duplicate of a lost child, which is plausible but naive of her.

You can't replace an individual in this way. Twenty years later, the uterine environment would be different to that experienced by the lost child – diet would be different; stress levels in the womb would be different. As the brain starts forming in the womb, it makes neural connections that are unique. This Sarah would be a unique individual at birth, and then receive more different stimuli thereafter. She would have a personality and identity of her own so the aspiration of replacing a lost individual with a clone is an illusion.

I'm a philosopher not a scientist, though I do need

to understand the science. I address ethics. The question of 'Should we do this?' is best answered before things happen, rather than end up saying afterwards 'Wish we hadn't done that.' There is a responsibility to scan horizons, and see if we wish to move towards them. Reproductive cloning is unproblematic from an ethical perspective but like many human projects is riddled with contradictions and misunderstandings.

There are a lot of ethical myths around cloning, fatuous statements like one that came out of UNESCO stating that, 'The human genome is the common heritage of mankind and must be preserved.' The only reproductive method that would preserve the genome WOULD be cloning. Ordinary reproduction mixes genomes and introduces mutations, continually changing the genome. It is as though UNESCO wanted to find literally any argument against human cloning and hit on the least plausible argument available.

We should remember that we humans have a long experience with reproductive cloning. One in every 270 births produces identical twins – true clones if ever there were any – without ethical catastrophe. The problems are the ones Michael Arditti refers to: the failure and abnormality rates. But normal sexual reproduction has a failure rate of 80% and an abnormality rate over 6%. If sexual reproduction were a new technology it would never have been licensed because it is simply too dangerous.

So cloning makes a good story but like so much in human affairs the tragedy is of our own making, not inherent in the science nor in the technology but in the human failures of understanding and of sympathy which so far, despite science and technology are as frequent as ever.

Zoology

Simon Ings

Since its foundations were laid, less than a year ago, the new Life Sciences building has been rising smoothly, steadily, and quickly enough to pique the faculty board's paranoia: 'And the catch is...?'

The new building and its predecessors form a striking architectural triad. The Past is a handsome, fussy Victorian redbrick near the trunk road. The Present is a serviceable Eighties glasshouse. The Future is an Ayn Rand wet dream, an artfully 'unplanned' assemblage of geometrical figures. Clever windows. Passive-aggressive air conditioning. A truncated cone. The corner of a cube. A dome. The building's elements imply the solids from which they have been cut. In this way, the building promises more than itself. You pause a moment to admire the building and you glimpse a vast, expensive Platonic idea.

Goodness knows how they will label its honeycombed levels and intersecting atriums. The university has a love of complex navigational nomenclature. I began my career here in the Past – '1860' carved into the brick above the main entrance – and they still somehow managed to find me a laboratory on Floor 3Ω. The room in which we're assembled this morning is almost directly below that old lab (now a multimedia facility) and the sign on the door says 5.5-B – 'B' a felt-tipped label stuck inexpertly over a raised plastic 'C'.

Most of this morning's meeting has been spent misunderstanding the floor plan of the new building. 'So,

Kevin, microscopy will actually be gaining space.'

Anja is right, as usual. Anja with a 'juh'. American by birth: surname Sinauer (no relation to the publisher). I try not to catch her eye.

There were no latecomers to this meeting. The marks of institutional preferment are ours for the taking now, in a catfight over square footage and parking space allocation. And I have behaved like a pig, fighting my department's corner with more fury than sense.

Part of it is frustration.

I got my PhD in 1982. Back then I described myself as an invertebrate physiologist. Each morning I arrived for work at the Department of Invertebrate Physiology. That's what it said on the door. Since then (and in this I am no different to thousands of others, caught in the headlights of the Molecular Revolution) I have watched as my discipline has been swallowed and swallowed again by dinky new labels, each more nebulous than the last. The moment I got my feet under the lab table, the Department of Invertebrate Physiology was ingested by the Department of Physiological Science. I left to work in France on a CNRC grant; returning ten years later, I found the words 'Life Sciences' drilled into a slab of Perspex mounted by the steps of the Present.

What will they call us this time? What have they left themselves? 'Studies'?

It took two meetings with Human Resources to establish that this year's mergers, and our staggered expansion into the Future, will be accomplished without redundancies.

'See?' Anja Sinauer uncrosses her 10-denier legs and leans across the outspread plan to tap a manicured nail against the edge of the uptilted pyramid. That pyramid is an effective piece of architectural self-aggrandisement. The administration, however, has been wildly underselling it. In HR meetings, Anja calls it 'the top floor'.

For those in the know, the name makes a kind of buried sense. These days the top floors of most new university buildings are left empty for at least the first couple of years of the building's life. It being cheaper to expand in an ad hoc way through an existing structure, than to build another annexe. 'Top floor' is code for 'empty'. The pyramid is wired and plumbed, but right now its mezzanines are raw concrete, and its rooms are simply metal tracks set in the floor.

All three edifices – Past, Present and Future – stand near enough to each other that (lest we miss the point) their upper storeys have been connected by big black tubes.

Last month a big black tube appeared above the window of the office I share with Joanne, blocking our already inadequate daylight.

From the outside, even up close, the tube's tinted plastic is utterly opaque. Anthony, our postgrad assistant, was with me in the office the day it appeared. 'What I don't get is why the tubes are so damned black.'

A corridor runs directly above our office. The tube carries it out into space. It slopes very gently over the Saabs and the Audis in the all-star car park below (stellar forces contest these bays: emeritus professors with desks in Zurich and lecture tours planned in the Southern States) and buries itself in the side of the off-balance pyramid which crowns the new Life Sciences building.

No-one is supposed to know about the sheep: descendants of Herdwicks that once grazed this land when it was moor, and the university was but a gleam in our charismatic founder's eye. A legal tangle over the deeds left the flock with grazing rights in perpetuity, at the same time granting the founders the right to build. Eventually, a secret compromise was reached. Today the sheep are driven unseen along the mirror-coated tubes from building to building, from Past to Present to Future, above the heads of the unsuspecting student body.

As puerile stories go, the one tickling the freshers this year does a better job than most of capturing the heady, deracinated spirit of Life Sciences: an institution that by sheer effort of corporate thinking has torn itself free from mere geography, repudiates in statements of steel and glass naive notions of useful land, and smothers beneath its over-complex signage any hint of home.

His metabolism comprehensively rewired by cannabinol, Roy Sennett weaves a smoky, sleepless, paranoid path from plane to plane, city to city, nation to nation, in the hunt for innovative footwear.

Roy being my last great passion. ('Not "last",' Joanne would say, '"most recent".' The top shelf of our office bookshelf has become, on her initiative, an unashamed shrine to the efficacy of high self-esteem and neuro-linguistic programming.)

Roy, a native of New York, was employed by a leading international baseball boot manufacturer to seek out and buy interesting tat, and courier it post-haste to the company's Brooklyn workshop. This was not stealing, he told me. This was *reverse engineering*. Having had one or two findings of my own reverse-engineered over the years, usually by ambitious Stateside labs, I took Roy's irony as a given.

Roy was cocky, loud, gorgeous, and already – less than six hours after flapping and flolloping his way like a stranded fish from the airport to the relative conviviality of Cable Street – stoned out of his mind. Landed in the dead of night by KLM Royal Dutch, he clearly had only hours to live. He was twenty-five. I girded my loins and, with more appetite than affection, I administered the kiss of life.

Incredibly, Roy took to me. We went shopping together. Picture it if you can. Kevin shows Roy around Ted Baker. Poor bastard. A Windsor princeling led through a refugee camp could not have tried to look more serious, more compassionate, more unshockable.

The next day Roy phoned to invite me to a friend's birthday party. I thought: friend? You've been in the country less than a week.

We met early on Cable Street, at a bar, and Roy, who never knowingly undersold anyone, brought me up to speed: 'She's the most magnificent monster!'

I understood what he meant as soon as we shouldered our way into the basement of the club. His monstrous friend, in a translucent black dress and killer heels, had seized the dais at the back of the dance floor, where the spotlight lit her up like Madonna as she swayed and tossed her head; not so much dancing, I decided, overcoming my first surprise, as miming what it was like to be herself. Her performance was gorgeously onanistic: a closed loop.

'I know her,' I shouted into Roy's ear.

'She's so *out there!*' he cried, his erudition crumpling against the sheer wall of her ego.

Anja herself seemed determined not to show the hit. When she could no longer avoid acknowledging me, she gave me the vaguest of have-we-met smiles. Only her eyes betrayed her, retreating into her skull for a second – a trick of the wheeling lights – as though tugged by a muscle.

Three doors down from our labs there is a cupboard. Or rather, an architectural oversight with a door. It doesn't appear on any of the blueprints, it doesn't have a room number, and for a while – the joke palling quickly under the onslaught of Harry Potter-related hype – it was nicknamed Room 9æ.

We didn't need a cupboard. We needed another workplace – so we made it into one. A wide fitted shelf doubles as a desk. There is room for someone to sit down in front of a computer, and for a colleague to peer over their shoulder at the screen. Communities of *Drosophila* maggots are stacked in petri dishes behind the base of the Anglepoise lamp, where even I can't contrive to knock them over.

Anthony takes a maggot from a dish and fixes it to the end of a matchstick, immobilising it with a strip of paraffin film. It's close work: the grey–white maggots are small, one could sit happily camouflaged on the milky rim of your fingernail. They are like balloons – the skin is tough but the insides are jelly. They burst easily. Even the best wrapping tends to distort a maggot's shape. It took Anthony weeks to perfect his experimental routine. By then he had figured out, pretty much by intuition, which end was the head and which the tail.

Next to Anthony's workstation, taking up fully half of our secret laboratory, stands a heavy trolley with lockable wheels. Its metre-square work surface floats on a bed of engine oil. In this way, things on the table are insulated from vibration. (The fan cooling the CPU under Anthony's desk. The hum of the fluorescent light. Sounds from the plumbing. Footfalls.) On it stands a heavy tripod. Anthony clamps the matchstick to the tripod and slides the Leica into place.

The electrode is mounted in a vice. Small adjustments bring it into line with the maggot's 'head'. Turning the final wheel brings the needle into contact with the maggot's skin. Though the tip is too fine to see without the aid of the microscope, still the tegument resists a moment, denting and buckling before it pops, and the needle is inside.

Only now does Anthony turn on the speakers mounted in the upper rear corners of the room. The din issuing from them is terrific. Gunshots. Mortar fire. This blitzkrieg is the electromagnetic spill from Anthony's hand, as he adjusts the position of the needle, easing it into the maggot's 'nose'.

When he takes his hand away, the noise diminishes. Half a cardboard box wrapped in bacofoil – our cheap-and-cheerful Faraday Cage – insulates the maggot still further: now, at last, there is peace.

The components of the smell of rotting fruit are well known. Aldehydes. Ketones. Droppered onto cotton wool and offered up to our maggots, singly or in combination, they tell us what the maggots can smell, and what scents they are attracted to. Anthony nudges a cotton bud into place, settles back as comfortably as he can, and listens in.

Waves crash.

Pebbles stir and sweep.

Once I was showing a group of schoolchildren around our rooms. I paused in the corridor, let them peer into Room 9æ (they loved that), and asked them to guess the meaning of this sound. The ocean swirl of raw sensation.

Invited to explain, Anthony caught my eye and smiled his malign smile. 'This,' he said, 'is the sound of a maggot's anguish.'

We've known for a long time that we construct, from confused evidence, much of what we see and hear. Smell, on the other hand, never seemed to require such complex explanation. The short-hand used in school textbooks really did appear to capture, with reasonable accuracy, what we thought went on. Differently shaped aromatic molecules fit into differently shaped receptors on the tongue or in the nose. Smelling is simply a question of matching locks to keys, and there is an exact, one-to-one match between chemical reality and olfactory sensation.

Drosophila maggots have just 21 olfactory sensory neurons, making them ideal experimental animals. There is even a laboratory-bred strain that has only one receptor. It was Anthony's job, having passed our rigorous round of interviews and reference checks, to sit in 9æ, hour after hour, week after week, listening to the roar and backwash of that single cell.

Sealed in his cupboard, Anthony toiled, trying to isolate the signal we were after: a maggot's quantum of sensation.

Drosophila doesn't lay its eggs on just any old piece of fruit. The female searches out the type of fruit she remembers from when she was a maggot. Smell and memory are connected in *Drosophila* as surely as they were in Marcel Proust, who unlocked, in the taste of a Madeleine dipped in tea (a filthy habit), seven unwieldy volumes of *roman à clef*.

One Friday afternoon, as Joanne was leaving, Anthony greeted her with a mordant 'Eureka', pulling at his cheeks and dropping his jaw in the manner of Edvard Munch's *The Scream*.

If different aromatic molecules latch on to different olfactory receptors, then Anthony's larvae, each boasting but a single receptor, should only have been able to smell one smell. Anthony had discovered otherwise. He reckoned his virtually noseless maggots were noticing every smelly cotton bud he put in front of them: a selection representing the entire spectrum of maggot food sources.

'The stunted little fuckers,' he said, 'are noticing *everything.*'

At 1pm, Anja Sinauer logs out of the admin server, pulls her tote bag from under her desk and heads for the women's toilets.

Behind the locked cubicle door, she sheds her shoes, rolls down her tights and knickers, and drops them into her bag. She undoes her bra through her sweater. She disentangles herself easily, used to this routine, and draws the bra out through her left sleeve. The brassiere follows the rest of her underwear into the bag.

Leaving the lavatory, Anja climbs the stairs to the top floor, takes a magnetic card out of the front pocket of her bag, and swipes her way through a fire door and into the tube.

The incomprehensible blackness of these postmodern footbridges is nowhere apparent from the inside. Here the tubing is bright and clear – the Lord only knows how quickly the sun's ultraviolet will fog, smear, cloud or otherwise ruin such exotic material.

The tube slopes very gently down towards the pyramid crowning our new Life Sciences building. The view from here is spectacular, vertiginous, and very subtly blue-shifted, glamorizing the car park, the annexes, and the trunk road beyond. The walkway itself is the only part of the tunnel that is not transparent – a narrow strip of non-slip rubber, down which Anja cannot help but stalk, hips a-sway with the effort of landing one high-heeled foot precisely in front of another: a gymnast treading the beam.

The pyramid is empty, raw, without coverings or furnishings: the arena for a sport yet to be invented. A while ago I swiped two stacking chairs from the back of a lecture hall. In a space meant eventually to house a hundred people, these chairs are the only furniture.

Anja and I say very little to each other. Whatever needs we satisfy here are sufficiently dissimilar that discussing them would only engender boredom.

Away from the windows (though these too are mirrored) Anja takes off her clothes. The red compression marks left by her underwear have virtually disappeared. This detail hardly matters to me, armed as I am with a mere handful of sweaty HB pencils. But it is a habit she has acquired: a bit of professional business.

Roy and Anja went to the same art school in New York. Modelling Roy's graduate show was Anja's first 'gig'. I would like to be able to say that this was only the beginning of Anja's confidences, the night of her birthday; that, having left the club with Roy and me and a couple of her other friends to find something to eat, she warmed to me. As it is, her smile, whenever we pass each other in the corridors of Past and Present, is perceptibly no less chilly than it was when she started working here.

Still, there must be more than professional courtesy behind her agreeing to this arrangement. To stand and sit and recline here, in the cavernous and none-too-warm spaces of the Future, unclothed, self-abandoned, and oh, so closely observed.

The last thing she is, is naked. She is no more stripped by taking off her clothes than a cannon is stripped when the screen of camouflaging branches is pulled clear of the muzzle. Naked, she is fully armed. I am not so far gone that I cannot remember that feeling: the body as a source of power.

I would like to pretend that some of these important insights into Anja Sinauer's character and motivations will make it into my sketches. But I cannot claim much capability. By sheerest intuition, I can just about make clear on paper the difference between the front end and the back end. I draw what I see, which is to say, I get everything wrong.

Studying an early effort, Joanne's tight-lipped comment was: 'I suppose you don't like women very much, do you?'

It was a portrait of Roy.

Seeing the amateurishness of my work, Anja would be well within her rights to call a halt to this: 'Are you drawing? Are you looking? Or are you just *staring?*' Luckily, and thanks to Roy, I come to her pre-vetted: a harmless queer whose difficult ideas teem like lice beneath terrible hair: '*Indulge* him, Anja darling, everybody else does.'

We have called our paper 'Peripheral OR Response Profiles in larval *Drosophila melanogaster:* a Fuzzy Approach'.

I am almost apologetic when I explain to people what we've found: the way a *Drosophila* smell receptor reacts strongly to one aroma, mildly and intermittently to others. If I were an ambitious thirty-year-old I'd be completely brash and self-confident about the complexity we've unearthed. I'd make it my career. 'We construct what we smell!' I'd bore everybody's pants off. On the other hand, if I was an embittered old git, I'd probably feel the same, but with a huge dose of desperation stirred in. As it is, and from the equivocal vantage point of middle life, my best bet seems to be to play up my dull, English embarrassment.

Anthony feels more reserved still. He has spent weeks, on his own, in a cupboard, listening to the neural meanderings of dying maggots. I know what he is afraid of. He is afraid that, come publication, we are going to be killed. Our experiments will be repeated – most likely by some hostile rival in the States – and it will turn out that our fuzzy peripheral responses possess no more reality than Lovell's Martian canals. Our careers will be over, and it will be Anthony's fault, and everyone will know.

'Can anyone tell me why the damned thing has a nose at all?' He swirls the dregs of his Frobisher's Red Orange around in its bottle. It catches the low afternoon light: a little liquid sun, aflame against the thick brown ground of the varnished table where we sit, hunched towards each other, like conspirators.

I am too old for shame, and am working my way

through my second San Miguel. Joanne has already downed her caffe latte.

'It hatches out onto its food source. It's small enough it will never exhaust its food source. What does it need a nose for?'

The maggot does not need a nose. The fly does. The fly must lay its eggs on the same food source that sustained it when it was a maggot. In this way, good moves are perpetuated from generation to generation.

All the same, the maggot's sense of smell, as we have modelled it – so complex, so sensitive, so responsive to circumstance – seems worryingly ornate. Our elders and betters – professors whose theories of lock and key have won them enviable parking spots in universities bigger and better than this one – will not be slow to comment.

At least *Nature* has come on-side.

We have nailed down our findings as best we can. But we have to remain realistic. Far from generating knowledge, at this early stage we are simply adding to the uncertainties troubling the field.

'Of course, it could be that *Drosophila* has a really lousy sense of smell,' Joanne says. 'Really shoddy, I mean. Hopelessly unreliable. God, what if we've spent the last three months of our lives trying to systematize its *mistakes?*'

Anthony laughs. His time with us so far falls into equal halves. Weeks spent in a cupboard trying to scrub the white noise off an elusive signal. Weeks in the same cupboard analyzing the shape and frequency of the very noise we had asked him to erase. No wonder Joanne's idea delights him. That the maggot knows no better than he does, what it is smelling, or why. That maggots, too, are prey to the hopeful artefact.

I keep my sketches zipped into a separate compartment of my briefcase. I know myself too well. It is well within my declining powers to substitute life sketches for hand-outs at an inopportune moment.

At home, I lay the drawings out.

Anja Sinauer is an American. A native of New York. An arts school graduate. An exuberant dancer. A dyke, or at any rate, a fag-hag. An ex-model. A manager in the human resources department of a major English university. An exhibitionist. A glorious monster. An unfriendly person. Prejudices, truisms, misinterpretations, assumptions and guesses. And as for the drawings!

The art manuals say that the feeling of not being able to draw is merely the sensation that accompanies the act of drawing. Biology teaches a very similar lesson, as poor Anthony has discovered. Biologists know virtually nothing about anything. They hurl themselves giggling into the muchness of things and return – when they return at all – with buckets brimming over with half-truths, experimental artefacts and doubts. Anthony had better get used to the feeling. If he's any good, it is going to become his constant companion. His compass, and his conscience.

Were I to devote every hour of the rest of my life to capturing the truth about Anja Sinauer, I would fail. If I substituted oils for pencils, or learned how to be a better artist, or took a magic pill that turned me into a great artist – it still wouldn't make any difference. The outcome, the failure, would be the same. The truth is real enough. But truth is a seam too rich to be exhausted.

Last year, after twenty years spent tracing the activity of single cells, and listening to the ecstatic rush and curl of another animal's being, and prompted, perhaps, by my boyfriend then – Roy, for whom human surfaces were the walls of his pleasurable world – I felt in need of reassurance. I needed to know that the uncertainties I worked among were not mere artefacts. I wanted to be sure that the difficulties I faced were, at their core, general and ordinary. A professional observer, I needed a way to return, now and again, to simpler processes, more natural, more direct ways of working. So I picked up a pencil, and started to draw.

I am by now, jokes aside, tolerably competent. You

would recognize her, from the drawings I have made today.

In one, Anja is sitting with slumped shoulders, her legs apart, her elbows resting on her knees. It is an attitude of exhaustion.

There is an intelligence in her look that I recognize. It is a look I steer away from in those dreadful HR meetings of hers. (And after all, how are we supposed to take seriously a woman who says – by way of invitation to her lair – 'I'll arrange sandwiches'? A woman whose annual report was entitled 'Enabling the Delivery of Excellence with Impact'?)

Recorded here, too, there is an appetite I am not built to match, any more than her other friends were, that night on Cable Street. I wonder now, thinking back to how magnificently she grandstanded under those lights, whether anywhere but Cable Street could have tolerated her. Had there been enough other women there they would surely have torn her limb from limb.

What else? There is a softness to her jawline – but that is all wrong, an artefact, I see now, of my tentative technique.

My hope is that, with practice, the many misfirings of my mind and hand and heart may yet come to an accommodation, so that I may capture – just about, and almost purely by chance – the spark of life.

Afterword: Exceptions

Dr Matthew Cobb, Programme Director Biology, the University of Manchester

When Simon came to visit Manchester, my colleague Catherine McCrohan and myself were trying to get a scientific paper published. This involves submitting a draft to a journal, and then waiting for other scientists – our 'peers' – to review it anonymously, recommending whether it should be accepted and making suggestions for changes. This process is frequently quite stressful – referees are often irritating and seem not to understand the point of it all. The fact that we, too, are referees on other people's papers, and can be just as irritating and obtuse, seems to escape us.

'Anthony' – our PhD student, Derek Hoare – had been working on this paper for three years. To our surprise, it ended up challenging some of our basic ideas about how the sense of smell works. Smell neurons are supposed to respond like a lock when a key (the smell) is turned – they either respond or they don't. 'Anthony' had found that although this was true for some examples, in many others, smell neurons sometimes responded to an odour, and sometimes they didn't.

This was annoying not only because it challenged what everyone thought (including us), but also because it went against the whole point of doing an experiment. Science is about trying to turn squishy reality into hard numbers and consistent effects. This is relatively straightforward in physics, but in biology it is difficult. Laws of physics that were worked out 300 years ago can put a satellite in orbit around Jupiter, but we cannot accurately predict which way a maggot will turn. Our findings showed that the sense of smell has an important random element, the meaning of which we still do not understand.

Our paper was published in a leading neuroscience journal, with Derek as the lead author, and we have presented its findings at two international scientific meetings, one on smell, the other on maggots. At the smell meeting, people came up to me afterwards and said 'We've seen that kind of thing before, but always ignored it.' We also tried to ignore it – or at least to get rid of the unexpected variability. But we could not, and we eventually found that the maggot's nose had boxed us into a corner. We could not escape this 'noise', so we had to embrace it, explore it, and try and understand it. The lesson is simple – as the pioneer geneticist William Bateson put it: 'Treasure your exceptions'.

Temporary

Frank Cottrell Boyce

Pa,

Been fretting over me? Cease that now for I am in the ascendant and hope this finds you likewise. Caine most like told you how I was plucked from class. Two real live Auditors come in and asked how if anyone had been out to see the new star. I told them me and Caine had been out both to look, but how we hadn't seen a glimmer of it on account of all the clouds. And I went on to tell them how when we got home, you tried to cheer us up by letting us fry the onions for the omlette ourselves but they said that was not relevant. They said, nobody hardly seen it with their eyes as yet but that there it was sure enough in our house, Capricorn. He asked if any of us was born under that sign. And everyone was of course, except for the two Chentoufi boys who are Virgos. They was throwed out of Virgo school on account of playing around in a not-very-Virgo like of manner. So they ended up down here in Capricorn school.

'A new star in the sky is always interesting. A new star in your Zodiac House is a cause of great hope and rejoicing,' is what the Auditors said. They'd come all the way from the Auditorium so that we could hear what was going on in our heavenly home. They showed us papers with jagged lines jumping around and said they were the radio waves the star was making. They said our star was a new note in the music

159

of the spheres.

Everyone put their hand up and started in to asking what the new star meant. Some said it meant our pa's would get new jobs or that we'd all be getting better houses.

'No one knows yet, what it means,' said the Auditor. 'But something good.'

'Maybe we'll all go to Virgo school,' said Caine.

'Maybe you definitely won't,' laughed Anwar Chentoufi, 'Virgo school is for Virgo people, not for goat folks and fools.'

'That's true,' said the Auditor. 'But the star might mean a great improvement in this school. How would you like that?'

I said, 'And when the star goes away again, will the school still stay good?'

Everyone went real quiet and everyone was looking at me and in the end, my Teacher said, 'Child what are you chatting? Stars don't go away again once they appear.'

'Once a star has joined the Cosmic Orchestra,' said the Auditor man, 'it plays for ever and more.'

'Not this one, though,' I said. 'This one's coming brighter and then it's going to go.'

My teacher told me to sit down and that smartly, but the Auditor pulled me by the arm, saying, 'What makes you say such a thing, little girl?'

'Badness,' yelled Caine. 'Tell her to hush it, saying bad things about our star and wishing us bad fortune. Just because we went out everywhere looking for it and never saw a glimmer.'

Everyone was booing and throwing things. The Chentoufi boys were laughing out loud and calling our new star a useless star, a temporary star. 'Goat folks can't even afford a permanent star.'

The teacher yelled and everyone else yelled louder until the Auditors took me out to their transport and asked me what made me say what I did. I said, 'It's the plain sad truth, that's all. Can't you tell from those papers?'

'How would we tell, do you think?'

'The sound it's making. The sound the star was making was getting louder and louder, then it wobbled, and now it's starting to dip down already.'

'You can tell what sound the star is making just by looking at those charts?'

I said, 'What are they for, otherwise?'

They said, 'Come with us.'

They took me straight off in their transport to the Auditorium, Pa. One of them said he believed I was the first Capricorn child to walk into that place.

Once inside, a whole bunch of other Auditors came to meet me. They showed me more charts from our new star. They asked me what I thought they meant. I didn't know how to explain. I just looked a little at the charts and then hummed out the noise they seemed to be describing. It was so plain to me. They seemed pleased enough and they showed me round the whole place, all the maps they have there of space, and models of the nine spheres themselves, showed me where the noise from the radio receiver comes in, even let me move the radio dish around a little while. They seemed pleased with me. The one who came to school said, 'She's an instinctive interpreter.'

At least one did. The other one said, 'We don't know that she is right of course. She could be just...' something I couldn't understand. I think he thinks I'm maybe crazy.

After that I said, 'Thank you very kindly and can I please now go home.'

They said, 'Best not to.'

They explained that because I'd said that about the star disappearing again, people might not like me any more. I had best stay here in the Auditorium with them and they would show me more charts and I could be useful to my people.

So, Pa, this is where I am. I am not punished. I am being kept here for my own safety until I am proved right.

It's kind of an honour. I am a guest. You can come and see me, I'm sure of it.

Pa,

Yesterday the star did disappear. I said to the Auditors, 'Don't that just show that I was bang right, all along? And can I now go home please?'

They said, 'Best not. Capricorn people are uneducated. It may be they believe you caused the star's disappearance.'

You don't think that, do you, Pa? No on thinks that do they? And if they did, you'd put them straight. How can a girl make a star do anything. Stars control us, not the other way round. I said so to the Auditors. The one who came to school said, 'We don't know we are only just beginning to understand the balance between above and below.'

The other one who came to school said, 'Tycho Brahe said, As above, so below. That's all we can be certain of.'

Pa, I don't believe that I caused the star to disappear. But maybe you do. Maybe you are mad at me for that.

I know that bad things happened to Capricorn people after the star disappeared. I know that some of our land was taken and our schools closed and we paid more taxes. But the fault is in the stars, not in me. Maybe you don't believe that. Maybe that's why you don't come here and try and get me back. Or even say hello.

Dear Father,

They have encouraged me to reassure you about my happiness and general condition. I have nothing to complain about here. I am well fed and lodged. I spend the days looking at the radio wave print outs and humming them. I'm not sure how this is useful but I am kept busy all day. Because I was right about the star disappearing, I command some respect and I am treated like someone. Even the one who said I was maybe crazy brings his print outs to me.

I am telling you this because when you finally came

to see me yesterday, after all this time, you seemed to think I would be coming home with you. At least that is the impression I got when you finally finished eating all the biscuits and drinking all the juice which is left in reception for visitors while they are waiting. These things are meant to be shared, by the way, and not consumed by one individual, as was pointed out to me, more than once, by people also making remarks about Capricorns, and forgetting that I am a Capricorn.

This is not something I have forgotten myself.

When I am not working I go into the archive where they keep all the old print outs. Pa, people from the other star signs watch their constellations and write down everything that happens. But Capricorns don't do that. I'm doing it now, for all our sakes, and I have made a discovery, Pa.

The star that came and went, came and went before. Many times. Not much more than twenty years ago, and twenty years before that, and twenty before that, going right back to the time of Tycho Brahe.

Tycho Brahe is the one who first found out how all the World works. He built the first Auditorium – only he called it an Observatory because he was only looking at the stars, and not listening to them. He had a pet elk. It died because he got it drunk and it fell downstairs. Also, he was the first to say, As Above, So Below. It's from him we learnt that Capricorns can't marry Librans, and the Virgos should never hold public office and everything in fact. But all he learnt was lost and forgotten until after the War. Then it was all found again in his secret condominium in Uraniborg. As soon as everyone read them, they could see that here was a way to end unhappiness. Here was a way to stop inappropriate people doing important work or marrying incompatible people, or breeding at random times of the year – in the past a Virgo might have a Capricorn child or vice versa. Here was a scientific, rational way to order things. And so the great Auditoria were constructed and peace reigned. It is unfortunate of course that Capricorns have not distinguished themselves or prospered in this World. But perhaps that will change and perhaps I will help it change!

If the star came and went many times, that surely means it was not my fault that it disappeared, or that things went badly for Capricorns. If a star comes and goes throughout the ages, then perhaps it is not a bad sign when it disappears. Maybe we have misunderstood it. Maybe I can come to understand it and maybe if I understand it, things will go better with our people.

I liked to see you sitting there in front of me, even if only eating biscuits.

My Dear Father,

It has been exactly sixteen years and three months since I last saw you. I wrote in the past because it was pleasant for me to think of home – of you, of Caine, of our night time walks and of us cooking together. Me pushing the onion round on the pan with a wooden spoon, while you stood next to me and chopped and so on. I do not have to cook here. I realise that while I like to recall you, perhaps you do not like to recall me. Perhaps you are trying to forget me. Although I have no news of you, I know that things have not gone well for our people. When I try to picture you in a Capricorn settlement – with the high glass walls around it and no real occupation, and no permission to leave, I know that you must be unhappy. Here, it is considered impolite to remind me that I am a Capricorn, that I am your daughter.

So I am writing to you today to tell you that I believe, truly that your – our – unhappiness will soon be over. That the Capricorn people will rise into their Ascendant now.

For our star is returning.

I came into the Auditorium this morning and found on my desk a message from an Auditor in Siberia. He has seen it. Maybe you will see it yourself tonight.

Today I am the ears of the World. For more than ten

years I have explained and propounded and sort to prove my theory that the star will return. Now I am vindicated. In a moment I – your daughter – will send word to every radio telescope on the planet. In the plains and on the mountains, in the deserts and on the backs of great ships, the dishes will rotate and attend to our constellation. In the higher orbits, and at the far edge of our solar system, the listening probes and satellites will alter their trajectories, to lean into the tracks of our star's remote disturbance. They will strain for and store and transmit, its ancient whispers – ancient because it has taken a hundred million years to reach hear. A hundred million years of travelling that will end in my mind. For every dish, satellite and microphone is connected to me. I am where it all ends and begins. I am Earth's ears today.

This time when I listen I will hear much more than last time. This time I will hear the truth of our infrequent star.

I do not interpret. I cannot tell you what the star means. I can only tell you it is back. But surely it must be something good.

I did try to interpret when I first came here.

When the other Auditors first heard my theory of the infrequent star, they asked me how a star can appear and then disappear if it is attached to one of the harmonious spheres.

I posited an answer – that perhaps the harmonious spheres are not entirely transparent, perhaps they contain dark patches which obscure what lies behind them. Of course if this were really the case, then there would be swathes of stars that would become infrequent. As far as we can tell, our star is a singularity.

In seeking an answer to the question, however, I was brought to asking other questions. For instance, it seemed to me that almost all the stars whose sounds I could interpret were moving not only across the sky, but away from us, further into space. As if the whole cosmos were expanding.

Pyth said this was consonant with wisdom – it meant only that the spheres of harmony themselves were expanding, like balloons.

But if the spheres expand, then the constellations which are written on them are distending and will one day no longer resemble the emblems of the houses of the Sun. One day they will be meaningless.

No, said Pyth, they expand for a while and then shrink again. As if they are breathing. The universe is a living thing after all.

And when I examine the print outs it is clear to me that some of the objects which we have called stars on our charts, are not single stars, but clusters and crowds of stars, and maybe even other universes, as full of stars as our own — so vast that their signal can be heard though they must surely lie beyond the furthest of the spheres of harmony.

'And, Pyth,' I asked, 'What are the spheres made of that they are thin enough to permit light through, but strong enough to hold the stars in place, and never to burn?'

'We don't know. But we know that they are there. We have measured the weight of all the stars, against the weight of the Original Singularity and discovered that there is matter missing. The missing matter is the material of the spheres.'

'And beyond our spheres, are there more spheres?'

'Perhaps.'

'And our spheres are so vast, Pyth. The light that comes from them takes centuries to reach us. Does that light really come so far really to tell us where to live and what tax to pay and who is amorously compatible with whom?'

'If it doesn't come for that, why does it come? Who would fashion a giant goat of stars and place it in the sky for no reason?!'

'But one day it won't be a goat — and in any case it's not all stars...'

Pyth put his hand on my shoulder and said quietly, 'Amy, you are an Auditor, an excellent Auditor, not an interpreter. Let the interpreters interpret. Do not trouble your head.'

'But my head is troubled.'

When he had gone, Tycho came to me and said, 'Keep all that you learn. Keep it in your head. Build your own cosmos in there. As above, so below. Do not interpret. But do not forget either.'

This is another thing I must tell you. I married him. I might have preferred to marry Pyth but he was a Virgo and therefore not compatible. Tycho is a Taurean. Almost on the cusp. We have a daughter called Amy.

On our wedding night, I asked if we could leave the Auditorium and walk around in the dark and look at the stars. Tycho said this would be unwise. 'You are building a picture of the cosmos inside your head. Looking at the stars in the sky will only confuse matters. You don't need to see the instruments to hear the music. In fact, seeing them distracts from the music.'

So I walk around with a tiny universe inside my head. And at night, when Amy falls asleep, I close my eyes and allow myself to float through its effulgent structures and wander along its brilliant complexities. Strangely, in my mind, when I come to rest, I do so always up on the ridge.

They allowed me to name the new star. I named it Neary, after you and the Ridge. Eyebrows were raised and remarks were made about the name. But it is my star and today is my day.

So I do not try to interpret. And I do not peep. I simply listen and describe what I hear. And nurture in my mind an image of the cosmos as I hear it. And today I hear a new sound. An explosion of joy. A lost star returning. I do not interpret, but I do hope. For you, Pa, and for all of us. And when it comes, maybe I will go out up onto Neary Ridge and look up and see it for the first time. Maybe we could meet up there.

For now I am going to listen.

Father,

Moment by moment as the printouts came in, I came to understand what was happening. Even from the first I knew that it was not a single star. I could see that there were two objects. Two objects interacting like two people conversing. Or fighting.

I am telling you this so that you understand. It is not a star at all. There are two objects. A huge, dark one. And another, nearby, much smaller and infinitely dense. The smaller one is destroying the other. It pulls material from the larger one's surface. The large dark object is unravelling and the smaller one is wrapping itself in the material, as though it were a scarf. Sometimes – every two decades it seems – there is so much material that there is an explosion. An explosion so huge that looking at the printouts made my ears hurt.

I believe the large, dark object is a dying star. I believe that stars can die, like people, like childhood, like memories. And when they die, they are torn apart by smaller objects, that these smaller objects gorge on the star and then spew the remains of its glory into space. Only the spew is visible.

I learned this, piece by piece, minute by minute as the printouts came in.

I did not tell at first. I pretended that it was harder to interpret than it was. I pretended that I needed time. And all the while, outside somewhere the light was blazing. But it was not starlight.

When I went to bed, I placed the two objects in the little universe I carry in my head. I travelled to them. I stared at them. I tried to will the explosion to continue, to burn forever. I tried to rekindle the star. I did not want it to die.

But this did not happen. What happens in the little universe in my head does not resonate in the big one above my head. Because 'as above, so below' is not true.

I talked to Tycho about it. I wanted to hide it. I said, 'A visiting star is something. Perhaps a sign of hope, a cause for celebration. But this, this is the twitching of a corpse. This is the incineration of rubbish. There is no way to interpret this well.'

He said, 'We are not interpreters. We are only Auditors. If we do not tell what we hear then what hope can there ever be? If you do not tell the way things are, then all humanity will be cloaked in a darkness you created.'

I had still not told. Snake Bearers were still full of hope and celebration. They brought tour parties into the Auditorium itself to see the printouts and listen to the clicks and whirrs and noises which they call the Musica Universalis. I watched them come and go, from the bridge across the atrium, hoping that you would come with them and I could explain everything to you. I think I was hoping that if I told you everything, you could somehow make it better. When I told you my troubles before, you could always make them better.

You didn't come.

It was a foolish hope anyway. Why would you be able to do what I with all my knowledge could not.

Besides, in the Auditorium it was already obvious that the new star was fading. It was pointless and painful to conceal the truth. I filed my report. The Head Interpreter himself came to our quarters to compliment me on its thoroughness and clarity. I had only seen him on his platform before and here he was at my door, crossing my threshold. He was shocked to see me chopping onions and frying them on a fire.

'Is the food we prepare inadequate?' he said.

I explained that I found the smell of frying onions comforting and he nodded and made a remark about my Capricorn parentage. It was not meant to be unkind. I said, 'Interpreter, yes my people are Capricorn. They are good people...'

'Good and bad, we all dance to the Musica Universalis,' he said.

'But if there was anything, any kindness...'

He looked blank. As though he did not understand.

The next morning's printouts showed me that the star

was all but gone. It would probably not be visible that night.

I watched the tour parties arrive. Already the mood was quieter. Even the Capricorns among them were beginning to feel uncertain. They shuffled in, in their ragged clothes, many carrying bags with all their possessions in, as though perpared for any eventuality. You were still not among them.

I shouted to them. I wanted them to understand. I shouted all I knew. I shouted that stars die, that the universe is exploding, that the constellations were temporary and arbitrary. I shouted the whole of the miniature Cosmos in my head, I spewed out knowledge like a dying star, I shouted, 'As above, so not below!'

They looked up at me. One of them pointed and said my name. Then they all applauded and continued with their tour. One of them asked to have his photograph taken with me. They seemed pleased to see me but indifferent to what I said.

Afterwards, when the Chief Auditor and some Interpreters took me to task about this, they said, 'It is a mercy that you were speaking in Latin. It is unlikely that any Capricorn might understand you.'

My own tongue has become my second language.

If we did meet, I would speak haltingly and you would have to speak slowly. In any case, you did not come, though so many Capricorns did.

And now the light – it is not a star – has gone out.

I am still held in some esteem here but because of my outburst – which did no good to anyone – my duties have been restricted. Also until now I have been educating my daughter myself. This is no longer permitted and she goes to school here in the Auditorium. Because of her Capricorn heritage, she is somewhat mocked.

My own movements are restricted. It is doubtful that I will ever leave the Auditorium again.

Father,

Today in the post I received a parcel from you. A handful of stones. They do not seem remarkable in any way. They seem to have no value and are not attractive. I showed them to my husband and my daughter. She said, 'Perhaps it is a Capricorn custom?'

He said, 'Perhaps it is a Capricorn insult.'

I said, 'I would know if it was. I'm a Capricorn.'

'Then what does it mean?'

In fact, I do not know many Capricorn customs and have no idea if a handful of stones is praise or insult.

Tycho, my dear,

You've woken up and found this note where my head should be, on the pillow next to you.

Don't fret I will not be gone long.

I read printouts last night and realised that the recurrent nova in Neary will be visible tonight for the first time in twenty years. In a lifetime of studying it, I have never seen it. Maybe it will be the last time it will be visible in its recurrent form. Surely sometime soon it will supernova. Tonight I am going to Neary Ridge to look at it.

I'm giving you the details in case something goes wrong. The ridge is on Capricorn administered land, which would be bad enough for anyone but I have been led to believe that I have become a hate figure for them.

Tycho'

This comes to tell you that I am well. I am in the ascendant almost and hope this finds you the same. Perhaps you have been fretting. If so, sorry.

I climbed the ridge in daylight, not knowing the paths, and determined to wait there till star rise and maybe watch all night the transit of the recurrent. I walked carefully. It was the first time I had left the Auditorium since I constructed the model universe inside my head. I had the ridiculous notion that if I did not walk carefully, I might trip and spill it.

The top is mostly broom, and away from light pollution. A good place to watch.

In the dusk, bats chased moths just above the tops of the broom, appearing and disappearing in my line of vision, twisting and fleeing in their corridors of sound.

Then I heard a sound. There was someone there. A big Capricorn male, a hood on his head. I stood my ground. I warned him that I had a weapon and a phone and that if he touched me he would pay.

The man grinned and said, 'So it will be here tonight! Pa was right!' and he took down his hood.

Which is when I recognised him as my brother, Caine.

I said, 'Pa is here? He is coming?'

'Pa is dead. Don't you hear anything up there in that Auditorium?'

'No. Seemingly.'

'Died years back. That's him yonder.'

He pointed to a pile of stones. Stones like the ones he posted to me. 'We brought him up here. Where he felt most comfortable. He spent most all his time here last few years until he passed. He worked out how to tell if the star was coming back. Some laughed at him. But seems he was right. It is coming back, isn't it? That's why you're here?'

'Yes.'

'He worked it all out in that head of his. Wanted to know when it would come back.'

'Because he thought it would bring good fortune to our people?'

'Because he thought it would bring you back home.'

I did not reply. A silence seemed to wrap itself around me like warm arms. Caine and I looked up at the sky together and I felt that he was wrapped in it too. After a long while he said, 'Last time it came, he was up here every minute,

172

waiting for you to show. He swore you'd come. I told him. She'll be busy listening to that thing, more than ever while the star is here. And then it went and I told him, maybe she did plan to come to see it. But she weren't to know it was gonna just come and go so quick. That's right, isn't it?'

'He came up here?'

'Every night. Buried him up here now. We each brought a stone to put on the place. You're here now. That's all he cared about. The star took her, he said, and one day it will bring her back. He was right there, too. Just a bit late, is all.'

'Yes.' I felt a need to defend myself. I said, 'He never wrote.'

'He never knew what to do for the best. The time you was plucked from school like that, he took hisself straight up there and just waited till they let him see you. Days and days he had nothing to eat but what he brought along with him. Days they kept him waiting till he was like to starve to death. Then they let him in and there was nothing there but a plate of biscuits and some Fanta. That's what he said. Don't know that it was the case.'

'It was the case. He was starving last time I saw him.'

The Sun sank, removing the cloak of its brilliance from the air, and the first stars fell into our sight like slow confetti. The stars I had listened to but rarely seen.

'You look at them and you know all that they're saying?' said Caine.

'I did not even know what my father was saying,' I said.

'Well he never said much,' said Caine.

But everything he did say, I kept with me and studied and puzzled over and in the end, misinterpreted. I said, 'No one knows what the stars are saying. No one knows if they're saying anything at all.'

It was dark now and the stars were bright atoms scattered across the sky. It didn't look like anything I had studied or knew. I thought perhaps there was something wrong with it. Caine said, 'You're looking in the wrong place, have to say.'

I had no idea where to look for the Neary recurrent. Caine took my head between his hands and moved like a telescope till it was positioned correctly. Then he pointed.

'There she is,' he said.

And I could see it! I looked across a hundred centuries and a galaxy and saw its dying spasms of radiance. And for an instant the stones on my father's cairn seemed to flash in its light.

And as I watched, the Neary recurrent, dropped like a word into the tiny universe I had carried there inside my head. As though the one was a continuation of the other, as though as above, so it was below. And as I looked I knew that of course it was speaking to us, some vast word that we could never comprehend or repeat, but only watch as its syllables enfolded us.

Afterword: A Star the Size of the Earth, Covered in H-bombs

Dr Tim O'Brien, Senior Lecturer & Head of Outreach, for the Jodrell Bank Centre for Astrophysics.

One of the key elements of Frank Cottrell Boyce's story is a crossover between astronomy and astrology, science and pseudoscience. Out of this mix appears a new astrological sign in the horoscope, the Serpent Bearer Ophiuchus. Although Ophiuchus is a real astronomical constellation it isn't counted as one of the astrological signs of the zodiac despite the Sun spending more time in Ophiuchus than it does in Scorpius.

Whilst working with Frank I told him about my connection with this constellation. Every twenty years or so, a nova – a bright new star – appears in Ophiuchus. Historically it was thought this marked the birth of a new star. However we now know the sudden brightening results from explosions on a pre-existing dead star called RS Ophiuchi, a star I've spent a long time studying. The explosion takes place on the surface of a white dwarf, the dead core of a star which has collapsed to the size of the Earth but which weighs more than our Sun. This white dwarf is in a binary orbit around another star, a red giant perhaps a hundred times larger than the Sun. Gravity causes material from the red giant to rain down onto the surface of the white dwarf. This material, mainly hydrogen, builds up on the white dwarf until the pressure is so intense and the temperatures so high that nuclear fusion begins and the layer of hydrogen explodes like a gigantic hydrogen bomb. It is impossible to imagine the intensity of these events. It's as if the whole surface of the Earth were to be covered in H-bombs which were then triggered to explode simultaneously.

RS Ophiuchi is usually so faint that we need a telescope

to see it, but the explosion renders it briefly visible to the unaided eye before it fades away again. We observe these cataclysmic events with a huge range of instrumentation which Frank refers to in the story – telescopes working right the way across the spectrum, collecting not just visible light but radio waves, X-rays and so on. As in the story, we even occasionally turn the signals we receive into sounds, an engaging alternative to visually interpreting the data.

Despite its intensity the explosion of RS Ophiuchi doesn't destroy the white dwarf. Matter is ejected into space but then it begins to gather fuel again, until twenty years or so later it explodes again. The most recent explosion was in 2006, but before that astronomers noticed explosions in 1985, 1967, 1958, 1933 and 1898. We think that the explosions have been going on for hundreds, maybe thousands of years, but have just not been recorded. However, if in each cycle the white dwarf does not eject all the matter it has collected from the red giant, then it will increase in mass. When it reaches a critical point at 1.4 times the mass of the Sun it will trigger a supernova. The white dwarf will explode, ripping itself to shreds and ending the cycle of explosions in one final titanic bang.

At the end of the story Frank mentions Tycho Brahe. He was a real, pre-Galileo astronomer who accurately measured the positions of stars. His work allowed Kepler to develop his laws of planetary motion. There is no evidence that Tycho ever saw RS Ophiuchi explode but in 1572 he did observe a supernova explode in the constellation of Cassiopeia. His observations showed the supernova to be farther away than the Moon. Such a dramatic change in this previously assumed fixed and immutable realm caused another crack in the existing cosmology which held the Earth to be at the centre of all things. Strangely enough, Tycho did apparently keep an elk as a pet. He also had a metal nose, a prosthetic to replace a part sliced off in a duel.

Tycho was born on 14th December, 1546, so Frank

makes him an Ophiuchan. This would be correct, except for what astronomers call precession. The Earth's axis wobbles like a spinning top. It now points toward the North Star but over 26,000 years the spin axis moves slowly, describing a giant circle on the sky. So, in December 1546, the Sun was actually in Sagittarius. It also means that astrologers should probably have changed the names of their zodiacal signs... if they were being as generally scientific as Frank has been.

Doing the Butterfly

Kit Reed

Today I meet Tesla. It's our first date. She and I are scheduled to hook up bimonthly for… 'Well,' the clerk says brightly as she takes my particulars, 'it depends on you.'

In the cubicle where Tesla's subjects wait, each new aide takes me down the MRI checklist. By the time the kid with the gurney comes to wheel me to my assignation, I know the questions by heart. 'Yes,' I answer before he can choke out the first one. Anything to get in, get done, get it over with and get out. 'No.' I tick answers off on my fingers. 'No. No, no and no. OK?'

In another minute he'll start to cry, so I have to let him ask all ten by the numbers as the gurney rolls along to the bay where the row of Department of Corrections Teslas wait.

'Are you claustrophobic?'

Are you kidding? Do you know where I've BEEN? He does, of course. Which cellblock. Which tier. It's on my chart. 'No,' I say, although my year in jail took me apart and some pieces rolled away forever. 'I'll be fine.'

He's already asked did I remove my ring, belt buckle, what else did you have in mind, kid? Concealed weapons? Prosthetic leg? In a lab where six MRIs crouch like grazing beetles, you have to think ahead. The M in MRI stands for Magnetic. They claim the test is noninvasive, but these next-generation suckers are strong enough to yank shrapnel out of your gut.

179

I thought: If I claimed I had a steel skullcap underneath all this hair, would they let me off? Then I thought better of it. These people will take any reason to put you back in the slammer.

He bends over, fixing me with watery blue eyes. 'Are you OK?'

'Fine,' I say, wiping where he dripped on my face. Tense, probably. Freaking, but determined to beat this thing. With an MRI, first impressions are so important. I need to come across as earnest, attractive and straightforward, a not-a-cloud-in-the-sky kind of guy. Tesla has to see a man clean of evil intentions, one you'd trust with your new puppy, kid sister, family fortune. That you'd feel good about unlocking his anklet alarm with the GPS, electrodes to jolt him if he strays. The kind of guy you want to release, so he can walk free in the world.

I've been quiet for so long that he says reassuringly, 'There's no pain.'

'No prob,' I tell him. *Fluffy thoughts, Anderson. You need to think nice, fluffy thoughts while Tesla cross-sections your brain.*

I scare him so he rattles on. 'Everybody's anxious the first time. Don't worry, they don't judge you on this one, even if the wrong parts of your brain light up.'

Careful, Peter. 'Which parts?'

'That show anger, um. Arousal? The thinking parts and. Er. The primitive parts. Stuff you may not know that you feel lights up parts of your brain that you don't even know about, stuff that makes you look...' He gives up and starts over. 'They're looking for what's working and what's... You know. Shrunk.'

I ask one question too many. 'To find out...'

Which makes him frantic. 'Whether you'll do it again! Look. This is only a dummy test. To establish a base line? Like, what's normal for you? You'll see scary stuff during the procedure, but don't worry, the images aren't loaded this time.'

This makes me wonder which images, exactly, the D.O.C. thinks are loaded for me. So, what, do they start with something innocuous, like sunbeams and reindeer? Follow with Dumpsters full of body parts? Or is it belly dancing centerfolds, after which... My mind goes places you don't want to know about. That Tesla must never see. Wherever that is, my grimace scares the kid. He claps a damp hand on my arm and I jump. 'Don't do that!'

'If you want Valium, I can ask Dr. Green,' he offers. 'Since it's your first time and all.' Then, 'But, just so you know? Once you're in the program they screen for tranquilizers, like, every time you come in for a scan? And if you don't test clean...'

'No thanks, I'm fine.'

'This session is just to get you used to the procedure,' he babbles, 'so there's nothing, like, at stake here? Tesla 12 is cutting edge, so don't worry about getting sent up the river by mistake. In the Beta testing period these scans were, like, a hundred per cent accurate, so it's all good...'

He hits bullet points like a metronome but all I hear is, *She knows when you are sleeping, she knows when you're awake.* TMI, asshole, *too much information,* I think but do not say. 'Fine.'

'This time.'

'Fine.' *Chill, Anderson. Work on it. Can't show them what you're really thinking, ever.*

'OK then, um... Ah. OK. So, the technician will tell you all this before she starts the scan, but just so you know? Inside Tesla, it gets loud. They give headphones to shut out the racket, you can pick your favorite CD, and there's a panic button. In case you...'

'I told you, I'll be fine.'

Poor kid is too young to keep it impersonal. 'You're not the type we usually get in here.'

Please shut up.

'You know, the criminal type? Don't worry, you'll do fine.'

If I shut up, will you shut up?

He's also too young to have opinions, but he can't

181

stop. I am a captive audience. 'Really. It's a clean test, you won't feel a thing. With probation, the government has to be careful, given recidivism and all. The T12 tells them who's in the right head to go loose in society. Some people object, but you've gotta admit it's cleaner than a gazillion probation officers.'

For the criminal justice system, it's also cheaper. 'I wouldn't know.'

'You don't feel a thing.'

'I wouldn't know.' I do know, magnetic resonance imaging is just that; I don't think it can read thoughts, but these Tesla 12s are sophisticated machines, and this is my first time. It's my first time for everything: jail, probation. Hell, the trial. Attempted manslaughter, charged at my first-ever and only arraignment. The public defender tried to get me off after what I accidentally did to Tad Seaver. It was, after all, an accident. I wasn't trying to kill the guy, I just wanted him to pay for yanking my girl Stephanie out from under me like a rug in a cheap magic trick. I didn't even want him to pay for screwing her on his lunch hour at my place, on my Egyptian cotton sheets, I just wanted him to stop.

But that was before.

'No music, thanks,' I tell the technician who taps in the code that unlocks the D.O.C. anklet, produces headphones and slides me onto the tongue of the machine. She's maybe too young and too, er – never mind. How does a girl like that end up in a cold, techy job like this? I'd like to sit up and start over but she's belting me to the platform that will slide me into the belly of the MRI. The machine is tremendous: smoother than the early Teslas, less like a cigar case and more like a beetle configured to cradle me inside its sleek carapace.

All business, the girl positions my head on a block to keep it steady and hands me headphones to shut out the noise.

'Are you sure? Music helps.'

I need the racket to

keep my mind focused so it doesn't wander off and fall into one of their traps. Can't let the wrong parts of my brain light up. 'I like the noise.'

'Well, that's a first.' Wow, look. I surprised a smile out of her. Lovely woman, I wish we were meeting somewhere else. Maybe something about natural blonde hair and a modest top that doesn't quite disguise the figure? 'You may feel queasy going in; if you get twitchy, I can slow things down.'

'Don't worry, I'll be fine.' I'm beginning to feel good about this. At least I'm in the right head. Forget bureaucracy, invasion of privacy. Focus on that pretty face.

'OK, then. We're going to show you a lot of images in fast-forward, and we need you to tell us how they make you feel. Ugly things. Lovely things. Things that are going to make you mad. Use the buttons on this handset to rank your emotions – whether for you, the pictures you're seeing are good, bad or neutral, OK?' Our moment has ended. She's in high professional mode. 'If goggles make you claustrophobic, we can always use the mirror.'

'Goggles will be fine.' So she can't tell whether my eyes are open or not. I may peek, but since I've decided to choose *neutral* no matter what they show to arouse me or piss me off, who's to know?

'Don't worry, I'll be watching from the booth.'

I slide into the maw of the giant beetle and the pounding begins. Cha-cha-cha-cha/cho-cho-cho-cho. I imagine a giant engine, pistons going up and down, until the racket intensifies. I'm surrounded by Einsteinian streetcars coming and going, gangs of them, that hypnotize. I fix on the noise and slip into the zone, humming under my breath until the tech's voice comes into the speaker, 'Now. In this sequence. Good? Bad? Neutral?'

I don't care what's showing inside the goggles, white fluffy kittens or raping and pillaging, I keep my eyelids clenched so the bastards will see nothing unusual inside my head, just Anderson, being completely calm. *There.* Button under my thumb registers my first N.

'Wow.' It's soft, inadvertent.

Never mind. I am safe inside the engine – not Tesla, which is imaging my head, slice by slice, serving up cross-sections of my brain for the D.O.C.. I mean the one inside my head, where I let the racket drown out thought as I keep pushing N. N. N. Then the light assailing my closed eyelids turns red. Some new image. Push Neutral, dude. And don't peek.

Her voice is loaded. 'What about this one?'

Chill, Anderson. Keep doing what you're doing. N. No, I'm not pissed, I'm not angry or lustful or anything that will light up my brain. N. I'm just a neutral, nonviolent kind of guy.

'OK. Responses to this montage?'

Don't look. Neuropsychologists have a way of telling you you're doing one thing when they're really looking for something else. Sometimes they deal you a wild card; I ought to be wary, but I'm beyond thought.

The sequence must have been a ringer.

I hear it in her gasp. N is not, apparently, the expected response to what she's showing me. The goggles render images up close and personal, 3-D high-definition LCDs. I'm scared to look. I have to look. Naked bodies tumbled in heaps. More bodies stacked like cordwood in filthy pits. My heart jolts and my belly trembles. What perverted assholes designed this test?

So much for the orderly's 'unloaded images.' The goggles fill with atrocity photos from a dozen old wars, including one I was in: twisted bodies, montages of torture and mutilation; I want to struggle, scream, anything to make it stop.

Lovely as she is, my handler's voice turns cold. 'And these?'

Now that I see them, I bite the inside of my mouth to keep from howling with grief. Holocaust photos. B. Hiroshima. B! I hit the button like a radioman on a sinking ship. My Lai, Darfur. B. Horrors segue into warped, sadistic, ugly porn, followed by... Again, Anderson. B. again, again. Anything to tell her *What you are showing me is BAD.*

I'm so shaken that somehow, she knows. My handler's voice softens. 'Are you all right?'

With my left hand, I give a thumbs-up for the mirror: *fine.* I am. I have to be. I will be fine, I vow, until – does she feel sorry for me? – the slideshow slows down and turns benign. Farmland, fields of wheat. Beaches, prairies, for God's sake sunsets. Cloud formations almost pretty enough to obliterate what I just saw and then, weirdly, photos of me in kindergarten, getting beaten up in high school, in the college pool doing the butterfly, outside a bar the day I beat up a guy – wait, did I really beat up that guy or is it... With Mom and Dad; I twist inside, miss them still. OK then, Peter. Settle. You can handle everything they pitch and anything they invent, so let it play. I focus on the racket, which changes timbre as Tesla slices deeper into my brain. Don't think about Stephanie marrying rat-bastard Tad Seaver – Don't go there, Peter, no. Nice Seaver, genial, OK person, that Tad. N-i-i-ice. Rank the images, not how you really feel, and do it fast, think *bland...* Remember girls before Stephanie, lovely things we did to each other and how good it felt, don't think too hard, *you are standing in a field...*

At last it ends. I slide out into the light, drenched and groping, steadied by my handler's touch. Gently, she lifts the goggles; is she new at this? She looks shaken. 'Are you sure you're all right?'

'Fine.' I manage to sit. Standing? Not so fast.

She replaces the security anklet. 'I'm so sorry.' It locks with a spiteful *click.*

'You didn't do this to yourself.' She means the anklet, testing, the works. I'm not ready to tell her that in fact, I did, or that right after it happened, I was glad.

'I'm sorry about all of it. Duane? Duane!' She hits her beeper. 'Damn kid's supposed to wheel you back. Don't get up. I'm sorry it hit so hard. It's because you're not the type.'

My inner demons leap for joy. 'No problem. I'll be fine.' But I'm staggered by *all that stuff*. The goggles produced horrors intercut with porn, and – weird, photos from my life – at least it looked like my life. Some scenes, I remembered being there and it happening. Others? I'm not so sure. I saw pictures of me doing stuff that I don't remember, things I don't know about, but I was in them, so I must have... It's confusing, it's....

She checks her phone. 'Hell with Duane. You're my last for the day. Let me take you.' She offers her elbow. Is this S.O.P. or does she really like me? It's too soon to tell.

'It's OK, thanks. I can walk.'

'You need caffeine, something. I'll have Admissions send your valuables down to the caf.'

We sit over coffee in the fading light until I stop jittering. I haven't said much. Neither has she, but we linger. 'You don't do this for just anybody.'

Her smile says: *you're not just anybody*. 'No.' I'd like to move into this girl's head and build a house in the part that lights her smile. 'Most of our subjects don't...' She starts over. 'You're not the usual type.'

'So. Ah... Did I pass?'

'It isn't that kind of test. The computer calibrates, but somebody has to read the scan. Our psychoneurologists don't come in until Friday, and you only hear if your reading's...'

She doesn't need to finish. I only hear if Tesla tells the D.O.C. all the things I'm trying so hard to hide, and they start the drugs. Careful, I have to be very careful, or they'll bypass drug therapy, and lock me up. 'What. Agh. What are they looking for?'

'You know how this works, right? When you're angry, aroused, depressed, activity lights up different parts of your amygdala, and Tesla knows. The images are prompts, and with...' she chokes. 'With our ex-convicts, Tesla looks for flareups. What angers you, exactly how angry you are —'

'That's creepy.'

'It's to keep everyone safe.'

'Oh.' I tent my fingers, trying for a neutral tone. I can't tell her the lie, so I do what I can. 'That's great.'

Too late. She knows I'm dissembling. The shutter clicks behind her eyes. 'Two weeks, then.' She gets up with an official smile. 'See you in two weeks.'

Once I clear the installation, I let go. It helps to curse them all as I kick an empty beer can along the sidewalk, once for the judge, once for the Department of Corrections, once for the guards on our cell block and once for the sanctimonious doorman in the complex where parolees live until they scan clean. I'm stuck here inside the perimeter until I convince Tesla that anger management classes have purged me of evil intentions and I am fit to walk free. As for Tad and Stephanie, well... That has to wait.

My apartment's not bad, but it's depressingly beige. Walls, generic furniture, carpeting, it's all beige except the display on the flat screen TV. Defying *feng shui*, everything's bolted down. It needs my own, humanizing stuff, books and photos and art, but my place is outside the perimeter where, until I'm off probation and because of the anklet and the restraining order, I can't go.

Vile Tad moved in with Steph the day I got sent up, and at this stage in my probation, the least offense... They're probably in there right now, just back from Walmart, taking down my oils and engravings to nail honeymoon pictures onto my walls and crapping up the decor with flowered everything, which is Stephanie's tragic flaw.

Because my old office is within the perimeter, I could actually go back there except that I no longer have a job. As that video of me and Tad outside the Oyster Bar migrated from UNI-TV to NuTube and went metastasized, I'm no longer welcome there. I didn't mean to shove him, I was just trying to make a point. I didn't even shove him very hard. It's not my fault the window broke, although I do wish the plate glass he got hung up on had finished the job by cutting off his head.

Oh, yes. I have a lot to keep from Tesla. As I'm basically trapped in beige limbo, terminally bored, I've done a little research. There are ways, I think, to fool Tesla; I just don't know what they are. Fail and I spin out my life inside the perimeter, on Public Work details, to be assigned after the next session, when they start measuring my progress. Unless they put me back in jail. I'm in stasis until the MRI, my new lover and – if I'm not careful – life partner, either declares me unfit for life anywhere but prison, or decides that my intentions are pure.

It's all about my responses; Google tells me so. The MRI's been used as lie detector (results questionable), mood detector (demonstrated), even a mood enhancer (proved). For the D.O.C., it's become a gauge of criminal potential which is, I guess, where I come in. Now, if I can just present as sweet-natured, innocuous...

They slide me onto the platform and Duane leaves. My handler says, 'If you're thinking what I think you're thinking, Peter, don't bother. Don't even try.'

'How did you...'

'Everybody does,' she says as she positions my head on the block.

'...Know my name?' I build a smile that makes her smile.

She taps my chart. 'They all want to get even, it's natural.'

'I thought I was good at...'

'Nobody's that good. OK, today we're going to count you down from two hundred, watch the numbers, every single one.'

'No more Dachau.'

'Promise.' Her tone as I slide into the machine is warm, almost intimate. 'It will help you get into the right head.'

The numbers dwindle to one, but no amount of preparation will put me into the right head. The images go from general to specific, from innocuous to what I'd have to call occuous: photos of childhood disasters that I thought nobody knew about, things I didn't know, battle scenes from my time in the service, phone screen shots of Tad and Stephanie kissing outside my front door. Surveillcam digis of them having sex.

I don't have to ask my handler how well I did when the intolerable slideshow stops and the goggles go dark. She lifts them and I sit up so fast that my head spins. 'That was harsh.'

'It's meant to be. Sorry, Peter.'

I don't even know her name! 'I'm sorry too. So, if you're done for the day, errr...'

She replaces the anklet. 'Maia.' *Click.*

Pretty name. 'Can I buy you a drink?'

After the third session Maia's so worried about me that she lets me buy dinner. Until I lose the omniscient anklet, this is as far as it can go. An alarm sounds somewhere if you interface with a person from the D.O.C., Maia warned as we got into her car. 'We can't see each other in any real way, but I just feel so *sorry* for you.'

'This one was pretty bad.' It was. The scenes between Steph and Seaver are tight close-ups now, painful to see, fueling the urge to kill.

She taps my hand. 'Get used to it, Peter.'

'I'm trying.'

'You have to, or they'll never let you go.'

I cover her hand with mine. 'And when they do let me go,' I say with no intention of finishing the sentence.

She flows against me, just a little bit. 'Then we'll see.'

On our fourth − it isn't exactly a date, it's more like decompression after you come to the surface too fast and they're scared your blood will boil − on our fourth date she says, 'You'll be OK, you just have to...'

'What, Maia. What?' Crap. How can I control this when I can't even control my voice?

She doesn't exactly answer. 'It gets better, I promise.'

'You mean, they stop showing...'

'No. That just gets worse.'

I slam my fist on the table.

'You start to get used to it.'

My heart goes out to her. 'Maia, I love you.'

'You can't,' she says, and then my heart flies up because she adds, 'Yet.'

Maybe six weeks in, I'm almost getting used to it, but I can tell from Maia's greeting that last week's results weren't that great. We've progressed to exchanging life-stories and hand-holding at dinner, but it's not enough. She's the only person I've been close to since I almost killed Seaver and they cut me off from everyone in my old life. We've told each other everything, at least almost everything. Now Maia addresses the truth head-on. She's known from the beginning what's really going on inside my head. 'You want to get out so you can go back and kill him.'

Nodding, I tap the anklet. 'Are you sure these things aren't bugged?'

'Like, they'd bug you when your scans tell everything they need to know?'

'Do they know...'

'That you want to kill him? Yes.'

I swallow hard. I need this girl! 'What else do they know?'

'That you have a sleeping libido and the fastest temper in the west.'

We're not bugged, but I pencil my next question on a

napkin, in case. WHAT AM I GOING TO DO?

She thinks it's silly but instead of answering, she prints: IMPULSE CONTROL. Then she says, 'Do you run? Play tennis? Any all-body thing?'

'I used to be a swimmer.'

'Imagine you're swimming. Freestyle?'

'Butterfly. It's better than flying. I love the pool.'

'Do this for me, Peter. For an hour tonight and every night until your next scan, get back in that pool inside your head. Perfect your butterfly,' she says, and she wants me to read this on two levels. She wants me to beat this thing! 'Any time you're upset, start swimming. No matter what Tesla shows you next time, imagine the pool.'

— 'Pretend harder,' Maia says. It's been two weeks. 'One more reading like this and they'll give up on you and start the drugs.' Is that good or bad? Is it: if you don't improve, you'll be in the compound forever?

She waits to tell me the rest until we're installed in a corner booth in a place where nobody goes. She slides a package across the table. 'We're not supposed to do this, but I want to try something. These are the goggles. With today's memory card. Go home and do the butterfly while you run the sequence, OK?'

'You're a lovely woman,' I tell her. She is. 'Butterfly.'

Our code word for whatever is between us. 'Butterfly.'

— Progress. At ten weeks, the psychoneurologist who likes to hit on Maia as they go over the week's readings lets it slip, and she tells me. 'He thinks you're getting a grip on the anger.'

'Does that mean I'm cleared?'

'No matter what you see, keep doing what you're doing.' Her smile makes promises. 'Maybe by spring.'

'That seems like forever!'

'Compared to life back in the joint, it's a walk in the park.'

'I love it when you talk tough.'

'No matter what Tesla shows you,' her fingers are crawling up my arm, a sensation I don't mind in the least, 'Do the butterfly.'

Lulled. I haven't been in the water since the day I came back from the gym and found them fucking, but I slide in and out of the MRI each time I'm tested as refreshed as if I'd just come out of the pool. Knots inside me unsnarl. A few more sessions like this and I can spend the time inside Tesla unmoved.

'Better, you're doing much better,' Maia tells me, and ticks off a note on her pad. 'Whatever you're feeling, the anger's under control.'

When you're doing the butterfly, it's all you think about. I want to butterfly through the next session and into the zone but I can't, exactly, although freedom is close. The powers have slipped in ringers to wake me up. The usual is intercut with digis of A-list women, not stars, real people but so pretty that I can't help wishing they were here. Class portraits from high-end universities, or girls too pretty to need the online dating site they were posted on.

'This is interesting,' Maia says, and I have to wonder how much she sees on the screen inside her booth. Fresh activity in the amygdala. 'Your libido's back.'

And the whole time, I thought she was just tending the machine. *You watch Tesla as she scans?* I see the finish line receding. 'Is that a bad thing?'

Her voice turns to satin. 'Not to me. See you next week, Peter.'

My heart staggers. 'Next week?'

Satin, lace and velvet. 'We can move a little bit faster now.'

I can't help what happens when I stop doing the fly; the flood of new photos makes me roll over; I have to glide along on my back and let them wash over me. Maia naked, Maia in a silky shift, and the hell of it is – and these sweet surprises are scattered among the usual – for each Maia they show, there is a Stephanie. Now, I'm used to seeing Steph striking infuriating poses with Tad Seaver in these sessions: both of them clothed, naked, screwing this way, that, and I've learned to control my responses. That part of my brain stays cool, but now! Here's Steph without Tad: Stephanie when we first met, Steph and me in the pool that spectacular night, doing it naked; never mind Maia, I fix on Steph and me, just the way I want it, with Seaver dead, it's all planned. I don't want much. Him dead and Steph and me forever, that's all I want.

I try to keep my heart level.

Maia's face as she jerks off my goggles says it all. She snaps on the anklet. 'I'm sorry. I tried to help you, but there's an irregularity. I'm afraid we'll need to start the drugs – which ones will be up to your psychoneurologist – your appointment is tomorrow, 6 a.m.'

Make up with her, Peter, you've got to make up or you're here for life. I open my chest and rip out my heart to give her. 'But tonight it's dinner together, right, Maia? Next week, the Rooftop Glade – great band. We can see the whole city from there.'

She gives back nothing. 'About next week. The trial period is over. Starting next week, you get a new handler. Goodbye, Peter. We're done.'

Afterword: The Sensitivity of the Technique

Dr Steve Williams is a Professor working in the Imaging Sciences Research Group, in the Faculty of Medical and Human Sciences, University of Manchester.

Kit Reed's story is credible, but not currently do-able, and may prove not to be. Magnetic Resonance Imaging can do remarkable things, but what we normally do now in research is compare one group of people with another, for example control groups against groups of psychopaths, depressives or schizophrenics.

MRI might show you that in general as a group, depressives activate the brain differently in response to stimuli. We present pictures on a video screen while they are lying in the magnet, exactly as Kit describes in the story. They might view a scene with emotional content such as a crime scene or children or shots of drug paraphernalia while we image the whole brain. An output of that work might be that a test group of depressives react differently to images of sad faces than the control group, or that habitual drug users respond differently to a picture of an empty syringe than those who don't use drugs.

What we can't really do now is look at an individual's response and say for certain that this person has a history of depression, or schizophrenia or some other mental disease. Every depressive person does not have the same response. There will be an overlap with the control group and a range of responses in a bell-shaped curve.

Much of my current research is into psychiatric disease. We've just finished a study funded by the Medical Research Council into anti-social personality disorder. We imaged people from Rampton, a secure hospital. We didn't expose them to strong images. We were able to see clear differences in the way that as a group their brains tended to respond to photographs of happy, sad or fearful faces.

We're also interested in imaging the action of drugs in psychiatric diseases. Someone is given an anti-psychotic drug while in the scanner, and we can see what part of the brain the drug is acting on. That gives us clues as to how the drug works and what brain systems it's interacting with.

People will try to use MRI in individual criminal cases. A couple of companies have set up in the United States claiming that they can use MRIs as lie detectors. A series of programmes on Channel Four broadcast last year showed MRI being used as a lie-detector in cases which had been in the news. I have been approached by a solicitor in the UK to do a lie detector test on his client.

The most we could say now is: given this individual's response, there's a 75% chance that he has a history of depression, or schizophrenia or some other diagnosis. Of course we wouldn't use that probability in a court of law as proof. But as Kit's story predicts, that won't stop people trying. The final aspect to comment on, is that Kit has placed her story in the future and is using equipment which operates at a higher magnetic field than we currently use. This will increase the sensitivity of the technique, though it will require technical challenges to be met. In addition to advances in the equipment, we would also expect our methods for analyzing the data to have improved and for us to have developed more subtle tests. On that basis, her flights of imagination may not be so fanciful!

White Skies

Chaz Brenchley

We live in the world we made, and it doesn't matter.

These are the lessons of the skies, says 'Mester Truman. They are white by day and fit to be written on, fit for the hand of man, just as the hand of man has made them; and at day's end red and rotten, the sun-sink like a promise of a bloody closure. Every day the same promise, whatever the weather, and nothing we can say to that. We can do as we like, says 'Mester Truman, because in the end there's nothing we can do.

Maybe you get to be cynical – or realist, pragmatist, whatever he would call himself – when you must sail from township to distant township, a semester here and a semester there, never let stay a full year together. Never let in.

Maybe something else happens, something worse. That's what Dad says. He says all that exposure, staring at the skies and sleeping under them, he says it makes you unsteady in the world, it snaps your keel. He says you can turn turtle. Turtle Truman we called the 'mester for a while after that, Mish and me. It didn't catch on, but wouldn't matter if it had. No one else would understand it, only us.

My dad's a keelman, he likes to make out he sees us all in terms of hulls and sails. At the world's mercy, needing skill to survive. Luck and skill together, but skill mostly. By his reckoning your hull and keel are nature and nurture both; they are what you're given but you have to take care of them or the sea will get you sooner or later, worm or rot or that sudden snap in a storm. Your sailing skills are nurture all the way, the ways you're taught to get by.

I don't think motors have much place in his metaphor. If they did – well, the guys with motors would be the streaky ones, high-powered, top deck. Not like us.

Definitely not like 'Mester Truman. A 'mester isn't bilge, no, far from that. True 'mesters are almost legendary in the schoolrooms and in our parents' talk, but even so. Folks like us, Dad says, we're at the mercy of the wind, except for how we learn to use it; he says that and he means it, but I think even more he means folks like the 'mester. Metaphorically he means it, and literally too. He likes that, when something he says strikes absolutely true.

'Mester Truman's sailboat measures five metres, stem to stern. He had us down to measure her and map her in the dock, the whole class of us together.

'My kind are not so common any more,' he said, 'that you should miss this chance. You might not see another. Another like me, I mean,' tall and lean, we thought he meant, with his long black hair caught back in a silver ring, 'a sea-gypsy with knowledge to trade. I know every township does exchanges, you swap teachers regularly and call them 'mesters too, but that's a different thing.'

Oh, it was, a very different thing. Teachers are teachers, but he was a wild man, dark and dangerous and bold. Someone to love, and we thought we half loved him already, Mish and I. How not, when he sailed this tiny fragile cockleshell craft ocean-free, out of sight of land and townships both? On his own under the dreadful blank of the sky, into the dreadful blank of an empty future that he would have to write for himself, find a 'ship willing to sign him, willing to let him stay one semester for the sake of their young generation. He'd need to be persuasive. Persuasive first, and then good. And even then, good as he was, as he proved to be, he'd still be sent free again at year's end, sailing off again, untrusted, unretained.

He took us aboard to let us chart his boat, in twos and threes together. There wasn't room for more. Waiting our turn, Mish and I sat on the wharf and kicked our heels above the water and said, 'It's so *small...*' And the world so big, we meant, and the sea's temper so swift to turn. Mish and I rarely needed to say so much aloud. We lived in each other's pockets, almost in each other's minds; in each other's hands and trust entirely.

Maybe everyone needs someone they can trust, just the one? I had Mish and he had me and we were sufficient together, against all the caution and doubt of the edifice that is a township, through all the turbulence and question of a shared adolescence.

Maybe 'Mester Truman was still looking for his one to trust. Or maybe he was sufficient unto himself, content to lay his trust where he could see it, hold it close. For sure he must trust his own abilities, from basic maintenance to higher navigation. The sea has a thousand ways to threaten a man alone. His simple survival was a testament to his skills; he hardly needed a reference else.

'You two, is it?' he said as we stepped aboard, last of the class, magnificent in our patience. We'd actually waved other kids ahead, to be sure of this final slot. There might be advantage in it. He'd sent the others away once their time was over, not to have them hanging around on the docks annoying the grown-ups; with no pressure and no one waiting, now that we had him to ourselves perhaps he'd let us linger, ask questions, slip curious fingers beneath the skin of him. We'd bury our romantic hearts within his blood-beat, maybe. If there was profit in it. 'Are you actually inseparable, or does it just seem that way?'

'Oh, totally,' we assured him. 'There are rumours that the world will end, if anyone ever contrives to separate us. Like splitting the atom, only more so: all the energy there is, released in one great vengeful cataclysm. It's all right, though, we're very careful. Always have been. No one gets between us. Our parents will confirm.'

'I'm sure. Nevertheless, I'm going to put this sail between you. There's only room for one at a time at the winch. This boat's designed that way, optimised for my life, a man alone.'

Nevertheless he was glad to have us there, I thought: two bright boys pliable and attentive, swift to learn and eager to please. Devoted, almost, very much his slaves for the hour. Not practical slaves, as there was nowhere actually to go and no work to do, but welcome none the less. We rattled sails up and down and flung the tiller to and fro in response to his commands, to various imagined winds and sets of sea, storm and calm and steady swell, while this isolated pool actually stirred hardly at all beneath us.

He had to duck through the hatchway to the cramp of the cabin below. Neither Mish nor I was tall enough to worry, but we both ducked anyway, in possessive imitation. 'Now,' he said. 'With the stars and planets hidden as they are, how do you imagine I find my way from one township to another?'

'GPS, of course,' we chorused, with a flourish at the bank of electronica, all dark here in dock, all silent but still blackly gleaming with potential, the promise of data. We loved data.

'What, would you trust your life to satellites not under your control?'

That brought us up short. No, of course we wouldn't. They could be switched off at any moment; they could be sabotaged. Worse, they could be corrupted, they could corrupt their own data, feed us misinformation, lose us in an ocean of lies...

He told us about the old ways, ready reckoning, which sounded to us little better than blind guesswork and nothing to chance your life on; he told us about new ways that were more reassuring, alternate data, the salinity of ocean currents and flux in the magnetic field, mappable through time, fluid but secure. If anything could ever be secure, out at sea.

We asked the right questions, expressed a proper admiration, flattered his ego and his boat together. He did brew chai, and he did let us squirm among his wiring, turning this on and testing that, taking the backs off his boxes to learn how they were linked, what languages they spoke, what they said to each other and to him.

We didn't leave until he chased us out. What we really wanted, of course, was what all the class had wanted: a trip out of the dock into open water. Teach us to sail, why not, when he was teaching us so much? We did ask, but that turned out to be the wrong question at last.

'I can't do that,' he said. 'Not without your parents' consent,' which he knew and we knew that he would not get. Dad with his talk of white skies and how they unsettle a man, falling down to the horizon like a solid wall ahead; and the township churning away from us towards that wall, and only the various wind to fetch us back if it ever could get us up to speed again? No chance.

He told us to forget pleasure-jaunts and learn from his life, the truth of him, his solitude. Without that, he said, we'd never understand the 'Mester Truman that we saw, nor what he tried to teach us. Then he sent us away.

We kicked along the dockside, looking at all the other boats, the tenders and speedboats and barges that never get to sail while the township's moving, and yes, of course we were both thinking the same thing, talking about the one thing, how we could sneak down here some evening and take the 'mester's boat out by ourselves, now that we'd learned the ropes...

And how we couldn't, because the dock doors are locked up tight when we're in motion, there's no way out without a pass key and a code. Which kids don't get, of course, and would they give them to a transitory 'mester? We didn't know. All that talk about our parents might be bluff. He might be locked up too, as tight as any of us, no way off until his strict term ends.

So then we shrugged off dreaming and compared treasures, actuality: the little things we'd contrived to filch, one of us helping himself while the other held 'Mester Truman distracted. Fuses, cables; chips and tools. Mostly taken from his box of spares, nothing he would miss until he needed it, nothing he would need aboard the township.

They used to call us seedships, because we made the oceans bloom. Maybe they still do, back in the dry. I wouldn't know. Would anyone? We don't talk much any more, the dryfolk and us.

We do still seed the oceans with iron, we do cultivate the algae, we do our bit. Welcome or otherwise.

That's what they tell us, that's what we're taught: that what we do is right, regardless of what other nations think. Someone had to do something. So we cast iron dust into the sea where the plankton it spawns will sequester the carbon dioxide they munch on, and drag it down into the deeps. They tell us it's a mission. Mission-critical, they say.

'Plankton' comes from the Greek and means 'wandering', that's what 'Mester Truman told us. Which is what we do: we wander the oceans and spread the dust and tend the algal blooms, harvest the fish that feed on them. It's what he does too, he says. He wanders the ocean and spreads the knowledge that he carries, and tends the young minds that grow on it. That's us. The township harvests our future, he said, his metaphor breaking down around him but never mind.

These days 'townships' names us better. We grew around the seeding, and we do still seed, but that's not what we are any more. We grew. The ships grew into argosies, because why go back and forth sowing iron dust and doing nothing else when we could be bigger, carry goods, offer services to ports and provinces and nations? Ports, provinces, even nations that might see little traffic else by the time we'd finished growing, by the time we'd eaten all the small fry?

And then the argosies grew into manufactories, because why buy goods when we had power and raw materials and personnel, everything we needed to turn them out ourselves?

And the manufactories made weapons, first thing they did make, because there's always a demand and we demanded them ourselves, we had to defend the 'ship. We'd been hated from the first, because we soured the oceans and some people, some *peoples* could never settle to that; and now we were taking trade from the mercantile lines and they loved us not for that either. And there were regular pirates too, who might have thought us easy – bloated wealth, the softest of targets – if we weren't so conspicuously otherwise.

History. Old history, mostly. People don't touch us now. Not us, nor any of our sisters. The townships are a nation, and we protect each other.

Still make weapons, though, and sometimes it seems like half the township is barracks, half the folk aboard are soldiers when we come to land. Everyone has another job at sea, which matters more; but why sell weapons when you can hire them out with the personnel trained to use them, a strike-force ready made? We don't linger for long wars, but mercenary missions are just one of the services we offer. In and out, and no one left behind.

They double-check on that, the drysiders, that no one's been left behind. Of course they do. Paranoia is the fuel that runs us all, so says 'Mester Truman, since oil came up short. They count us off the 'ship, and count us on again. We do the same. And guard our flanks as carefully at sea, let few folk aboard at all and fewer stay. No one looks kindly on strangers any more; they might too easily turn out to be spies and saboteurs.

That's why we take teachers for a term, a semester, no longer. How can you trust an itinerant? They see too much, they go too far, they might have come from anywhere.

Cross-fertilisation is good, everyone knows that. New tech, new insights come from all over, and 'mesters spread them around. It's all about control, though: we let them on, we do not take them in.

Mostly we take them from other townships, known quantities, already tried and tested. Still not trusted. We are a nation but not entirely one people, never quite at ease even with each other. Paranoia sits too deep, 'Mester Truman says. Every township sets its own course, listens to its own counsel, never lets a stranger be alone and unwatched anywhere that matters.

'I guess we don't matter, then,' Mish said later, after we'd talked it through in class. 'Nobody watches the 'mesters while they teach.'

We'd come up high like good boys, to spend an hour standing an unofficial and redundant watch in our favourite spot just forward of the main bridge, just where we could be best seen to do it. The 'ship has electronica, of course, to scan seas and skies and far horizons – but tech can always be superseded, machines can be subverted. Watchfulness is an unshakable tradition, deep-laid: *Don't waste the good years, while your eyes are sharp. If you've nothing else to look at, look out.* It was our own creed, our common sense that added *be visible about it*, not to waste the effort, or the credit that ensued.

'Don't be dry,' I said, grinning at him sideways, just to catch his profile against the muted glare of sun behind the sky. We stood under the shelter of an overhang, always, but the skies fall like curtains, all the way to the water. 'We all do, the whole class of us.'

'Oh. Yeah...'

Chagrin: it's a beautiful thing. We think so much the same, Mish and I, we each of us hate it when the other one thinks ahead, is faster or sharper or better prepared.

Either our parents and governors trust us entirely, individually – the 'ship is ours, after all, our life today and our floating future: how could any of us ever wish it harm?

— or else they trust us collectively, practically. If any 'mester ever tried to subvert us, someone among us would be sure to report it; which being true, of course we would all report it, because who wants to be singled out as the one who didn't? The slowest, the driest-thinking of us could see the danger in that. We'd fight to be first. And be watched ourselves thereafter, of course, for fear we'd been subverted anyway; and submit to it with a careful grace, because we knew the alternatives. One way or the other, our elders could be sure of us. Thought they could be sure.

And of course the 'mesters know that too, every detail of that, and so would never try to subvert us, not in class.

Even so, 'Mester Truman took us out of the classroom when he could, up on deck when the weather let him. On deck and not in shelter, under the sky, white sky. He was used to it, I suppose.

So were we all, used to living beneath it; but our way kept us below as much as possible, taught us to eye it askance and distrust what it concealed.

We seed the oceans and some people hate us for it, teach against us, declare boycotts and threaten what sabotage they can.

Other people seed the skies.

It's an evil, but what can we do? We can't even see them at it, let alone come at them. There were raids once, 'ship to shore, but now they build their airfields far inland, beyond our reach.

They strew sulphates into the atmosphere, to turn back the sun's rays, they say: to raise our albedo, and so cool us all down. We should all of us be grateful, they say.

We've heard them, Mish and I, on the propaganda channels. We're not supposed to listen, but we do. We built our own receiver, three semesters back.

They say their plan is better, they're not poisoning the planet the way we are. It isn't true, of course; we're not fool enough to believe them. We know what harm they do, we've been taught it, year on year. Besides, we can see: or rather we can't, because it was them who turned the skies white, so we can't even see their planes as they fly overhead.

'Mester Truman says it doesn't matter. They do what they do, and we do what we do, and neither one of us can save the other. Or ourselves, or anyone else. It's gone too far, and the world will kill us all in the end, soon now, sooner than we think. So he says. So it really doesn't matter what we do.

Mish and I, we pretty much do what we like outside of school. Our parents are working, neither of us has sibs and everyone knows who we are. We're good boys; we've been very careful about that. No wild stuff that anyone might notice, no bad reps, no public trouble.

We have places to go, people to be seen with, pictures of innocence. Schoolkids aren't allowed to work, but we work anyway: fetching and carrying mostly, a bucket of chai to the engine room, bento boxes to the bridge. If you want to know the 'ship, work from the galley outwards; if you want the 'ship to know you, start with the junior officers and let your reps trickle up. The commodore knows our faces, the engineer knows our names. We know everyone. And everything. How safe the pile is, how many years'-worth of fuel is stored in lead-lined bunkers deep, deep in the hull; how much is stowed secretly on distant rocks far from any shore. Where we're due to sail next, where after that. Who's up for promotion, who's going the other way, who's not trusted at all.

It's all currency, it's negotiable, though mostly we just hoard it. Spend wisely, and always have more in reserve; never tell everything you know. People think we're strictly small-scale, just kids, barely understand the use they make of us; they think they pay us in sweets and baubles and petty cash, they think we're content with that.

They have no idea. No *idea* what we know, how much

there is of it, how it makes a webwork of information from mast to keel, from wind to lee and stem to stern.

Once, just once we did spend big. We tipped a woman off that she had been listed as subversive. She wasn't a 'mester, not an incomer at all, she was born on board and we liked her, rather; we didn't want to see her go. She put her name down to trans'ship at once, of course. If you're quick, if you're lucky — if they can't prove anything against you, if it's only suspicion that they have — you can start again with a clean record on another hull. No new captain would believe whatever record came with you, anyway. How could they trust another 'ship's judgement? It might be unreliable, dishonest, subversive itself, any of a hundred ways of wrong.

She left, swift and sudden, as people tend to do. Properly, her cabin should have been reassigned, but there's always more space than crew. Too many solo berths, and who likes to sleep alone? Couples sometimes look for privacy, that may be only natural; what's truly natural is to draw together, to bunk together in dormitories and barracks, look never to be left alone. Never to be caught alone. Common sense goes hand in hand with nature: if people see you acting solitary, holding yourself apart, how can they help but be suspicious?

That was her trouble, perhaps, or the start of it, that she'd taken a single cabin. She actually took it to bundle in someone she wasn't meant to be bundling — we knew! — but of course that wasn't on the record. Of course people would look at her askance, when she moved out of the common dorm and set up on her own. And wasn't around, wasn't available for her old friends in the way she used to be. Perhaps they heard she had a secret lover — but lovers have been used before, as excuse for espionage. Sabotage, even, the unforgivable sin.

So she left, just ahead of the rising wave, because we tipped her off. Perhaps she was glad to go, glad to leave the lover with all the other trouble at her back. We were sorry, but still: there was profit in it.

We were known quantities, people thought they had the measure of us. If we offered to spend half a shift helping in the purser's office, doing routine admin, they assumed we were storing up treasure in heaven, accumulating credit to be cashed in later. We did it all the time. Nothing different now, except for letting one minor call on the system – the availability of an undesirable single cabin, say – be slipped aside all unheeded, action taken, never mind.

So we had our own space, with our own doorcode, so buried that no one official would ever dig it up. Nor anyone unofficial, by any chance that we could reasonably guard against. If people saw us in that corridor, anywhere on that hull, we always had a reason to be there. It was usually visible in our hands: we were fetching supplies up from the hold, running an errand to the commissariat, bringing a mop to a pool of vomit, something. Someone else's vomit, obviously. We would be conspicuously acquiring merit, and very likely dodging school. People liked to see that written so clear on our transparent, innocently guilty faces; they found it obscurely reassuring. The world was as it was, and boys were being boys. School was being dodged. All was well.

No one ever, ever saw us going in and out of the cabin. We were scrupulously careful about that. First thing, we tapped a line into the 'ship's security, so that we could watch the corridor and be sure.

Second thing, we diverted that camera's feed only to our own monitor, so no one else could catch us by unhappy accident or random check.

We had our space, securely; then we had to fill it. The bunk was built-in, but we weren't there to bundle. We did our courting in the common rooms like wise boys, transparent, innocently carnal. The mattress went out and in came furniture, as much as we could fit: two hard chairs and a table. The stripped bunk made more and better surface-space. The door came off the closet and went for recycling, which made those shelves more handily available for servers, comms units and the like.

Everything we had was cannibalised or reclaimed, almost all of it hand-built with our own tender hands, but that's just the way a township works. Everything gets used and used again, nothing is ever wasted or thrown away. It's cool to be in school: chips, cables, redundant circuitboards and sockets find their way to the classroom playbox, for science lessons and experiments. We could take what we wanted, Mish and I. We left a few builds big and obvious in the labs, and never mind if they didn't actually work; teachers need something to criticise, something to misunderstand besides their actual pupils. What we actually wanted was smuggled back to our own place where it was repurposed, conjoined with whatever fresher gear we could beg or more likely steal, and so incorporated into the masterwork.

If you'd asked us what it was, that masterwork, what we were eventually making, I don't believe either one of us could have told you. It grew as we did, day by day. It had no name. Our old receiver was a part of it, that mattered, that it could listen to the world; now there was a transmitter too, we could talk back to the world, if we'd only had anything to say. That was still only an aspect, only a functionality of something far broader and deeper.

We thought it was deep, at least. We thought it was art, as much as engineering. We loved it, almost as much as we loved ourselves for making it, for the achievement of the thing. It was a way to say – in code and electronics, in solid matter and transient current and immeasurable ideation – how we felt about the world and our place within it. It was a machine that started from the same place every day, that couldn't be reprogrammed; but it could reach out into the world, it could listen and learn and reply in kind. We had made it, we could use it, and it wasn't us but very much itself, the perfect spy: alert to others, honest to itself.

It wasn't us, but it was ours and we were mighty proud.

Did we give ourselves away in some kind of rash joint enterprise, not quite oblique enough, or did we say something directly, one of us? I don't know, Mish says he doesn't either. I guess I can believe that. We're made of the same stuff, Mish and I. Unique together. We've been told so all our lives. Uniquely sinful, is what they usually say. We like that.

Uniquely exposed, once 'Mester Truman knew our secret.

It had to be him, of course; we'd have wanted it to be him. Which is why I wonder if either or both of us let something slip deliberately, or halfway that. Half wishing that he knew, so letting it happen, letting him learn...

Anyway. It was just our careful secret, and then suddenly it wasn't. One way or another, he knew.

'Show me,' he said, 'show me what you boys have done.'

We didn't really have the choice. Once that was true, of course, we wanted to show it off, every detail: our fabulous network of links and interlinks, all the subtle coding, the engineering hard and soft, the sneaky attack modes and sneakier defences...

We've never seen it since.

Next we knew, men came and took us out of our beds, middle of the night, nightmare time. Our parents wept and shouted, which did them no good at all. At least, our mothers wept, in fear or fury or helplessness, all three. Mish's father, he shouted. I could hear that, clean down the corridor. My own father looked at me silently, watched me taken away, wondered I think what tangle I had in my lines, whether my hull was breached. Had my keel snapped?

If I'd said this storm was none of my own making, he

would have shrugged and waited, to see if I said true. A fit vessel and good seamanship would survive whatever honest weather came, he would be sure of that. He must be. He needed it. If I sank and was lost, it must necessarily be my own fault.

As it was, of course, but I didn't mean to sink.

They wouldn't let Mish and me see each other, except for one glimpse in the corridor, so that we both knew the other was taken too. They wouldn't let us speak at all.

No matter. I could trust him. I thought I could trust him. I had to; that was my own need this night.

All I needed. Everything else was ready.

They said, *this system that you've built with stolen parts, tell us of its purpose, what it does.*

I said, 'It taps into the township, quiet as a cat. It listens, it reads, it measures. It remembers everything.'

And it talks, too?

'Yes, of course. It could talk to the world, and you'd never hear it: microbursts on frequencies that shift according to a shifting algorithm...'

The innocence of youth, doubled up with arrogance. It's hard to overplay it, when that's just exactly what they're looking for.

And to whom have you been talking, lad, who has this precious algorithm? Who's listening to all our secrets?

'Why, no one, of course. No one except 'Mester Truman. He promised that. This was just a test, he said, a project, see if we were as smart as we thought we were, could we subvert the 'ship's security, like that...'

Did he think, did he really think we wouldn't have defences in place, beyond whatever we'd shown him? Not protect ourselves, in all our youth and arrogance?

If township life has taught us one thing, *one*, it is to watch our own backs, and each other's.

If he'd spent more than a semester on this 'ship or any other, he'd have learned that too. It seeps into your bones, but not I guess when you're always shifting, always moving on.

He hadn't thought to check, hadn't stopped to wonder who we might have set up for the fall, if that fall ever came. He just betrayed us, handed us over like the hired servant that he was.

Perhaps he thought it might win him citizenship, see him invited in.

I took them down to the dock and showed them the receiver on his boat, with its clever little patch that knew our algorithm and could listen in to everything we sent. I let them look further on their own account, didn't even try to point them to the equally clever little patch on his transmitter, that could shuffle all our data into other people's codes and send it on, still in those undetectable bursts. Now I'd brought them this far, they would find it.

That, and more. They'd find the data hidden in the class computers, everything he might have sent already, stored behind our own most obvious passwords that we would never have been so stupid as to use for such a purpose. A transient 'mester trying to cover his own back, though, thinking himself almost caught and so throwing his own pupils to the wolves to cover his escape, he might easily be so clumsy...

They'd find a stolen passkey and its codes on board his boat, ready for a swift illegal leaving if it came to that.

Best, worst, they'd find his sabotage, and all the records of it.

What boy doesn't like to make explosions?

He'd had us making bombs, his hidden records said: so much of this chemical, so much of that, all requisitioned for lab lessons, just with the two of us. Pipes and welding gear, electronics.

'Of course,' I said, when they asked me; just as Mish would be saying, when they asked him too. "Mester Truman wanted to put on a display before he left, I think maybe he was hoping to persuade you to let him stay? Sort of fireworks, he said, only with a serious intent. He wanted to float targets in our wake and blow them up, sort of a son et lumière...'

A township isn't quite one ship, it isn't quite a dozen. At one time, I suppose it used to be a fleet. Now – well, you can still find records of the separate hulls under their separate names, there are charts and our lovely spy-thing will have captured them, but nobody thinks that way. It's not a unit, it's a unity.

Someone sometime understood that if they bound the fleet together, they'd have the bonus of guaranteed, chained loyalty – no one ship could go sliding away in the night, bearing secrets to the dry or to another fleet – and the bonus too of stability: with more breadth, they could build higher superstructures and never risk a capsize.

Catamarans, trimarans can be stiff, but not us, we cover acreages: all our links will flex when they need to. Still, we are one thing of many parts. And have reasons, yes, more than one reason to fear sabotage. Nobody could sink us, but cut those links at crucial nodes and half the township would be suddenly unseaworthy, turning turtle.

Turtle Truman's bombs, that we had made him – we had told them that nickname by now, we told them everything, how not? – would be found at all those crucial nodes, live and ready, waiting only the electronic order to erupt.

They'd find him guilty, and us not. That was written. We had written it.

Us? We're just boys, foolish boys: foolish but loyal,

demonstrably loyal. We gave him up as soon as we understood what he'd done, what he'd had us doing. We'd be watched more carefully, that's all. We'd learn.

We'd learn to be more careful. Trust no one but each other. Watchfully.

Him? He's a saboteur. All the evidence is there. He is all the proof they need, why we can never trust a 'mester. Or any stranger else.

They'll snap the mast of his boat, cut all the sheets and crack the keel. Short out the electrics, jam the winches, shred the sails; leave him helpless and adrift in our determined wake. No food, no water, no succour, no hope.

He'll be a lesson to us all, a dot against the glare, lost soon enough as we churn on under white skies into a red sunset.

This is the world we made, and it doesn't matter. He taught us that.

Afterword: Skies and Sea

Dr Sarah Lindley, Lecturer in GIS, School of Environment & Development, University of Manchester

There may be a lot of uncertainty about global climate change and its impacts but one thing is certain, greenhouse gases are essential for life on Earth. Without the greenhouse effect, the Earth would be a very inhospitable place. Evidence of past climates shows us that concentrations of greenhouse gases are not static over time and changes can result from a range of natural causes. However, what has mobilised scientists and governments the world over is the knowledge that recent rates of change appear to be unprecedented and that they cannot be explained by just considering natural causes alone. The consensus is that by introducing enormous quantities of additional greenhouse gases into our atmosphere, human society has unwittingly begun a global experiment and we are now beginning to see its first results.

Future climate change is the backdrop to Chaz's story. He allows us a glimpse into how the results of our global experiment may look further down the line. His world seems very different, but interestingly it is society itself which appears the most changed. The people at the centre of the story live and work around an activity which has been receiving a lot of interest as a means to mitigate future warming. The idea is that carbon can be removed from the atmosphere by artificially stimulating biological productivity in the oceans through the addition of iron. Experiments have shown that fertilising the ocean in this way does indeed increase phytoplankton production, something which can also be observed as a natural process. However, it remains a controversial idea for wide scale and commercial exploitation. The controversy stems from our lack of understanding of its long term efficiency and wider ecological impacts, in other words the worry that this is a second global experiment, this time associated with the oceans.

In the story such ocean fertilization is commonplace and supports an ocean-dwelling community made up of floating townships, rather like the floating phytoplankton communities they are centred on. These townships are clearly not thriving. Rather they seem isolated, regressive and mistrustful communities eking out a subsistence-based existence. Our main character tells us of the dryfolk, land-based societies whose solutions and lifestyles are different. These 'others' carry out cloud seeding practices, one of a number of plausible reasons for the white skies of the title. It is these white skies which could, in part, be leading to the decline and decay that Chaz portrays given that phytoplankton requires light as well as nutrients.

Another strong theme in the story is the demoted role of learning and the suspicion and distrust of initiative and development of ideas. In this world 'Mester Truman is a transient and excluded visitor, and one who is ultimately betrayed by our narrator and his friend Mish. Technology is also treated as a necessary evil, something capable of causing great harm in the wrong hands and which must be tightly controlled for the survival of the township.

Chaz's vision of the future is both fascinating and thought-provoking. Being a lecturer, researcher and at least a partial technocrat, I prefer to have a more optimistic view of our ability to use technology to help make the right decisions for the future. My own work centres on climate adaptation, what has been termed as 'managing the un-avoidable' while others work to 'avoid the un-manageable'. I'm looking at ways that our own towns and cities can be made more climate proof so that human society, the most fragile element of Chaz's future world, will, I hope, continue to thrive.

Enigma

Liz Williams

Cambridge

I asked that this room, my current truth, should be crafted
to resemble the room in which we sat then, and I suppose
they have done their best. But they've put me in King's,
not Trinity, and there has been no need for me to line the
windows with paper to correct the proportions, as I did at
my old college, for these are already perfect.

The light is golden, the stone grey. Fluting arches taper
to a point above the windows, which appear in austere
Gothic harmony at intervals along the wall. If I half-close
my eyes, their substance looks more like bone than stone, as
if I sat in the body of some great beast, lumbering down the
meadows towards the water. My desk is covered with neat
piles of paper and pens in regimented lines. Everything is
orderly, except for an apple core sitting on the mantelpiece.
I frown, and frowning, carry it to the bin and throw it away.
I don't remember eating an apple. In fact, I don't remember
what it's like to eat.

In this room, it is always summer. The sun falls heavy on
the grass, as if illuminating it from within; it seems to glow.
Above, the sky is a pale, bleached blue, not the intense azure
that covers the city in winter, the Fenland cold sparkling
off the windows of the colleges. I have visitors, but perhaps

not as many as you might expect; I understand that they are carefully screened by the relevant authorities. None of them are frivolous: I suspect it costs too much money for casual enquirers. Some are players in this particular game, some are from outside, and then of course I like to have my little joke and tell them that I can't possibly understand what they're talking about. They are from a span of times and I enjoy conversing with them. They speak of remarkable things: mined moons far beyond the asteroid belt, communications from the denizens of the far past, veils of bone and blood that can convey information to their hosts. *Darkware*, someone called it.

I suppose they are telling me the truth, but I have no way of verifying this. And all truth is an invention. I know this to be true – or rather, I believe that this is a fact that I have conjured out of the games that fill our lives. My friend disagreed with me, during our discussions on this matter in the long summer afternoons before the war. But what else can you expect from a mathematician? I used to watch him as he leaned forwards in his chair: a young man, then, with a face that was to me – the non-Englishman – very English, with its short nose and pronounced chin. I recognised him for what he was, of course, but neither of us could speak of it. You did not, in those days – or at least, not in those circumstances.

My young mathematical friend sought to replicate intelligence in a machine. Nowadays – if that is a word that makes any sense – I understand that this is no longer regarded as a solution. Naturally, I told Alan at the time that he was on the wrong track, but he did not agree with me, pigheaded as always.

'Imagine this,' he said, in that rather didactic way of his. 'You are on the other end of a telephone, there is a voice that sounds human. How would you know that it was not?'

'Because a false note would be sounded. It would say something that no human would say.' I remember that I smiled. 'But then, who is to say what that might be? Imagine that you are speaking on a telephone. The person on the other end tells you that there is thunder in the sky and that this means that a spirit has been angered. Do you think you can understand what this means?'

He bridled. 'Of course. I understand the concept of *god*.'

'But do you really? You know what *you* mean by *god*. But how far would this hypothetical individual have to go in order to convince you that you understand what is meant by *his* god?'

'What do you mean?'

'Do you understand what is meant by "thunder"?'

'Of course.' My young friend was now convinced that I was an idiot. 'The expansion of air along the path of an electrical discharge, that releases sound.'

'Of course. And to you, it is. But to our tribesman it is the footstep of a mighty god, it is the harbinger of disaster, the herald of woe – you may know what *you* mean by these things, but can you properly understand what it means to him?'

Alan was silent. I was not sure that he really understood the question, let alone what it implied.

And as I sit here, remembering, there is a rumble of thunder from the perpetual summer of the Cambridge lawns, and looking out of the windows I see that the perfect sky is black.

★

Diary Entry, August 25th, 1939

There's a war coming, an old man at a bus stop told me this morning.

'So there is,' I said, very solemn. You'd have to have been living in a cellar not to know that, but I didn't want to make him feel a fool – or to say that I was already part of it. They've told me to go to Bletchley, under the aegis of a department who are a sub-division of a branch of a part of the War Ministry. It's all very Gilbert and Sullivan. Cracking codes, that's what I'll be doing. Or to be more precise, making machines that can crack codes – because the mechanical mind can work a great deal faster than this puffy sponge of grey cells that we call the human brain. I know something of how fast that is, because I've started to dream in code: heading to some mathematical heaven every night to converse with numbers. They flit past me with dizzying speed – really, one might call it hallucination rather than dream.

And *she's* there, in the dream. She has a cold face, between wings of black hair, like a witch herself rather than the fresh faced little girl in the Disney film. She's holding out an apple, as red as her lips. She's German, in the original story – they didn't say that in the film. How ironic, given what's been happening in Europe. And she chants, as I used to chant at King's:

Dip the apple in the brew
Let the sleeping death seep through.

But that was the witch's chant, not Snow White's. I only remember this when I wake up. At the time, it seems quite natural.

*

Cambridge

I can manipulate the symbols, but I do not understand them and this, with its accompanying irony, frustrates me. The awful thing is that the answers I am able to give are apparently convincing. The people who have constructed the room, the college, the view across the Backs, are pleased with this. They come to see me – or perhaps it is only one of them who comes. I have seen two of them together, but cannot tell them apart. They are luminous, almost spectral. They tell me that they are constructs of numbers, but I have confessed that I do not understand this. They tell me that understanding is not, in this case, relevant.

So I sit, frustrated, and manipulate the symbols in response to the questions that come in. The questions themselves appear on a wide pale screen, situated at the back of the room. They concern the nature of reality. Whoever is asking them is, I think, building an ontology, and of course it has occurred to me that this is the very same as the one I myself am currently inhabiting.

I can display the correct symbols – via a smaller screen and a pointer – because they have explained to me the rules but I do not know what the symbols represent. I have been trying to work it out, however. But then there is the question of whether I am able to understand – would a comprehension of the symbols be a true understanding, after all?

On the day that the sky turns black, I have been playing with the symbols. They have explained to me that the hexagon must always be placed in conjunction with the sphere, but why should this be so? It seems random to me, entirely arbitrary. So, in the middle of the quad, I take the physical models with which my guides have supplied me. I take the hexagon, but instead of the sphere, I take a cube and a small, glistening pyramidal shape, which has always appealed to me for purely aesthetic reasons. I place them in the middle of the quad, on the grass which I don't remember being quite so green, when I lived in the original version.

★

November, 1939

A handful of months later I have my bombe.

The name always makes me laugh – a bombe to fight bombs. But it's needed and there's no time to waste: the German war machine rumbles on across Europe, swallowing villages and towns and people in its wake. We intercept their transmissions at Bletchley and we can't understand a fraction of it.

But sometimes I wake and it seems to me that I am somewhere else entirely. There's a vast black space, spangled with stars, and the numbers that I converse with are real, figures encased in a strange armour. I don't know who, or what, they are, but they converse with me in a kindly way, as one might pet a stray cat. One night, however, during one of these dreams, *she* comes to me and asks me what I am. It seems to me that they have raided my head, and found someone whom I understand, someone with whom I can communicate. She's wearing the same clothes as in the film: the puffed sleeves with the big collar, the blue blouse and yellow skirt. But in the dream she is a real person, not a cartoon. Her face is still cold.

'I am a human being,' I tell her. She simpers.

'How do you know?' she asks me.

'Why, because –' I pause. How best to answer this?

'This is what you believe yourself to be,' she says. Her face is pinched and intent. 'But do you really know?' And she begins to ask me questions, about all manner of things: some childish (my favourite colour, what I like to eat), some more abstract (do I believe in a god?) I do not understand why she should wish to know such things, but I answer her nonetheless, night after night, until I become quite reconciled to her presence. Outside, the war machine rumbles on and my work at Bletchley becomes increasingly engrossing.

Then, one night, she does not come and question me, and I wake with a curious sense of anticlimax and disappointment. But Bletchley and my bombe and the war soon swallow it up and I don't think about the dreams and my visitor until it's all over and we are spat out into a new European day.

★

Cambridge

I open the door and walk back onto the quad, under the black sky. Overhead, the storm clouds are racing in. The hexagon and the pyramid are still where I left them, sitting innocently upon the grass, but something has changed. Around the symbols lies a line of faint light, as if the grass itself has started to glow. I stare at it for a moment, then glance towards the Backs. This is a walk I often take – I find it more peaceful than the town itself. Outside King's, this version of Cambridge changes too much, as though they're experimenting with it. Perhaps they are. Perhaps we'll get a final version one day. But the Backs themselves do not change, even though what lies beyond them is no more than a wall of mist. I look up at the unnatural sky and think I shall take a chance on seeing what else might be altering. It occurs to me that the whole thing is finally breaking down, but if that's the case, I'd either have due warning or none at all. So I head down the quad for the river.

It's not quite like real water. It's fine if you look at it directly, but if you glimpse it out of the corner of the eye, it sparkles like hot silver coals. Maybe visitors have the same experience with me: how are we to understand our own nature, after all? The bridge, however, looks exactly as it did when I lived here before: old stone, lichen-covered and weathered with age. Ahead, the mists shimmer – but as I cross the bridge, they begin to fade.

I stop. I've never seen beyond the mist before. In the real Cambridge, the Backs led onto a road, and then to the rhododendron-fringed grounds of the University Library. But now there are only woods – beech and oak and ash with tangles of briar in between, leading to rows of fir and pine.

I pause. This looks more like Germany than England, the kind of forests I'd hiked in as a boy, old and unkempt and impenetrable. There's a path, narrow and snaking. I cannot discount the possibility – in fact, I am compelled to entertain it – that manipulating the symbols in the quad has caused the reality around me to alter. But anything that creates change is interesting.

'If you're experimenting with Cambridge,' I say aloud, 'then why shouldn't I?'

I set off down the path. I look back once and Cambridge is no longer visible; there are only the woods.

Within perhaps a quarter of a mile, the landscape begins to change, becoming more wintry in appearance. The last rags of leaves hang on the trees and the bare sky above me has the yellow-grey of impending snow. The stormcloud blackness is gone, and snow lies on the ground in heavy drifts, creating hills and hummocks over the bushes. I pause and smell the air. It reminds me of the woods outside Vienna, also of Skjolden. I've asked them if I could have a Skjolden here; they have been non-committal, perhaps perceiving too great an irony in providing me with a retreat from what is already a retreat. Or perhaps it's just too much work to create that as well. Perhaps, in this far-future world where everything else has changed, there are still budgets to justify.

A short time after that, I hear the sound of hammers. I go quickly on through the snow, hastening towards the sound. Soon the woods open out and I find myself looking down over a steep drop. On the opposite side there is some kind of mining operation, with small figures moving up and down the hillside. Children, for the most part, in rough sackcloth clothing. Their faces are filthy and they move slowly. The hammers ring out rhythmically, like church bells. A voice says, 'It's copper.'

I turn. A young man stands on the path behind me, shabbily dressed, in a cap. His hands are in his pockets. His eyes are a cold blue, the colour of moonlight on snow.

'You mean the mine?' I ask.

He nods. 'Her brother owns it.'

'Whose brother are you talking about?'

The young man smiles. 'He always loved the story. Did he ever tell you that? You're German, after all.'

'No,' I say. 'I am Austrian. I was born in Vienna.'

'Ah,' he says, with a shrug as if it is all the same thing. 'Then I am wrong.' He holds out a hand and the snow comes down in a flurry. I blink and he is gone. So are the children and the mine. Only the woods remain.

I do not feel the cold, of course. Nor do I hunger and thirst. Just as well, because the dusk is falling over the winter woods now and if I'd still been human, I'd have been flagging long before now. I keep walking, not knowing what else to do, on the assumption that this is some kind of test. It also occurs to me that I might have damaged the system in some way – created an anomaly and then caused the thing to enter some kind of iterative loop. I seem to remember Alan saying something – but without further symbols to manipulate, it's impossible to make any further changes.

So I walk on and at last I glimpse a light through the trees. Its homely glow is almost offensive. I used to despise myself for that secret yearning for company, tried hard to stamp it out. Largely, I'd succeeded. But we are all beasts at heart with that soft need for comfort and warmth. So I head for the light.

★

September 1948

Manchester since the war is grim and grey, a city of warehouses and mills. But there are surprising green spaces in between the streets and the stones. I arrived here in September, in a chilly drizzle. Outside the station, everyone was muffled up against the rain but as I made my way through Piccadilly I passed a young man in a cap, his eyes a startling light blue and set too wide. He reminded me of Ludwig; there was something German about his face. But the war is over now. I turned, once, and found that he was looking back at me. For a moment, I felt as though the woods were closing in on me, the grey streets melting.

I thought of saying something, but of course I didn't. That would be a good way to start my lectureship, I thought, with scandal, arrest, God knows what else… But the memory of the young man in the cap stayed with me, all the way back to my lodgings.

★

Cambridge

The house has a path leading up to it, snaking through briars. I make my way to the door and pause for a moment before knocking. Behind me, the woods are silent: no birdsong, as if the snow has swallowed all sound. When I knock, the noise echoes through the trees.

I am not expecting anyone to answer, somehow. When they don't, I push the handle of the door. It opens easily and I step inside. Within, the house is no more than a cottage, with whitewashed walls and a stone floor. My footsteps are loud as I walk down the passage and into the single room.

There is a fire in the grate. A lamp has been lit. When I look at the flames from the corner of my eye, they sparkle like sunlight on water. A man is sitting in the armchair, staring into the fire.

★

1952

Maybe I shouldn't be surprised it's all come crashing down. It has been growing harder to conceal and I never really see why I should. They seem to think you ought to be ashamed of this kind of thing – even though it goes on in every public school across the country. And it's not as though I'm unaccustomed to keeping secrets.

I won't name him. It's bad enough that they've found me out. We were lovers for some months; he's a local boy. A stupid thing to let happen, but what am I supposed to do?

After the trial, they offered me a choice – pretty much a poisoned chalice either way. I could go to prison, or I could accept a 'cure', which would take the form of oestrogen injections. I couldn't face prison, so I chose the 'cure.'

And this is why I am in hell.

★

Cambridge

'Alan?' I say. He does not turn his head.

'I've been expecting you,' he murmurs.

'How long have you been here?'

He gave a short bark of laughter. 'I really don't know. Does that even make sense?' He turns his head to look at me, finally. He has aged from the broad-faced, confident young man I had known and has become physically heavier. He wears a shapeless tweed suit.

I smile. 'It occurs to me,' I say, 'that you are answering my questions in a perfectly satisfactory manner to convince me that you are, in fact, Alan Turing.'

'And that you are Ludwig Wittgenstein. But if you are a programme, which in some sense you must be, then it is all illusion anyway. I may prove satisfactory to you, but if neither of us is human in the first place, then it's irrelevant, isn't it?'

'It seems to me that we must be the same form of life, otherwise we would not be able to understand each other.'

'If a lion could talk, you said, we would not be able to understand him. Am I a lion talking, then?'

'No, because I can understand you. Where are we, Alan? *What did you do?*'

He holds out something round and red. An apple, with a bite out of it.

'Now I really don't understand.'

'Snow White,' Turing says. 'Always was my favourite fairy story.'

'It smells like almonds,' I tell him.

He nods. 'Poisoned apple. I didn't want – that is, my mother couldn't know. It had to look like an accident. Something I'd picked up in the laboratory.'

'You killed yourself?'

'A few years after your own death.'

'They explained that to me.' I frown. 'At least, I think they did. I have a faint memory –'

'They are us,' Turing says. 'Centuries in the future, this is what they've built. We're nothing more than ghosts in a machine – if you can call it that.'

'They mentioned something called Darkware. I don't know what that is. I suppose I'm in the wrong form of life.'

'It's the human mind. All of it. Everyone's linked into a thing called the Veil: there aren't separate bodies any more. Instead of creating intelligent machines, they went the other way, to a biological system.'

'So really, there is only one form of life, now?'

'I suppose so. You know me, Ludwig. I always was a little impatient with philosophy. Mathematics, that's the answer. That's the one truth that crosses your forms of life.'

I shook my head. 'Even that, Alan, must have its

limitations. You attended my lectures, I remember.'

'Yes, but I didn't understand them!' Finally, he laughs. 'If this is a single form of life, Ludwig, then it seems they are experimenting with others. And we are part of that experiment.'

There's a sound at the door. I look up and to my surprise, given what I know of Alan, I see a woman. She's young, but her face is gaunt and her eyes hollow. Lank black hair falls in wings on either side of her face and she wears an old fashioned dress with puffed sleeves.

'Who are you?'

'She's Snow White,' Turing says.

'What?'

Turing speaks wearily. 'It was my favourite film. So the apple – do you see now? I wanted to pay a little homage to it. When they brought me here, they wanted to use symbols that are meaningful to me, that others would have to try and interpret. She is one of them.'

'Does she speak?'

'She used to. Not any more.'

Out of the corner of my eye, I see a sparkle of light. 'Alan, the system –'

'Do you remember, Ludwig?' He is eyeing me warily.

'Remember what?'

'Coming here before.'

'I have never been here before, Alan.'

No,' he says, sighing. 'That's what you always say.' He hauls himself out of the armchair. 'Ludwig, I know you don't remember, but we've tried this before – if I give you something, will you take it back with you? Try to do something with it?'

'Of course, Alan,' I say. By now I am sure that his mind – if that's a word I can use – has become affected, but he is visibly distressed, shaking and pale-faced, so I say, 'I'll do whatever you want me to do.'

'Then take this. It's my death. It's the feelings I –' He

breaks off, and thrusts something round and cold into my hand; it burns my skin like ice.

'Alan, what —' I start to say, but the mist is swirling all around, the cottage and Alan Turing and Snow White becoming fading and faint, until I am standing once again in my summery chamber at King's. The grey stone walls are honeyed by light. Everything is as I left it. There is something I am supposed to do. I am holding something. I look down at my hand and in it is a crisp, half-eaten apple, its skin as red as blood, its flesh as white as snow, and its pips as black as night. I can feel a memory, or maybe a dream, draining from my mind like water: my friend, and a woman… I stare down at the apple and the dream is gone.

There is something I am supposed to do, but I do not know what it is. At the far end of the room, the screen is blank. I put the apple on the mantelpiece, then I sit down at the table and pick up my papers.

Afterword: Artificial? Intelligence?

Steve Furber, ICL Professor of Computer Engineering, the University of Manchester

Liz Williams's story draws the reader into a discourse between Turing and Wittgenstein that takes place in a virtual world in the distant future, but revolves around their contemporaneous existence around the time of the Second World War. The virtual conversationalists appear fully conscious, to the extent that they are aware not only of themselves but also of the infidelities of the virtual world they now inhabit compared with the physical world of their former existences. The conversation is about artificial intelligence and the 'Turing Test', with allusions to Searle's 'Chinese Room' (in which a non-Chinese-speaking human passes the Turing Test in Chinese simply by following algorithmic instructions: since the human passes the test without understanding, so could a computer). The story focuses on the distinction between symbolic processing by automata (such as computers) and by intelligent beings. An intriguing association is also made between Snow White and the cyanide-laced apple that ended Turing's life.

Turing thought that computers might lead rapidly to the creation of artificial intelligence (AI), but this was not to be. It has turned out to be much more difficult to create machine intelligence than early AI researchers thought. Today's computers are better at chess than the best human Grand Master, but they don't play 'intelligently' – whatever that means – they use brute force and very high-speed search. They are better than humans at many things, but they still don't strike us as intelligent. What is the problem?

Part of the difficulty is that we do not, even today, have a good definition of what it means to be intelligent. We don't know how human intelligence works, and we don't know how our brains work. But we are now within sight of computers powerful enough to model substantial parts of the human brain. These computers are a million million times more powerful than the machines available to Turing, which perhaps explains why progress was so difficult then. We can begin, with these machines, to explore the principles at work in our brains, and through that gain an understanding of our own intelligence.

In my own work I am developing chips for a massively-parallel computer specifically for brain modelling and similar tasks. The machine will ultimately incorporate a million microprocessor 'engines', each responsible for its own small part of a very large 'program' that simulates the spiking language of biological neurons, the components from which our brains are constructed. It is intended to provide a computational platform that will enable neuroscientists and psychologists to test their hypotheses of brain function on very-large-scale models. This work, or perhaps similar work elsewhere, may one day give us the insights needed to fulfil Turing's vision of intelligent machines.

Or should we pursue a completely different path, as Liz suggests in her story?

The Bellini Madonna

Patricia Duncker

The light wavered, hesitant before the upraised hand of the woman who stared out from the gilded frame. There she sat, hieratic, magnificent, and serene before her adoring multitudes. Her indifferent gaze encountered the vacant air above three women skulking in the Lady Chapel. Rachel Webster, sitting bolt upright and craning her neck in the first pew, struggled to glimpse the Bellini Madonna, her magisterial shoulders and gleaming crimson robes. The painting shrugged back into shadows, awaiting another euro in the electricity box to animate the dimmed spots. The security lasers flickered like dragons' eyes, guarding the Madonna on loan from the museum in Venice, where the thing was rumoured to have worked a miracle. Miracles should happen in churches. The museum authorities stifled the newspaper reports and sent her to Rome for a cooling–off period, before their stately rooms could be overrun with unwashed cripples seeking comfort and sanctuary.

Rachel Webster, in attendance for artistic rather than religious reasons, and completely unaware of the Madonna's recent activities, found herself trapped in the middle of the bench. On one side kneeled a black and white nun, head bowed, face masked, her fingers moving stealthily over the gleaming pearls of her rosary. *Santa Maria, madre di Dio, prega per noi...* Her muffled murmur rose up into the dim scented vault of the chapel. On the other side, further away, but still firmly blocking off the end of the pew, knelt a pale curled perm, all the waves awry, as if a great wind had ruffled them. The woman's cheek, an evil yellowish white, and her clothes, synthetic camel-coloured jacket, cream shirt with a lop-sided bow instead of a collar, and quite hideous scuffed trainers, suggested an American. A tourist. Probably one who has just discovered she has terminal cancer, and intends to sit there, praying, for hours and hours and hours. Rachel's English manners forbade her disturbing either set of devotions, but did not preclude resentment and impatience. She was unable to move; worse still, her view of Bellini's immaculate Madonna was curtailed by a monstrous nineteenth-century horror, which had been left bang in the centre of the chapel aisle, cemented no doubt to its stone plinth.

The plinth sported another Madonna, but of a very different order; a mass-produced plaster statue of Our Lady of Compassion, her arms outstretched and her cloak of stars spread wide, to gather in lost souls. The pious face, bland, sugary and offensive, suggested a girl barely older than Rachel, who now announced to anyone who asked that she was twenty-one rather than nineteen. The plaster statue wore the usual blue and white robes, a little dusty and blackened with candle-smoke; her golden halo of sun's rays bore up bravely, despite numerous cracks and missing flecks of colour. Her sandaled feet balanced on the crescent moon and, illuminated by the mass of candles placed before her, the gilded stars, painted on the belly of her dark cloak, danced and flickered. Here were all the constellations of the middle heavens, glittering, unstable, embedded in her grimy plaster folds.

Hail Mary, full of grace, blessed art thou amongst women, and blessed be the fruit of thy womb Jesus. Hail Mary Mother of God, pray for us sinners now and at the hour of our death, pray for us now, and at the hour of our death.

But you are masking my view of the Bellini Madonna. And you are vulgar beyond belief. Rachel hissed her own frustrated prayer at the apparently innocuous idol, towards whom the death's head tourist and the musty old nun were directing all their adoration, wonder, love and praise. She eyed the black electricity box and dug her purse out of the money belt that encircled her waist like a castle wall.

And at the very moment, almost as if she had pressed a button or shouted ACTION, the chapel shadows gave birth to two importunate shapes scrabbling down the pew, pushing, crying out, shoving a placard with an ill-spelt sob story in English and Italian into her resisting arms. MANGERE! MANGERE! NO EAT! NO EAT! GIVE MONEY! GIVE MONEY! Two scrawny children stuck out their tongues; the little girl, no more than seven or eight years old, pushed one filthy hand into her mouth. The other hand closed around Rachel's purse and snatched it away. She fumbled for the vanishing leather pouch, which contained all her library cards, her Barclays connect card, her membership of the Opera Club, her MasterCard and three hundred euros. The children had already backed out of the pew, ducking under the bench, the nun's rosary twirling around an enterprising wrist. They screeched at one another like baboons, then ran for it, still clutching their cardboard back-story.

'Stop thief!'

Rachel trampled over the nun and belted after them, yelling in outraged Dickensian English. The square white light of the distant church door framed the racing children, who hurtled out into the midday glare and the rush of spring sunshine. Rachel crashed out of the west door, still shouting, to find herself accompanied by a pounding mass of enraged worshippers, who now constituted themselves into an impromptu lynch mob. The smaller of the two children vanished, but the little girl who had captured the rosary, still glittering upon her wrist, stumbled within her grasp. Rachel plucked the child out of the air as she leaped for the steps. Immediately, they were surrounded by unintelligible screaming, but two phrases emerged, viciously clear, even to

Rachel's rudimentary Italian.

Gypsies! Beat her! Hit her!

The child shrieked and kicked. Rachel caught her by the heels, whisked her upside down and shook her violently, so that her head skimmed the dusty stones. The ragged dress flew downwards over her writhing body, skinny as a clothes peg, muffling the shrieks; but the creature wore no knickers so that Rachel found herself looking down onto a naked brown bottom and a hairless slit that was anything but innocent. The lynch mob closed in.

Hit her! Little thief! They deserve it!

The pearly string of prayers and the silver crucifix splattered into the dust, but the purse had already been passed on or given to the younger child. Rachel dropped the girl, appalled and trembling, and snatched up the rosary. A man in the crowd tried to apprehend the fleeing gypsy, but the tiny thief sank her teeth into his wrist. He cuffed her ear, roaring, and she darted away, soared over the walls like a wild goat, disappearing between the line of parked cars and the passing crowds.

Rachel had lost all her library cards, both her credit cards and three hundred precious euros. But she still had her passport, her notebook and pencil, her mobile phone and the nun's rosary. And so back she staggered, into the twilight of the church, pushing through the dissipating mob, shocked and tearful. All her mother's gloomy predictions had come to pass. On your own in a foreign country? Where you can barely speak the language? You'll be attacked and robbed. But I haven't been murdered. Not yet. She crouched in the eerie dark of the Lady Chapel, waiting until her eyes adjusted to candlelight and her hands ceased to tremble. There in the distance sat the Bellini Madonna, rigid and crimson, still partially obliterated by the plaster-cast Virgin, who appeared to extend her dark, starred robes like bat's wings, in sympathy for the chastened young woman and her recent loss. The gilt stars shuffled and glittered in the night sky of her cloak. Rachel's tears drenched the firmament. She noted down time, place and date for the police report. I must be sensible, otherwise I won't get my insurance money. Then she felt her way down the aisle towards the first row.

And there she saw them, both the kneeling nun and the liverish tourist. Silent, bent, unmoved by the drama of the gypsies' attack. She stood still, astonished and enraged. Neither of them had lifted a finger to help her. Then she did what still seemed the right thing to do. She tapped the nun's shoulder.

'Excuse me sister, here is your rosary.'

The white skull face lifted towards her and the nun smiled, her teeth gleamed yellow and uneven, the voice a silken whisper.

'Thank you, my child.'

Santa Maria, madre di Dio, prega per noi.

The pearl beads resumed their gentle rhythm.

Dismissed.

Rachel glared at the tourist, the odious statue and the Bellini Madonna, which she had come especially to see, and stalked out of the church.

'Name?'

'Address?'

'No, not your address in England, your address here in Rome.'

A huge queue battled in the waiting room at the police station. She gave the clerk at Reception the same information twice and waited to be called. As the afternoon warmed, the waiting-room stench of unwashed bodies and cigarette smoke, drifting back inside the opened windows, became ranker and more pungent. Rachel squirmed on her plastic chair, her thighs damp and her sense of alienated distress rising. She had cancelled all her bankcards, but the precious library cards and treasured euros were gone forever. She rang her mother and grizzled for ten minutes, only to be told that a gap year art history trip to Italy all on her own at her tender age constituted a *folie de grandeur*. You've been asking for it, my girl, and now it's happened to you. Come home at once. Rachel hung up, chastened and snivelling.

'Signora Webster?'

Her turn.

The young, unsmiling policeman wore a blue shirt that matched his computer screen.

'Name?'

'Address? No, not your address in England, your address here in Rome.'

Rachel suddenly began to howl in grief and frustration. The policeman sat watching her for a minute or two. Then said in careful, slow-motion Italian, adapted for idiot foreigners,

'What are you crying for? OK. So the children got your money. That's a pity. But why are you so upset about your library cards. They won't use them. The gypsies can't read.'

Rachel blubbered into her handkerchief and gazed at his handsome olive face. Why indeed was she weeping?

'I couldn't see the Bellini Madonna properly,' she wailed, 'and I've come all this way just to see her.'

The policeman shrugged. 'Go back later. The Madonna will still be there.' He looked at her speculatively; a pretty English girl with schoolbook Italian.

'Listen. You shouldn't be crying. Nothing serious has happened to you. That lady over there has lost her husband.'

Rachel swung round to survey the distant row of chairs, and there, cowed, yellow-faced, mired in the stillness of shock, sat the death's head tourist, still wearing her frumpish camel jacket and her awful trainers. No dark glasses and no handbag, her reddened piggy eyes screwed tight with dried tears.

'Look. Will you help me? She can't talk. Not in any language. But she might talk to you. I'll ask the questions

238

and you can translate. Here,' he offered her a minor bribe, 'this is your certificate for the insurance and I've said you lost five hundred euros. That should cover the cost of replacing all your library cards.'

Rachel approached the lost middle-aged woman with the disastrous nest of collapsed hair, exuding cautious solicitousness. How was she to address this terrible, unspeakable grief? May I help you? I am so sorry. She regretted her resentment in the church.

'I'm here to translate for you.'

No answer.

'Where are you from? For the police report? Could you tell me that at least?'

The piggy eyes gleamed and the dried lips moved slightly. At first Rachel heard *prega per noi*, but gradually deciphered Southern Illinois. She stretched out her hand, which was immediately clutched by a gruesome yellowed claw, the rings loose around the dried knuckles. She lifted the woman to her feet and they moved across the tiles like a pair of dancing crabs, towards the young man lying in wait before his computer. But as they sat down the woman collapsed once more, speechless.

'Have you contacted the Embassy?' Rachel hissed at the policeman in a stage whisper. He shrugged again; the Embassy representative would turn up in due course.

They pieced the events together like a jigsaw, from nods and stifled murmurs. The reddened eyes remained blank and fixed, like a shattered doll. The woman was on a tour of Italy with her husband. They made trips to Europe every year now that he had retired, and visited all the things you have to see before you die. Last year: Paris, Chartres, Versailles. This year: Florence, Venice, Rome. They had arrived in Rome last night and checked into a hotel near the railway station.

'Why there?' The policeman looked at the address. 'They've got money. That's not their class of hotel.'

'Maybe they arrived late?' suggested Rachel.

But they hadn't. There was time for a shower and a stroll before dinner. They had taken all their valuables with them because there was no safe in the hotel and they didn't trust the lock on the door or the clientele in the corridors. Her husband had escorted her back to their room; she had locked herself in and gone to bed; he had assured her he would not be late and set forth once more into the warm evening and the passing traffic. He had been carrying: both passports, all their money and credit cards, the American Express card, the plane tickets home to Chicago, where their daughter intended to meet them, the keys to their car in the long stay car park, and all their travel insurance documents, luggage and medical. He never came back.

She had reported him missing at 11.30 on the following morning.

'Why so late?' The policeman looked hard at Rachel, who, enthralled by this sinister whispered tale, now held the shaking tourist's icy hand. 'Ask her if he often did this. You know, does he usually abandon her in hotels and disappear? Go on, ask her.'

Rachel stiffened, appalled. What sort of marriage did this woman have? Did he go out looking for prostitutes? Drugs? Transsexuals? Rent boys?

'I can't ask that!'

'You must. Ask her.'

But all they learned was the fact that he had always come back.

'Late?'

Yes. Sometimes late.

'The next day?'

The woman's unyielding, humiliated silence suggested that this was indeed the case. She gazed down at her scuffed trainers and spoke no more. Then she shuffled away to the toilets, leaning on Rachel's arm.

'You can go now. The Embassy will be here soon.

Grazie tante.'

'But what are you going to do?'

A small sigh accompanied the gesture of indifference.

'Probably nothing. Maybe put out a Missing Person Alert to all patrols and hospitals. These people usually turn up.'

'But what if he's floating face down in the Tiber!' Rachel imagined unspeakable things.

'Then he'll turn up,' smiled the policeman. He reached across the desk and shook her hand. 'Enjoy the rest of your stay in Roma.'

Dismissed.

Three days later Rachel plucked up courage to return to the Church and re-visit the Bellini Madonna. Sanguine and relaxed, she strolled down the nave and turned into the Lady Chapel. Her shining new Italian leather purse was now actually chained to her belt so that she resembled a medieval builder, burdened with valuable tools. There was the Bellini Madonna, her hand raised in blessing, and there too was the vile piece of plaster, her arms outstretched, her bent face floodlit by the dimmed spots. She was the chosen one, picked out by permanent lights, the candles blazing before her. Rachel paused to feed two euros into the electricity box, and behold! Before her gleamed the two Madonnas, bathed in light, like a team of consultants, open for business. She stood, transfixed, gazing at the incongruous images, one nudging the other into obscurity.

Then she realised that there were two other people in the sanctuary. The nun kneeled in her usual place: *Santa Maria, madre di Dio, prega per noi.* And right next to her, as if they were partners in the great race for the martyr's crown, knelt a fashionable older woman, wearing fabulous Italian clothes. Her padded green silk jacket with wide sleeves matched the smart slick trousers and gleaming golden heels. Rachel stirred in alarm as she noticed the glossy, red leather bag at the woman's feet. Where are the gypsies? They'll have that in seconds. She stepped closer, vigilant, guarding the bag. The Chapel smelt strongly of violets. Rachel looked up, straight into the mass of golden stars inside the Virgin's dark cloak.

And then something strange overtook her – a rushing movement, slight, distant, gathering. There in the unguarded deep of the night sky she saw the reeling stars, the pale glow of light that had taken two thousand years to reach her, the massed galaxies and planets, spinning outwards into eternity, hurtling away from the gigantic explosion of creation, the distant binary stars and their attendant planets, moving at fantastic speeds away from the centre, glorious, beautiful, unfettered, hurtling into the vastness of eternity. Her eye caught the whirling moons of Saturn, the miraculous trailing gas of the Crab Nebula, thousands of spinning pulsars, the great streaming winds of particles, belching forth from the mass of exploding stars. There, captured forever in the cloak of the Madonna blazed the universe itself, darkness visible; radio waves strong as lighthouse beams swept the church. Rachel staggered against the carved pew, sucked into the Virgin's cloak and the receding revelation.

'Are you feeling OK, honey?'

She was sitting in the pew beside the kneeling nun and the elegant American, a handkerchief bathed in violets pressed to her nose.

'Oh yes. Thank you. I feel a little faint, that's all.'

But I know this woman. And yet she cannot be the same. The woman I knew was a yellowed victim of failed matrimony. This woman is younger, beautiful, her coiffure poised, perfect, her nails manicured. Look, look at her blood-red nails. Rachel sniffed hard into the musky violets and looked again. Yes, this was the woman who had lost her husband, but now she was miraculous, transfigured. And at last, from this angle, breathtakingly close to the plaster cast

Virgin, she had a clear view of the painting. Rachel's blurred vision caught one tiny detail, something she had never seen before. There on the painted table beside an open missal lay a rosary of pearls, the same rosary she had rescued from the dust, now smuggled into safety from thieving fingers, painted back into glory at the right hand of the Bellini Madonna.

Afterword: A Cosmic Lighthouse

Dr Tim O'Brien, Senior Lecturer & Head of Outreach, for the Jodrell Bank Centre for Astrophysics.

In the final revelatory scene, Patricia Duncker captures the wonder and mystery that scientists themselves sometimes feel when contemplating the heavens.

When her character Rachel has a vision of 'the pale glow of light that had taken two thousand years to reach her,' there is a link to science. Since light travels at a finite speed, the farther out into space we look, the farther back in time we're seeing. I've spent a lot of time studying the repeated explosions of a star 5,000 light years away, events that actually happened 5,000 years ago. It is certainly possible to look at light that set off on its journey towards us 2,000 years ago.

Similarly, when Duncker writes of 'massed galaxies and planets, spinning outwards into eternity, hurtling away from the gigantic explosion of creation,' she is describing the expansion of space following the Big Bang.

In the 1920s we discovered that all the distant galaxies are moving away from us. The universe is expanding. Does that place us at the centre of the universe? In fact we're not so special. On large scales every point in the universe is moving away from every other point. Space itself is expanding, the billions of galaxies in the observable universe are hurtling away from each other.

We'd assumed this expansion should be slowing down as gravity acts to pull the galaxies back together. In fact, it's speeding up and we don't understand why. The question of whether the universe is indeed infinite or eternal as Rachel's vision suggests, is another which remains to be answered.

Rachel also sees binary stars, pulsars and the Crab Nebula. The Crab was first spotted in 1054 by Chinese astronomers as a new star so bright it was visible by day. When we now point our telescopes at the place they noted, we see a bright nebula. The glowing remnant of an exploded star, spreading into space, clouds of dust and gas.

In the heart of the Crab Nebula is a pulsar, the central core of the exploded star that has collapsed in on itself, compressed. It's the size of a city, but weighing as much as the Sun, spinning thirty times each second and sending beams of radio waves streaming away from its north and south magnetic poles. Like a cosmic lighthouse, we see it flashing as it spins.

When stars die the elements created in them are thus spread into space: the seeds of new stars, new planets. Oxygen, nitrogen, carbon, many of the elements that make up our world, were all made in stars billions of years ago. So Rachel's religious vision is accurate when she sees 'thousands of spinning pulsars, the great streaming winds of particles, belching forth from the mass of exploding stars.'

It is often assumed that science is all about certainty. In fact it moves forward through doubt, not faith. Scientists are trained to mistrust their theories and test them through observation and experiment. Although very different from religion, science offers its own wonderful vision of the universe.

Hair

Adam Roberts

1

It seems to me foolish to take a story about betrayal and call it
– as my sponsors wish me to – 'The Hairstyle That Changed
The World'.

All this hairdressing business, this hair-work. I don't
want to get excited about that. To see it as those massed
strands of electricity shooting up from the bald pate of the
vandegraaff machine. And whilst we're on the subject of
haircuts: I was raised by my mother alone, and we were poor
enough that, from an early stage, she was the person who
cut my hair. For the sake of simplicity, as much as economy,
this cut would be uniform and close. To keep me quiet as
the buzzer grazed, she used to show me the story about the
mermaid whose being-in-the-world was confused between
fishtail and feet. I'm sure she showed me lots of old books,
but it was that one that sticks in my head: the singing crab,
more scarab than crustacean; the wicked villainess able to
change not only her appearance but, improbably, her size – I
used to puzzle how she was able to generate all her extra mass
as she metamorphosed, at the end, into a colossal octopus.
Mostly I remember the beautiful young mermaid with the
tempestuous name Ariel. The story hinged on the notion
that her tail might vanish and reform as legs, and I used to
worry disproportionately about those new feet. Would they,
I wondered, smell of fish? Were the toenails actually fish-
scales? Were the twenty-six bones of each foot (all of which
I could name) formed of *cartilage*, after the manner of fish

bones? Or human bone? The truth is my mind is the sort that is most comfortable finding contiguities between different states, and most uncomfortable with inconsistencies. Hence my eventual choice of career, I suppose. And I don't doubt that my fascination with the mermaid story had to do with a nascent erotic yearning for Ariel herself – a very prettily drawn figure, I recall.

This has nothing to do with anything. I ought not digress. It's particularly vulgar to do so before I have even started; as if I want to put off the task facing me. Of course this account is not about me. It is enough, for your purposes, to locate your narrator, to know that I was raised by my mother alone; and that after she died (of newstrain CF, three weeks after contracting it) I was raised by a more distant relative. We had enough to eat, but nothing else in my life was *enough to*. To know that my trajectory out of that world was hard study, a scholarship to a small college, and the acquisition of the professional skills that established me in my current profession. You might also want to know where I first met Neocles (long final *e* – people sometimes get that wrong) at college, although what was for me dizzying educational altitude represented, for him, a sort of slumming, a symptom of his liberal curiosity about how the underprivileged live.

Above all, I suppose, you need to know that I'm of that generation that thinks of hair as a sort of excrescence, to be cropped to make it manageable, not indulged at length. And poverty is like the ore in the stone; no matter how you grind the rock and refine the result, it is always poverty that comes out. Thinking again about my mother, as here, brings her colliding painfully against the membrane of memory. I suppose I find it hard to forgive her for being poor. She loved me completely, and I loved her back, as children do: the beautiful mermaid, seated on a sack-shaped rock, combing her long, coral-red hair whilst porpoises jump through invisible aerial hoops below her.

2

To tell you about the hairstyle that changed the world, it's back we go to Reykjavik, five years ago now: just after the Irkutsk famine, when the grain was devoured by that granulated agent manufactured by... and the argument continues as to which terrorists sponsored it. It was the year the World Cup descended into farce. Nic was in Iceland to answer charges at the Product Placement Court, and I was representing him.

A PPC hearing is not much different to any other court hearing. There are the rituals aping the last century, or perhaps the century before that. There's a lot of brass and glass, and there is a quantity of waxed, mirrorlike darkwood. I had represented Nic at such hearings before, but never one quite so serious as this. And Nic had more to lose than most. Because I had itemized his assets prior to making our first submission before the Judicial Master I happened to know exactly how much that was: five apartments, one overlooking Central Park; a mulberry farm; forty assorted cars and flitters; more than fifty percent shares in the Polish National Museum – which although it didn't precisely mean that he owned all those paintings and statues and whatnots at least gave him privileged access to them. The Sydney apartment had a Canova, for instance, in the entrance hall, and the Poles weren't pressing him to return it any time soon.

He had a lot to lose.

In such circumstances insouciance is probably a more attractive reaction than anxiety, although from a legal perspective I might have wished for a more committed demeanor. He lounged in court in his Orphic shirt – *very* stylish, very Allah-mode – and his hair was *a hundred years* out of date. It was Woodstock. Or English Civil War aristocrat.

'When the J.M. comes in,' I told him, 'you'd better get off your gluteus maximus and stand yourself straight.'

Judicial Master Paterson came in, and Nic got to his feet

smartly enough and nodded his head, and then sat himself down perfectly properly. With his pocketstrides decently hidden by the table he looked almost respectable. Except for all the hair, of course.

3

I see-you-tomorrowed him on the steps of the courthouse, but he was staring at the sky. The bobble-layer of clouds on the horizon was a remarkable satsuma colour. Further up things were cyan and eggshell. The surface of the icebound estuary, which had looked perfectly smooth and flat in daylight, revealed under the slant light all manner of hollows and jags. Further out at sea, past the iceline where waves turned themselves continually and wearily over, a fishing platform sent a red snake of smoke straight up from the fakir's-basket of its single chimney. The ocean covered its nighttime depths with the firework sparkles of sunset.

'Tomorrow,' he replied absently. He seemed hypnotized by the view.

'Don't worry,' I told him, mistaking (as I now think) his distraction for anxiety about the prospect of losing some of his five apartments or forty cars and flitters. 'The J.M. said he recognized that some individuals have a genius for innovation. That was a good sign. That's code for: geniuses don't need to be *quite* as respectful of the law as ordinary drones.'

'A genius for innovation,' he echoed.

'I'm not saying scot-free. Not saying that. But it won't be too bad. You'll keep more than you think. It will be fine. Don't worry. Yes?'

He suddenly coughed into his gloves – yellow, condom-tight gloves – and appeared to notice me for the first time. God knows I loved him, as a friend loves a true friend, but he bore then as he always did his own colossally swollen ego like a deformity. I never knew a human with so prodigious a self-regard. His selfishness was of the horizoning, all-

250

encompassing sort that is almost touching, because it approaches the selfishness of the small child. His whim: I shall be humanity's benefactor! But this was not an index of his altruism. It was because his ego liked the sound of the description. Having known him twenty years I would stand up in court and swear to it. He developed the marrow peptide-calcbinder treatment not to combat osteoporosis – the ostensible reason, the thing mentioned in his Medal of Science citation – but precisely *because* of the plastic surgical spinoff possibilities, so that he could add twenty centimeters to his own long bones. It's not that he *minded* people using his treatment to alleviate osteopathologies. With a sort of blithe singlemindedness, he was pleasantly surprised at other useful applications.

Accordingly, when he did not turn up in the courtroom the following day my first thought was that he had simply overslept, or gotten distracted by some tourist pleasure, or that some aspect of his own consciousness had intruded between his perceiving mind and the brute fact that (however much I tried to reassure him) a J.M. was gearing up to fine him half his considerable wealth for property-rights violation. It did not occur to me that he might deliberately have absconded. This possibility evidently hadn't occurred to the court either, or they would have put some kind of restraint upon him. You would think (*they* thought, obviously) that the prospect of losing so many million euros of wealth was restraint enough.

The shock in court was as nothing, however, to the fury of the Company: his employer, and mine. I want to be clear: I had been briefed to defend Nic in court, and that only. I made this point forcefully after the event. My brief had been courtroom and legal, not to act as his minder, or to prevent him from boarding a skyhop to Milan (it turned out) in order immediately to board another skyhop to – nobody was quite sure where. 'If you'd wanted a minder you should have hired a minder,' I said. I was assertive, not aggressive.

The court pronounced in absentia, and it went hard on Nic's fortune. But this did not flush him out.

His disappearance hurt me. I was sent to a dozen separate meetings in a dozen different global locations within one week; and in the same timeframe I had twenty or so further virtual meetings. Flying over Holland, where robotically-tended fields shone greener than jade, and the hedges are all twenty-foot tall, and the glimmering blue rivers sined their paths towards the sea.

At Denver airport I saw a man with Parkinsonism – not old, no more than forty – sitting in the café and trying to eat a biscuit. He looked as though he was trying to shake hands with his own mouth.

The news was as full of people starving, as it always is. Images of a huge holding zone in Sri Lanka where people were simply sitting around waiting to die. That look of the starving: hunger has placed its leech-maw upon their heel and sucked all their fluid and solidity out, down to the bones. The skin tautly concave everywhere. The huge eyes, the aching face.

On Channel 9 the famine clock, bottom left corner, rolled its numbers over and over. A blur of numbers.

I flew to Iceland.

I flew back to Denver.

I was acutely aware that Neocles' vanishing put my own career at risk. Had I always lived amongst wealth, as he had, I might have floated free above the anxiety of this. It's easy for the wealthy to believe that something will turn up. But I had experienced what a med-uninsured hardscrabble life was like, and I did not want to go back to it.

He's gone rogue, I was told. Why didn't you stop him? The Company, which had been (to me) a dozen or so points of human contact, suddenly swelled and grew monstrously octopoid. A hundred or more company people wanted to speak to me directly. This is serious, I was told.

He has the patent information on a *dozen* billion-euro applications, I was told. *You* want to guarantee the company's financial losses should he try and pirate-license those? I thought *not*.

I thought not.

Not everybody scapegoated me. Some departments recognised the injustice in trying to pin Nic's disappearance on me. Embryology, for instance; a department more likely than most to require expert legal advice, of the sort I had proved myself in the past capable of providing. Optics also assured me of their support, though they did so off the record. But it would have required a self-belief stronger than the one with which providence has provided me to think my career – my twenty-year career – as staff legal counsel for the Company was going to last more than a month. The elegant bee-dance of mutual corporate espionage continued to report that none of our competitors had, yet, acquired any of the intellectual property Nic had in his power to dispose. I had a meeting at Cambridge, in the UK, where late winter was bone-white and ducks on the river looked in astonishment at their own legs. I flew to Rio where the summer ocean was immensely clear and beautiful: sitting on the balcony of our offices it was possible, without needing optical enhancement, to make out extraordinary levels of detail in the sunken buildings and streets, right down to cars wedged in doorways, and individual letters painted on the tarmac.

I flew to Alaska. I flew to Sydney, where the airport was a chaos of children – a flashmob protest about the cutbacks in youth dole.

In the midst of all this I somehow found time to begin, discreetly, to make plans for a post-Company life. My ex-wife was more understanding than I might have expected, more concerned to maintain medinsure for our two children than for herself. I scouted, gingerly, secretly, for other employment; but even with the most optimistic assessment it was going to be hard to carry five lots of insurance on my new salary. I could not of course deprive the children, and I did not wish to deprive Kate. That left my ex-wife and myself, and – truthfully – I decided to give up coverage for myself and leave my ex's in place.

Then, from the blue, news: Neocles had gone native in *Mumbai*, of all places. I was called once again to Denver and briefed face-a-face by Alamillo himself, the company enforcer and bruiser and general bully-fellow. It was not a pleasant tête-á-tête. At this meeting emphasis was placed on the very *lastness* of this, my last chance. The word last as conventionally used was insufficient to convey just how absolutely last this last chance was, how micron-close to the abyss I found myself, how very terminal my opportunity.

The very severity of this interview reassured me. Had they not needed me very badly they would not have worked so hard to bully me. For the first time since Nic had so thoughtlessly trotted off – putting at risk, the fucker, not only his own assets but my entire family's wellbeing – I felt the warmth of possible redemption touch the chill of my heart.

'My last chance,' I said. 'I understand.'

'You go *to him*,' said Alamillo. 'You have a fucking *word*, yes?'

I understood then that they were sending me because I was a friend, not because I was a lawyer. They already knew that *money* was no longer going to provide them with any leverage with Nic – that he had renounced money. He was easing himself into his new role as Jesus Christ, the redeemer of the starving. What can you do to a person who won't listen to money? What else does Power have, in this world of ours?

'I'll talk to him. What else?'

'Nothing else,' said Amarillo.

'Bring him home?'

'No, that's not what we're sending you to do. Listen the fuck to me. I don't give a fucking pin – just, just. Look. We're sending you to *talk* to him.'

4

I was flown out on a gelderm plane, its skin stiffening with the frictive heat of a high-inset aerial trajectory. I ate little medallions of liquorish bread, with shark caviar and Russian cheese paté; and then authentic sausages lacquered with honey, and then spears of dwarf asparagus, and then chocolate pellets that frothed deliciously inside the mouth. I drank white wine; a Kenyan vintage. The toilet cubicle of this plane offered seven different sorts of hygiene wipe, including a plain one, one that analyzed your stool as you wiped to check for digestive irregularities, and several that imparted different varieties of dotTech to your lower intestine to various ends.

I watched a film about a frolicsome young couple overcoming the obstacles placed in the way of their love. I watched the news. I watched another film, a long one this time – fifteen minutes, or more – based on the historical events of the French Revolution.

The tipping point of descent registered in my viscera, like a Christmas-eve tingle of excitement.

We plummeted to Mumbai.

Arriving at Chhatrapati Shivaji was like travelling back half a century in time: the smell; the litter; the silver-painted curved ceilings on their scythe-shaped supports. An all-metal train, running on all-metal rails, trundling me from the terminal to the departure room. Then it was a short hop in a Company flitter to the Jogeshwari beachfront – seconds, actually: a brief elevation over the peninsular sprawl of the city, its bonsai skyscrapers like stacked dishes, the taller curves and spires further south. The sky was outrageously blue, and the sea bristled with light. And, really, in a matter of seconds we came down again. I could have walked from airport to seafront, is how close it was. But better to arrive in a flitter, of course. When I'd called Nic he'd been gracious if laid-back in reply: no company men, just you, old friend. Of course, of course.

Of course.

There was a flitter park on the Juhu dyke, and I left the car, and driver, there, and started walking. Forty degrees of heat – mild, I was told, for the season. The sky blue like a gemlike flame. It poured heat down upon the world. The air smelt of several things at once: savoury smells and decaying smells, and the worn-out, salt-odour of the ocean.

I don't know what I expected. I think I expected, knowing Nic, to find him gone hippy; dropped-out; or a holy hermit chanting Japa. I pictured him surfing. But as I walked I noticed there was no surf. There were people *everywhere*: a rather startling profusion of humanity, lolling, walking, rushing, going in and out, talking, singing, praying. It was an enormous crush. The sound of several incompatible varieties of music wrestled in the background: beats locking and then disentangling, simple harmonic melodies twisting about one another in atonal and banshee interaction. Everybody was thin. Some were starvation thin. It was easy enough to pick out these latter because they were much stiller: standing or sitting with studied motionlessness. It was those who could still afford to eat who moved about.

The bay harboured the poking-up tops and roofs of many inundated towers, scattered across the water like the nine queens in the chessboard problem, preventing the build-up of ridable waves. These upper floors of the drowned buildings were still inhabited, for the poor will live where they can, however unsalubrious. Various lines and cables were strung in sweeping droops from roofs to shore. People swam, or kicked and splashed through the shallower water. On the new mud beach a few sepia-coloured palm trees waved their heavy feathers in the breeze.

Sweat wept down my back.

And then, as arranged, there was Nic: lying on the flank of the groyne with his great length of hair fanned out on the ground behind him. The first surprise: he was dressed soberly, in black. The second: he was accompanied by armed guards.

I sat beside my friend. It was so very *hot*. 'I think I was expecting beach bummery.'

'I saw your plane come over,' he said. 'Made *quite* a racket.'

'Airbraking.' Like I knew anything about *that*.

'I'm glad you've come, though,' he said, getting up on his haunches. His guards fidgeted, leaning their elbows on their slung rifles. They were wearing, I noticed, Marathi National Guard uniforms. 'Good of you to come,' he clarified.

'People in Denver are pretty pissed.'

'There's not many I'd trust,' he said. He meant that he did, at least, trust me.

'These boys work for you?' I asked.

'Soldiers. They do. The Marathi authorities and I have come to an understanding.' Nic hopped to his feet. 'They get my hairstyle, and with it they get the popular support. Of the poor. I get a legal government to shelter me. And I get a compound.'

'Compound?' I asked, meaning: *chemical compound? Or barracks?* The answer, though, was the latter, because he said:

'Up in Bhiwandi. All the wealth has moved from the city, up to the mountains, up east in Navi Mumbai. The wealthy don't believe the sea has stopped coming. They think it'll likely come on a little more. The wealthy are a cautious lot.'

'The wealthy,' I said.

'So you can come along,' he said. 'Come along.'

I got to my feet. 'Where?'

'My flitter's back here.'

'Are you allowed to park a flitter down here? I was told flitters had to be parked in the official park, back,' I looked around, vaguely. 'Back up there somewhere.'

'I have,' he said, flashing me a smile, '*special* privileges.'

5

'What is it we do?' he asked me, a few minutes later, as the flitter whisked the two of us, and Nic's two soldiers, northeast over the Mumbai sprawl. He had to raise his voice. It was noisy as a helicopter.

'Speaking for myself,' I said, 'I work for the company. I do this to earn enough to keep the people I love safe and healthy. I include you in that category, by the way, you fucker.'

'And,' he said, smiling slyly, 'how *is* Kate?'

I'll insert a word, here, about Kate. It is not precisely germane, but I want to say something. I love her, you see. I'm aware of the prejudice, but I believe it goes without saying that she is as much a human as anybody. She has a vocabulary of nine hundred words, and a whole range of phrases and sayings. She has a genuine and sweet nature. She has hair the colour of holly-berries. You'd expect me to say this, and I *will* say this: it is a particularly strange irony that if the *same people* who sneer at her personhood post treatment had encountered her *before* treatment, it would never occur to them to deny that she was a human being. In those circumstances they would have gone out of their way to be nice to her. And if before, why not afterward? Kate is happier now than she ever was before. She is learning the piano. Of all the people I have met in this life, she is the most genuine.

'She is very well,' I said, perhaps more loudly than I needed to. 'Which is more than I can say for your port*folio*.'

'A bunch of houses and cars and shit,' he said making a flowing gesture with his right hand as if discarding it all. His was, despite this theatricality, an untterly unstudied insoucience. That's what a lifetime of never wanting for money does for you.

'We could have saved more than half of it,' I said, 'if

you hadn't absented yourself from the court the way you did.'

'All those possessions,' he said. 'They were possessing *me*.'

'Oh,' I said. I could not convey to him how fatuous this sounded to me. 'How very Brother Brother.'

He grinned. 'Shit it's *good* to see you again.'

'This hair thing of yours,' I asked him, having no idea what he meant by the phrase but guessing it was some nanopeptide technology or other that he had developed. 'Is that a company patent?'

'You know?' he said, his eyes twinkling and his pupils doing that peculiar cycling moon-thing that they do, 'it wouldn't matter if it were. But, no, as it happens, no. As it happens.'

'Well,' I said. 'That's something.'

He was the hairstyle man, the saviour of the world's poor. 'I'm a benefactor now,' he boomed. 'I'm a revo*lution*ary. I shall be remembered as the greatest benefactor in human history. In a year I'll be able to put the whole company in my fucking *pocket*.'

He was polite after that: offered me lunch; held out a hand towards what might have been a government aircraft. At first he said nothing as we flew. 'That's my house,' he said pointing. All I could see were more bonsais. The flitter landed: a little series of bunny hops before coming to rest, that telltale of an inexperienced chauffeur.

We were inside his compound: a pentagon of walls thick-wreathed with brambles of barbed wire. It was crowded. People were lain flat on the floor, or lolling upon the low roofs, or sitting in chairs, all of them sunbathing, and all with their hair spread and fanned out, and everybody there without exception – men women and children – had long, inkblack hair. A central tower shaped like an oil derrick with a big gun at the top – impressive looking to a pedestrian, but like a cardboard castle to any force armed with modern munitions. It was spacious inside the walls, but it was crowded. Nic led me along a walkway alongside the central atrium, and the ground was carpeted with supine humanity. They were so motionless that I even wondered whether they might be dead, except that every now and then one would pat their face to dislodge a fly, or breathe in and out.

'Sunbathers,' I said.

And then, just before we went in, Nic stopped and turned to me with a characteristically boyish sudden spurt of enthusiasm. 'Hey, I tell you what I learnt the other day?'

'What?'

'Crazy that I never knew this before, given all the work I've done. Discovered it quite by chance. Peptides, I mean the word, *peptides*, is from the Greek. It means *little snacks*. There's something you never knew. Means nuts, crisps, olives stuffed with little shards of sundried fucking tomato. Peptides means scoobisnacks.'

'Extraordinary,' I deadpanned. 'And you with your Greek heritage,' I said, knowing full well that he possessed no Greek language at all.

At this he became once again solemn. 'I'm a citizen of the world, now,' he said.

We went through: up a slope and into a seminar room. Inside was a horseshoe seating grid with room for perhaps sixty people. The space was empty except for us two. The Auto put a single light on the front of the room when we came in.

I sat myself in a front row seat. Nic stood before the screen, fiddling with his hair, running fingers through it and pulling it. 'Why do *you* think you're here?' he asked, without looking at me.

'Just to talk, Nic,' I said. 'I have no orders. Except to talk. Man, we really ought to talk. About the future.'

'Hey,' he said, as if galvanized by that word. He flapped his arm at the room sensor and the screen lit behind him: the opening image was the Federal flag of India. 'OK,' he announced.

The image morphed into diagrams of the chemical structures of self-assembling peptides filling the screen: insectile wriggles of angular disjunction wielding hexagonic benzene rings like boxing gloves.

'Wait,' said Nic, looking behind him. 'That's not right.' He clicked his fingers. More snaps of his molecular tools–in–trade faded in, faded out.

'All very barnum–bailey,' I said.

'Calmodulin rendered in 3D,' he said. 'I always think they look like party streamers. Although, in Zoorlandic iteration, they look like a starmap. There's just so much empty space at the molecular level; our representational codes tend to obscure that fact. There, that there's lysine.' He danced on the spot, jiggling his feet. 'Lysine. A lot of that in your hair. NH2 sending down a lightning-jag of line to the H and H2N link, and O and OH looking on with their mouths open.' Images flicked by. 'One of the broken down forms of lysine is called cadaverine, you know that? The molecule of fucking decay and death, of putrefying corpses. Putrescine. Cadaverine. Who names these things?'

'Something to do with hair?' I prompted.

'Lysine,' he said. 'Hair.' He held his right hand up and ran his thumb along his other four fingers: the display flicked rapidly through a series of images. 'What is it we do?'

'You asked that before,' I said.

'Innovations, and inventions, and brilliaint new technological advances.'

'I'm just a lawyer, Nic,' I said. 'You're the innovator.'

'But it's the Company, isn't it? The Company's business. These technological advances to make the world a better place.'

I suppose I assumed that this was another oblique dig at Kate; so I was crosser in response than I should have been. 'So they do,' I said. 'Don't fucking tell me they don't.'

He looked back eyes wide, as if I had genuinely startled him. 'Of course they do,' he said, in a surprised tone. 'Man, don't misunderstand. But think it *through*. That's what I'd say. This is *me* you're talking with. Technological advance and new developments and all the exciting novelties of our science fiction present. It's *great*. You get no argument on that from me.'

'I've just flown from Denver to Mumbai in an hour,' I said. 'You'd prefer it took me three months sailing to get here?'

'You have grasped the wrong stick-end, chum,' he said. 'Really you have. But only listen. Technological Advance is marvellous. But it is always, ineluctably a function of wealth. Poverty is immiscible with it. People are rich, today, in myriad exotic and futuristic ways; but people are poor today as people have always been. They starve, and they sicken, and they die young. Poverty is the great constant of human existence.'

'Things aren't so bad as you say,' I said. 'Technology trickles down.'

'Sure. But the technology *of the poor* always lags behind the technology of the rich. And it's not linear. There are poor people on the globe today who do not use wheels and drag their goods on sleds or on their backs. Some armies have needleguns and gelshells; and some armies have antique AK47 guns; and some people fight with hoes and spades.'

'This is how you got the government of Marathi to give you this little castle and armed guard?'

'The hairstyle stuff,' he said.

'And that? And that is?'

There is a particular variety of silence I always associate with the insides of high-tech conference rooms. An insulated and plasticated silence.

'It's a clever thing,' he said to me, shortly.

'Of course it is.'

'It *is* a clever thing. That's just objectively what it is. Works with lysein in the hair, and runs nanotubes the length of each strand. There's some more complicated bio-interface stuff, to do with the bloodvessels in the scalp. When I said that none of this utilised Company I.P. I was, possibly, bending the truth a little. There's some Company stuff in there, at the bloodexchange. But the *core* technology, the hair-strand stuff, is all mine. Is all me. It's all new. And I'm going to be *giving* it away. Pretty soon, billions will have taken the starter pills. Billions. That's a big...' He looked about him at the empty seats. 'Number,' he concluded, lamely.

'Hair?' I prompted.

'I'm genetically *eradicating* poverty,' he said. And then a gust of boyish enthusiasm filled his sails. 'All the stuff we do, and make? It's all for the rich, and the poor carrying on starving and dying. But this –'

'*Hair...*'

'Food is the key. Food is the pinchpoint, if you're poor. Hunger is the pinchpoint, and it's daily, and everything else in your life is oriented around scraping together food so as not to starve. The poor get sick because their water is contaminated, or because their food is inadequate and undernourishment harasses their immune system. The future cannot properly arrive until this latter fact is changed.'

'So what does the hair...' I asked. 'What does... Does it, like, photosynthesise?'

'Something like that,' he said.

His avatar, frozen with his smiling mouth half-open, like a twenty-foot-tall village idiot, lowered over us both.

'And you – what do *you* do, then? I mean what does *one*. You lie in the sun?'

'The energy you previously got from the food you eat. Well you get that from the sun.' He did a little twirl. 'It's a clever thing,' he said. 'Actually the hair less so: that's easy enough to engineer. Peptide sculptors generating photoreceptive structures in the hair, and spinning conductors down to the roots. The clever stuff is in the way the energy is transferred into the – look I don't want to get into the details. That's not important.'

I looked up at giant 2D Nic's goofy face. I looked at human-sized 3D Nic's earnest expression and fidgeting hands. 'You don't need to eat?'

'No.'

'But you can?'

'Of course you *can*, if you want to. But you don't need to. Not once I've fitted the... fitted the... and I'm *giving* that away free.'

I tried to imagine it. All those supine bodies, laid like pavingstones across Nic's courtyard outisde. 'Lying all day in the sun?'

'Not all day. Not at these latitudes. Three hours a day does most people.'

'And what about, say, Reykjavik?'

'The sunlight's pretty weak up there,' he said. 'You'd be better off in the tropics. But that's where most of the world's poor *are*.'

'But,' I said. 'Vital amines?'

'Water, more to the point. You still need to drink, obviously. Ideally you'll drink water with trace metals, flavoursome water. Or gobble a little clean mud from time to time. But vitamins, vitamins, well the tech can synthesise those. Sugars, for the muscles to work. You'd be surprised by how much energy three hours' sunbathing with my hair generates. I mean, it's a *lot*.'

'Phew,' I said. The vertiginous ambition of the idea had gone through my soul like a sword. 'You're not kidding.'

'Imagine, in a few years,' he said, 'imagine this: all the world's poor gifted with a technology that *frees them from food*. Frees them from the need to devote their lives to shiteating jobs to scrape together the money to eat.'

'But they still *can* eat?' I repeated. I don't know why this stuck in my head the way it did.

'Of course they can, if they want to. They still have,' very disdainfully inflected tone of voice, 'fucking *stomachs*. But if they don't eat they don't starve. Contemplate that sentence and what it means. Don't you see? All the life that

264

has ever lived on this planet has lived under this precariously balanced axe, all its life. Eat or die. I shall take that axe away. No more famines. No more starvation.'

'Jesus,' I said. I was going to add: I can see why the Marathi authorities would seize on such an idea as a means of galvanizing political support among the masses. I understood the guards, the compound. And from Nic's point of view too: I could see why he might want this over a position as well-paid Company genemonkey.

'Why am I here, Nic?' I asked.

'I need a lawyer,' he said, simply. 'Things are going to change for me in a pretty fucking big way. I will need a team I can trust. I'm going to be moving in some pretty highpowered circles. Finding a lawyer I can trust – that's easier said than done.'

This, I had not expected. 'You're offering me a job?'

'If you like. Put it like that, OK.'

'What... what? To come here? To come and live here? To work in Mumbai?'

'Sure.'

'You're serious?'

'Why not?

I didn't say: *because in three weeks' time, the army of the Greater Kashmiri Republic is going to come crashing in here with stormtroopers and military flitters and crabtanks and many many bullets, to seize this extraordinary asset that the Marathi junta has somehow acquired. I didn't say what, come and work here and get very literally caught in the crossfire?* I didn't say that. Instead I said: 'bring Kate?'

He assumed a serious expression, rather too obviously deliberately suppressing a mocking smile. 'I've always had a soft spot for Kate.'

'The kids?'

'Surely. The ex too, if you like.'

'I can't bring the kids here. I can't bring Kate here.'

He caught sight of his onscreen image from the corner of his eye. He turned, flapped a hand as if waving at himself, and the screen went blank. Then he turned back and blinked to see me sitting there. 'Well,' he said, vaguely. 'Think about it.'

Later, as he escorted me back across that courtyard, so unnervingly full of motionless bodies, he said, 'it's not about my ego, you know.' Oh but it was. It was always about Nic's ego.

6

Things moved slowly at first.

The Company did not fire me, fearful I daresay of what I might take with me or whom I might take it to. There was a war in India. The news said nothing about him. There was an item on WNN about a new cult of sun worshippers, then a few more pieces about how the cult was spreading. We saw his disciples, their ascetic skin like a drumskin stretched on a coat-rack, saw how the cult was spreading northwards. Through all the Stans.

Once the technology was understood, it took off.

Nic was interviewed, obviously the 'guest' of the Indian league. Then a spectacular escape to Central Africa, and then another escape to Malyasia. Then I caught a posting: Nic was to be interviewed by Foss.

I watched the feed when Foss was flown out, and put through all the rigmarole of secrecy, to interview him. It really seemed to me the old Nic was trying to break out of what must have been an increasingly rigid carapace of popular, proletarian expectation. He cracked jokes. He talked about his plans. 'This is the future,' he said, in a twinkly-eyed voice. 'I'll tell you. My technology is going to set humanity free from their starvation. I'll tell you what will happen. The poor will migrate; there will be a mass migration, to the tropics – to those parts of the world where sunlight is plentiful, but where food is hard to come by. Some governments will be overwhelmed by this new exodus, but governments like the, er,' and he had to glance down at his thumbback screen to remind himself which radical government's hospitality he was currently enjoying, 'People's Islamic-Democratic Republic of Malaysia will welcome the coming of a new age of popular empowerment.'

'What about the rest of the world?' Foss asked.

'The rich can *have* the rest of the world. The cold and sunless northern and southern bands. The rich don't *need* sunlight. They have money for food. The whole global demographic will change – a new pulsing heart will bring life and culture and prosperity to the tropics. Over time the North and the South will become increasingly irrelevant. The central zone will be everything – a great population of *real people*, sitting in the sun for three hours a day, using the remaining twenty-one creating greatness for humanity.'

I scooped up my new contracts and got back to work. Kate was deliciously pleased to see me. She'd picked up a new phrase: long time no see! She had learned the first portion of a Mozart sonata, and played it to me. I applauded. 'Long time no see,' she said, hugging me.

'I missed you,' I told her. I tickled her feet.

'Long see, long time!'

7

But what can I say? It was a fire, and fire, being a combustion, is always in the process of rendering itself inert. I did consider whether I needed to include, in this account, material about my motivation for betraying my friend. But I think that should be clear from what I have written here.

The Company persuaded me. A message was conveyed that I wanted to meet him again. A meeting was arranged. I flatter myself there were very few human beings on the planet for whom he would have agreed this.

I had to pretend I had taken up dotsnuff. This involved me actually practising snorting the stuff, though I hated it.

But the dotsnuff was a necessary part of the seizure strategy. It identified where I was; and more to the point it was programmed with Nic's DNA-tag (of course the Company had that on file). That would separate us out from all other people in whichever room or space we found ourselves in – let's say, soldiers, guards, captors, terrorists, whomsoever – and in which the snuff would roil about like smoke. When the capture team came crashing in with furious suddenness their guns would know which people to shoot and which not to shoot.

He was back in the Indian Federation now: somewhere near Delhi.

I was flown direct to Delhi International. And we landed at noon. And I was fizzing with nerves.

From the airport I took a taxi to an arranged spot, and there met a man who told me to take a taxi to another spot. At that place I was collected by three other men and put into a large car. It was not a pleasant drive. I was bitter with nerves; my mind rendered frangible by terror. It was insanely hot; migraine weather, forty-five, fifty, and the car seemed to have no air conditioning. We drove past a succession of orchards, the trunks of the trees blipping past my window like a barcode. Then we turned up a road that stretched straight as a thermometer line, towards the horizon. And up we raced until it ended before a huge gate. Men with rifles stood about. I could see four dogs, tongues like untucked shirttails. And then the gate was opened and we drove inside.

I was shown to a room, and in it I stayed for several hours. My luggage was taken away.

I could not sleep. It was too hot to sleep anyway.

My luggage was brought back, my tube of dotsnuff still inside. I took this and slipped it inside my trouser pocket.

I informed my guards of my need to use the restroom – genuinely, for my bladder grew fuller, and bothered me more than my conscience. I was taken to a restroom with a dozen urinals at one wall and half a dozen sinks at another. A crossword-pattern of gaps marked where humidity had removed some of the tiny blue tiles covering the walls. The shiny floor was not as clean as I might have liked. I emptied my bladder into the white porcelain cowl of a urinal, and washed my hands at the sink. Then, like a character in a cheap film, I peered at myself in the mirror. My eyes saw my eyes. I examined my chin, the jowls shimmery with stubble, the velveteen eyebrows, the rather too large ears. This was the face that Kate saw when she leant in, saying either 'a kiss before bedtime', or 'a bed before kisstime', and touched my lips with her lips. I was horribly conscious of the flippant rapidity of my heart, the sense of blood perked with adrenaline.

A guard I had not previously encountered, a tall, thin man with a gold-handled pistol tucked into the front of his trousers, came into the lavatory. 'The Redeemer will see you now,' he said.

8

Had he come straight out with 'Why are you here?' or 'What do you want?' or anything like that, I might have blurted the truth. I had prepared answers for those questions, of course, but I was, upon seeing him again, miserably nervous. But of course he wasn't puzzled that I wanted to see him again. He took that as his due. Of course I wanted to see him – who wouldn't? His face cracked wide with a grin, and he embraced me.

We were in a wide, low-ceilinged room; and we were surrounded by gun-carrying young men and women. A screen was switched on but the sound was down. Through a barred window I could see the sepia-coloured plain and, wavery with heat in the distance, the edge-line of the orchards.

'Redeemer, is it?' I said, my dry throat making the

words creak.

'Can you believe it?' He rolled his eyes upwards, so that he was looking at the ceiling – the direction, had he only known it, of the Company troopers, sweeping in low orbit with a counter-spin to hover, twenty-miles up on the vertical. 'I try to fucking discourage it.'

'Sure you do,' I said. Then, clutching the tube in my pocket to stop my fingers trembling, I added in a rapid voice: 'I've taken up snuff, you know.'

Nic looked very somberly at me. 'I'm afraid you'll have to go outside if you want to snort that.'

For a moment I thought he was being genuine, and my rapid heartbeat accelerated to popping point. My hands shivered. I was sweating. When he laughed, and beckoned me towards a lowslung settee, I felt the relief as sharply as terror. I sat and tried, by focusing my resolve, to stop the tremble in my calf muscles.

'You know what I hate?' he said, as if resuming a conversation we had been having just moments before. 'I hate that phrase *body fascism*. You take a fat man, or fat woman, and criticise them for being fat. That makes you a body fascist. You know what's wrong there? It's the *fascism* angle. In a fucking world where one third of the population hoards all the fucking food and two third *starve* – in a world where your beloved Company makes billions selling antiobesity technology to people too stupid to understand they can have antiobesity for free by fucking *eating less* – in *that* world, where the fat ones steal the food from the thin ones so that the thin ones starve to death. That's a world where the fascists are the ones who *criticize the fatties*? Do you see how upsidedown that is?'

I fumbled the tube and sniffed up some powder. The little nanograins, keyed to my metabolism, thrummed into my system. Like, I suppose, fire being used to extinguish an oilwell blaze, the extra stimulation had a calming effect.

The talcum-fine cloud in that room. I coughed, theatrically, and waved my hand to dissipate the material.

'So you're free to go?'

'I'm not in charge of it,' he said brightly. 'Fuck, it's good to see you again! I'm not in charge – I'm being carried along by it as much as anybody. It's a tempest, and it's blowing the whole of humanity like leaves in autumn.'

'Some of it was Company,' I said. 'The ADP to ATP protocols weren't, legally speaking, yours to give away, you know.'

'The *hair* stuff was mine,' he said.

'I'm only saying.'

'Sure – but the *hair* stuff.'

I thought of the troops, falling through the sky directly above us, their boot-soles coming closer and closer to the tops of our heads.

'The photovoltaic stuff, and the nanotube lysine fabrication of the conductive channels along the individual strands of hair – that was you. But that's of no use without the interface to do the ATP.'

He shrugged. 'You think like a lawyer. I mean, you think science like a lawyer. It's not that *at all*. You don't think there's a moral imperative, when the famine in the southern African republics is killing – how many thousands a week is it?' Then he brightened. '*Fuck* it's good to see you though! If I'd let the Company have this they'd have squeezed every last euro of profit out of it, and millions would have died.' But his heart wasn't really in this old exchange. 'Wait til I've shown you round,' he said, as excited as a child, and swept his right hand in an arc, lord–of–the–manor–wise.

Somewhere outside the room a siren was sounding. Muffled by distance, a warbling miaow. Nic ignored it, although several of his guards perked their heads up. One went out to see what the pother was.

I felt the agitation building in my viscera. Betrayal is not something I have any natural tolerance for, I think. It is an uncomfortable thing. I fidgeted. The sweat kept running into my eyes.

'All the old rhythms of life change,' Nic said. 'Everything is different now.'

I felt the urge to scream. I clenched my teeth. The urge passed.

'Of course Power is *scared*,' Nic was saying. 'Of course Power wants to *stop* what we're doing. Wants to stop us liberating people from hunger. Keeping people in fear of starvation has always been the main strategy by which power has kept people subordinate.'

'I'll say,' I said, squeakily, 'how much I love your sophomore lectures on politics.'

'Hey!' he said, either in mock outrage, or in real outrage. I was too far gone to be able to tell the difference.

'The thing is,' I started to say, and then lots of things happened. The clattering cough of rifle fire started up outside. There was the realization that the highpitched noise my brain had been half-hearing for the last minute was a real sound, not just tinnitus – and then almost at once the sudden crescendo or distillation of precisely that noise; a great thumping crash from above, and the appearance, in a welter of plaster and smoke, of an enormous metal beak through the middle of the ceiling. The roof sagged, and the whole room bowed out. Then the beak snapped open and two, three, four troopers dropped to the floor, spinning round and firing their weapons. All I remember of the next twenty seconds is the explosive stutter-cough and the disco flicker of multiple weapon discharges, and then the stench of gunfire's aftermath.

A cosmic finger was running smoothly round and round the lip of a cosmic wineglass.

I blinked, and blinked, and looked about me. The dust in the air looked like steam. That open metal beak, rammed through the ceiling, had the look of a weird avant-art metal chandelier. There were half a dozen troopers; standing in various orientations and positions but with all their guns held like dalek-eyes. There were a number of sprawling bodies on the floor. I didn't want to count them, or look too closely at them. And, beside me, on the settee, was an astonished-looking Neocles.

I moved my mouth to say something to him, and then

either I said something that my ears did not register, or else I didn't say anything.

He didn't look at me. He jerked forward, and then jerked up. Standing. From a pouch in his pocketstrides he pulled out a small L-shaped object which, fumbling a little, he fitted into his right hand. The troopers may have been shouting at him, or they may have been standing there perfectly silently; I couldn't tell you. Granular white clouds of plaster were sifting down. Nic levelled his pistol, holding his arm straight out. There was a conjuror's trick with multiple bright red streamers and ribbons being pulled instantly and magically out of his chest, and then he hurtled backwards, over the top of the settee, to land on his spine on the floor. It took a moment for me to understand what had happened. He may have been thinking, either in the moment or else as something long pre-planned, about martyrdom. Perhaps the Redeemer is not able to communicate his message in any other way. It's also possible that he believed that he could single-handedly shoot down half a dozen troopers, and emerge the hero of the day.

I honestly do not know.

I was forced to leave my home, and live in a series of hideouts. Of course a Judas is as valuable and holy a figure as any other in the sacred drama. But religious people (Kate kneeling beside the bed at nighttime, praying to meekling Jesus gent and mild) can be faulted, I think, for failing imaginatively to enter into the mindset of their Judases. Nobody loved Nic as deeply as I. Or knew him so well. But he was rich. The poor don't want the rich to save them. What they want is much simpler. They want not to be poor. Nic's hair was, in fact, only a way of making manifest the essence of class relations. In his utopia the poor would actually become – would *literally* become – the vegetation of the earth. Without even realizing it Nic was labouring to make them *grass* for the rich to graze upon. I loved him, but he was doing evil. I had no choice. I had no choice.

9

Last night, as we lay in bed together in my new, Company-sourced secure flat in I-can't-say-where (though I'm the one paying the rent) Kate said to me: 'I am cut in half like the moon; but like the moon I grow whole again.' I was astonished by this. This really isn't the sort of thing she says. 'What was that, sweet?' I asked her. 'What did you say, my love?' But she was asleep, her red lips were pursed, and her breath slipping out and slipping in.

Afterword: Hair's Breadth

Dr Rein Ulijn, Professor of Chemistry, the University of Strathclyde,

This beautiful story revolves around a major real–life scientific challenge that currently faces the scientific community, the effective exploitation of *artificial photosynthesis*, or the ability to convert sunlight into useable energy. Artificial photosynthesis would provide a highly attractive (partial) solution to the energy crisis, as it exploits the sun as the ultimate renewable energy source while it also involves capture of CO_2 and is therefore actively researched around the world.

Plants' photosynthetic systems are outstanding examples of molecular self-assembly, with their ability to convert light into chemical energy optimized by evolution. These photosynthetic circuits show a number of unique characteristics that are made to look easy by biology, but pose significant challenges to scientists and engineers. These include: achieving very high levels of order in nanoscale assemblies; identifying effective mechanisms of self-repair or self-renewal; achieving high levels of conductivity; finding ways to direct and funnel energy with high precision and finally to effectively interface these systems with man–made devices.

The scientific community have made some progress in most of these areas: it is already possible to obtain highly organised molecular architectures that show effective electronic energy transfer; nanoscale materials have been effectively interfaced with biological materials and biologically inspired methods of defect repair are being developed. A group of researchers at MIT have effectively incorporated the photosynthetic system of spinach leaves, stabilised by peptide surfactants, into solid-state materials. Although currently of limited efficiency, this work has demonstrated that artificial photosynthesis may be possible when combining biological and synthetic components.

'Photosynthetic hair', as described in this story, is a conceptually very creative combined biological-artificial system where light capturing molecules are interfaced, via carbon nanotubes as conductive tracks, with human hair. The invention goes a step further in that it interfaces directly with human biology, by converting sunlight into ATP, the fuel that enables chemical transformations in biological systems. To make such a system a scientific reality, significant re-programming of mammalian cells would be required to adopt the characteristics of plant cells. This is certainly beyond the capability of today's genetic engineers and, as is clear from the story, it is questionable whether this level of nano-engineering of biology would be desirable.

References:
On artificial photosynthesis: Andrew C. Benniston and Anthony Harriman, 11, 2008, 26-34.
On MIT spinach photovoltaic system:
http://web.mit.edu/newsoffice/2004/spinach-0915.html
Ulijn research group: Ulijnlab.com

Carbon: Part Two

Justina Robson

My supervisor in this project is now talking in my head (I internalized him, so that it saves me actually having to talk to him). He's saying that the pathetic fallacy cannot be endured in a scientific atmosphere.

The elevator cable is a marvellous innovation and also it is just a piece of string and some glop. People will make it, use it, junk it regardless of my views. I am here to examine it with my little eye and see what's what – just leave it at that. It's atoms lined up. It's molecules clinging together. It's describable entirely without reference to anything else in the world except itself. So I should get on with it. Let others do the deciding of the meaning of things. They will anyway.

I wish that were true. I wish, as I wished on a star long ago, that science would forever remove the stupid foibled brainwashed delusional claptrap from the minds of those engaged with it and leave the crystal clarity of a factual, definite world. I didn't expect to be sitting at this monstrously expensive microscope staring at a cross section of infinitesimally small fibre and seeing the death of my dreams. Yet dead they are. I'd poke them, wake them up, but the longer I've sat here, the less movement they've made.

I'll tell you what I've learned out of all this. If you really look at anything, and I mean anything, even the structure of materials in their most intimate form, you finally start to understand that you don't see them. You see light, and then your mind interprets the image, and in that moment, even if it is wordless and autistic, what you see is yourself over and over again, endlessly thrown back from every angle. I'm not being poetic when I say I see voids, fractures. A void is a space. I could say I see a surrounding, an enclosure, a vacancy, an opportunity, a spheroid bubble; but I don't, I see a void because for me the materials are important, not the gaps between things. I can't see things without pouring myself into them and neither can you. Everything, even our most basic observations, are metaphors or down and dirty guesses or half-truths.

I think most of us are still afloat in the dream of science and its small, comforting world of confident testing, answers and explanations. I wish I were still there. It was a great place, you know. Even the food tastes better in the past.

It's still only ten thirty!

I try another sample, another, another, another. The day wears into afternoon.

I suppose it's my fault I can't invent a meaning in which the cable is a good thing. I see only death in it, like the search for diamonds and gold at the rainbow's end.

What's that you say? Because my dreams... oh, because I died right here in this laboratory, under the x-rays that penetrate everything, nearly, except the very dense. I have died here in the way that souls die while bodies live on. I've died figuratively, which is literally, of course, yes. Now I understand the source of my resistance. Who would want to serve as a slave to the very thing that had crushed their spirit? Well, nobody. I should've seen that.

Oddly, it is easier to write now. I'm free of having to agree, and so free from disagreeing too. I read my notes, form sentences, type them. I saw this. I found that. I measured these parts.

By three o'clock I am actually finished.

I close the microscope down, switch it off, turn out the

lights and look in to my supervisor to say goodnight. He is getting ready for a dinner. He is wearing a penguin suit and his oxblood brogues are replaced by slick new black claws.

His eyes are beady and attentive. 'How's it gone?'

'Fine,' I say. 'The lengths of the nanotubes are too short still but at least the polymer problems are getting better. Less voids. More adhesion. We might adjust the tension and the twist. I put it all in there.'

He nods. 'You worry too much.'

'I know,' I put my coat on, check my bag, look out my change for the bus. Tension and twist. There's mileage in that, I think.

Outside I look up. The moon is out in the daytime. I smile, safe in the knowledge I will never go there. I reach up and pick it out of the sky, a circular communion wafer of elven bread.

I put my hand in my pocket and the moon is still there, in the sky, in my pocket. It tastes a bit papery, a bit boring, like granola, but then it has this cool minty centre that is exactly like the white shine of reflected light and as I taste it I know everything is all right.

I am part of carbon's engine, the part that dreams and knows and longs. My mind and its fantasies, you my friend, are its furious speed, its eyes and glory. This cable may be the starter cord to something worthwhile, who knows? Surely not me. I am just a spark. But all sparks are essential to the running of the thing if it's to run at all along the road of light. And it does run. It does. Just listen to that roar!

Contributors

Michael Arditti is a novelist, short story writer and critic. He began his career writing plays for the stage and radio. His novels are *The Celibate* (1993), *Pagan and Her Parents* (1996), *Easter* (2000), *Unity* (2005), *A Sea Change* (2006), and *The Enemy of the Good* (2009). His short story collection, *Good Clean Fun*, was published in 2004. He was awarded a Harold Hyam Wingate scholarship in 2000, a Royal Literary Fund fellowship in 2001, an Arts Council Award in 2004 and a Leverhulme artist in residency in 2008.

Chaz Brenchley has been making a living as a writer since he was eighteen. He is the author of nine thrillers, most recently *Shelter*, and two major fantasy series; his most recent book is *Bridge of Dreams*. His novel *Light Errant* won the British Fantasy Award in 1998. He lives in Newcastle upon Tyne with a quantum cat and a famous teddy bear.

Paul Cornell is the author of two SF novels, *Something More* and *British Summertime*. His *Doctor Who* episodes 'Father's Day', 'Human Nature' and 'The Family of Blood' were nominated for Hugo Awards in the Best Drama: Short Form category. He's written widely in television, and is the author of 'Captain Britain and MI-13' for Marvel Comics.

Frank Cottrell Boyce is a novelist and screenwriter. His film credits include *Welcome to Sarajevo, Hilary and Jackie, Code 46, 24 Hour Party People* and *A Cock and Bull Story*. In 2004, his debut novel *Millions* won the Carnegie Medal and was shortlisted for The Guardian Children's Fiction Award. His second novel, *Framed*, was published by Macmillan in 2005. He also writes for the theatre and was the author of the highly acclaimed BBC film *God on Trial*. He has previously contributed stories to Comma's anthologies *Phobic, The Book of Liverpool*, and *The New Uncanny*.

Patricia Duncker was born in Kingston, Jamaica on 29 June 1951. Her novels include *Hallucinating Foucault* (1996), which won the Dillons First Fiction Award and the McKitterick Prize, *James Miranda Barry* (1999), and *The Deadly Space Between* (2002). Her short stories have been published in three collections: *Monsieur Shoushana's Lemon Trees* (1997), *Miss Webster and Chérif* (2006), which explores themes of desire, jealousy and revenge, and was shortlisted for the PEN/Macmillan Silver Pen Award and *Seven Tales of Sex and Death* (2003).

Simon Ings is an English novelist and science writer living in London. He was born in July 1965 in Horndean and educated at Churcher's College, Petersfield and at King's College London and Birkbeck College, London. His six novels include *Hotwire, Headlong, Painkillers* and *The Weight of Numbers*.

Gwyneth Jones was born in Manchester in 1952. She's the author of more than twenty novels for teenagers, mostly using the name Ann Halam, and several highly regarded SF novels for adults. She's won two World Fantasy awards, the Arthur C. Clarke award, the British Science Fiction Association short story award, the Dracula Society's Children of the Night award, the Philip K. Dick award, and shared the first Tiptree award, in 1992, with Eleanor Arnason.

Ken MacLeod was born in Stornoway, on the Isle of Lewis, Scotland, and currently lives in South Queensferry near Edinburgh. His novels often explore socialist, communist and anarchist political ideas, or extreme economic libertarianism, in SF contents, and include *The Star Fraction* (1995), *The Stone Canal* (1996) and *Learning the World* (2005), all of which won the Prometheus Award in the respective years.

Sara Maitland grew up in Galloway and studied at Oxford University. Her first novel, *Daughters of Jerusalem*, was published in 1978 and won the Somerset Maugham Award. Novels since have included *Three Times Table* (1990), *Home Truths* (1993) and *Brittle Joys* (1999), and one cowritten with Michelene Wandor – *Arky Types* (1987). Her short story collections include *Telling Tales* (1983), *A Book of Spells* (1987) and most recently, *On Becoming a Fairy Godmother* (2003). She also contributed a story to *The New Uncanny* (Comma, 2008) and is currently writing an entire collection of stories for Comma, with scientists, born out of this project.

Adam Marek's debut short story collection, *Instruction Manual for Swallowing*, was published by Comma Press in 2007. It was nominated for the Frank O'Connor Prize – the biggest prize in the world for a collection of short stories. His stories have also appeared in *Prospect* magazine and in anthologies including *Parenthesis* and *The New Uncanny* from Comma Press, two Bridport Prize collections and the British Council's *New Writing 15*. He is working on his first novel, and was recently longlisted for the Sundays Times EFG Short Story Prize.

Kit Reed is an American author primarily of fantasy, horror and and science fiction. Her first story was published by seminal mystery editor Anthony Boucher, and a good deal of her work could be classed as feminist SF. She has published 14 novels, including *Mother Isn't Dead She's Only Sleeping* (1961), *Armed Camps* (1969), *Magic Time* (1980) and most recently Enclave (2009). She has also published seven collections of short stories, most recently *Dogs of Truth* (2005). She has been been nominated for the James Tiptree, Jr Award three times..

Adam Roberts is an academic, critic and novelist. He also writes parodies under the pseudonyms of A.R.R.R. Roberts,

A3R Roberts and Don Brine. He also blogs at *The Valve*, a group blog devoted to literature and cultural studies. He has a degree in English from the University of Aberdeen and a PhD from Cambridge University on Robert Browning and the Classics. He has been nominated twice for the Arthur C. Clarke Award: in 2001, for his debut novel, *Salt*, and in 2007, for *Gradisil*.

Justina Robson attended the Clarion West Writing Workshop and was first published in 1994 in the British small press magazine *The Third Alternative*, but is best known as a novelist. Her debut novel *Silver Screen* was shortlisted for both the Arthur C Clarke Award and the BSFA Award in 2000. Her second novel, *Mappa Mundi*, was also shortlisted for the Arthur C Clarke Award in 2001. It won the 2000 Amazon.co.uk Writer's Bursary. In 2004, *Natural History*, Robson's third novel, was shortlisted for the BSFA Award, and came second in the John W Campbell Award. Novels since have included *Living Next-Door to the God of Love* and *Keeping It Real*.

Geoff Ryman has published ten books and won 14 awards. His novella *Pol Pot's Beautiful Daughter* is currently on the shortlist for the Nebula Award, given by the Science Fiction Writers of America. In addition to being an established author, he's the editor of several anthologies. Among his ten books is *Tesseracts 9*, an anthology of original Canadian science fiction and winner of the Prix Aurore. His most recent SF novel, *Air* won the Arthur C Clarke Award, the British Science Fiction Association Award, the Canadian Sunburst Award, and the James Tiptree Jr Memorial Award. He is the founder of the Mundane SF movement, which agrees to avoid bad–science tropes. In 2008 he edited the Mundane Special Issue of *Interzone* magazine.

Liz Williams' first two novels, *The Ghost Sister* (2001) and

Empire of Bones (2002) were both nominated for the Philip K. Dick Award. She is also the author of the Inspector Chen series. She has had short stories published in *Asimov's, Interzone, The Third Alternative* and *Visionary Tongue*. From the mid-nineties until 2000, she lived and worked in Kazakhstan. Her experiences there are reflected in her 2003 novel *Nine Layers of Sky*. This novel brings into the modern era the Bogatyr Ilya Muromets, and Manas, the hero of the Epic of Manas. Her novels have been published in the US and the UK, while her fourth novel *The Poison Master* (2003) has been translated into Dutch.

Special Thanks

The editor and publishers would like to thank Professor Dame Nancy Rothwell, Deputy President and Vice Chancellor of the University of Manchester, together with Dr Erinma Ochu, Director, Manchester Beacon for public engagement, for their support in putting this anthology together. They would also like to thank the following for their advice, help and inspiration: Tony Buckley of Daresbury Laboratory, John McAuliffe and the University of Manchester's Centre for New Writing, Michael Addelman, Media Relations Officer, Faculty of Humanities, University of Manchester, Charlotte Eley, Helen Hulme and Dr Jon Shaffer. Most of all we'd like to thank the scientists and authors who volunteered their time and energy to take part.